# THE GOVERNESS

## Sisters of Woodside Mysteries

### Boo

## A Regency Romance

# by Mary Kingswood

*The Governess: Sisters of Woodside Mysteries 1*

Published by Sutors Publishing

ISBN: 978-1-912167-18-0 (paperback)

Cover design by: Shayne Rutherford of Darkmoon Graphics

Author's note:

This book is written using historic British terminology, so *saloon* instead of *salon*, *chaperon* instead of *chaperone* and so on.

**About the book:** *A traditional Regency romance, drawing room rather than bedroom.*

*Miss Annabelle Winterton has become governess to the daughters of the recently bereaved Earl of Brackenwood. She has no idea how to teach, but her pupils can learn all they need from books, so how difficult can it be? She'll need all her ingenuity to cope with the rebelliousness of her charges, and the unwanted attentions of their father. But when her past returns to haunt her, she has to make a difficult decision.*

*Allan, the Earl of Brackenwood, is slowly getting used to life as a widower, but his mother is determined that he must marry again and produce an heir. He is determined that he won't, although the new governess is just the sort of woman he could fall in love with. But when a face from long ago reappears and stirs up suspicion, he has to consider the possibility that his wife's death was not natural. What is worse, he himself is the obvious suspect. If he can't prove his innocence, he may lose everything - his home, his new love and even his life.*

*Book 1 of the 5-book Sisters of Woodside Mysteries series, each a complete story with a HEA, but read all of them to find out all the family secrets!*

# The Governess: Sisters of Woodside Mysteries 1

**About the series:** *When Mr Edmund Winterton of Woodside dies, his daughters find themselves penniless and homeless. What can they do? Unless they wish to live on charity, they will have to find genteel employment for themselves. This book is set in England during the Regency period of the early nineteenth century. Book 0 takes place 5 years before books 1-4, and book 5 ten years later.*

**Book 0: The Betrothed (Rosamund) (a short novel, free to mailing list subscribers)**

**Book 1: The Governess (Annabelle)**

**Book 2: The Chaperon (Lucy)**

**Book 3: The Companion (Margaret)**

**Book 4: The Seamstress (Fanny)**

**Book 5: Woodside**


Want to be the first to hear about new releases? Sign up for my mailing list at http://marykingswood.co.uk.

# Table of Contents

# The Winterton Family

*Hi-res version available at http://marykingswood.co.uk.*

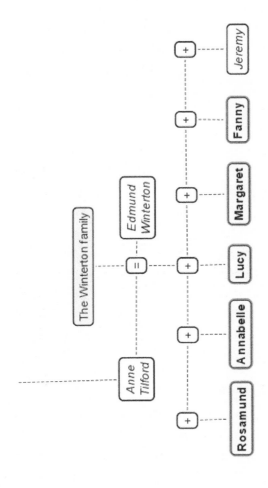

# The Dalton Family

*Hi-res version available at http://marykingswood.co.uk.*

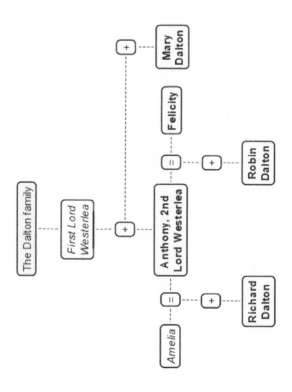

# The Skelton Family

*Hi-res version available at http://marykingswood.co.uk.*

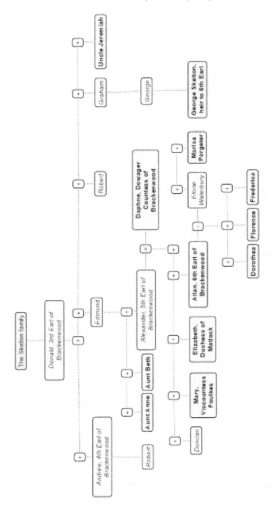

# 1: The Will (January)

'To Mrs Price, Miss Winterton, Miss Margaret Winterton, Miss Frances Winterton. My greetings to you, and sincere condolences on the sad demise of your esteemed father. If convenient to you, I shall do myself the honour of waiting upon you at noon tomorrow for the purpose of conveying to you the material contents of the last will and testament of your late lamented parent. Yours in deepest sorrow, Horatio Plumphett of Plumphett, Plumphett, Witherspoon and Plumphett, Brinchester, Brinshire.'

~~~~~

**JANUARY**

Annabelle huddled in her favourite chair in the morning room, too numb even to cry. In the matching chair on the opposite side of the fireplace, Lucy sobbed noisily. Margaret had taken her usual place at the worktable, but for once her hands were still. She stared into space, white-faced and wide-eyed with shock. Beside her, tears poured silently down Fanny's face.

Annabelle could hardly take it in. Whatever was to become of them? Their ignominy could not long be concealed from the world.

'Have you heard about the Winterton sisters of Woodside?' their acquaintances would say. 'Dreadful, quite dreadful.' And indeed it was dreadful. She had no idea what they were to do.

Out in the hall, a murmur of voices as the solicitor was shown out. Poor Mr Plumphett! The reading of a will was always a doleful business, but he must seldom have had such bad news to impart. His usual urbane voice was high with distress. "I am so sorry, so very sorry," he had said, over and over. Perhaps he was still saying it, even as he was ushered out of the house and into his gig.

Doors opened and closed, the gig rattled away down the drive and in the hall, more murmured voices. Then Rosamund and Robin came into the room, their faces grave. At least Rosamund was safe, and that was a mercy. She had been wife these five years to Mr Robin Dalton, heir to Lord Westerlea of Westerlea Park, and could not be harmed by the scandal. One sister, at least, uninjured by the catastrophe.

But four sisters remained at Woodside, with no brother or husband to shelter them from the disaster.

"Lucy, do stop weeping," Rosamund said. "Tears never helped anything."

"But we are destitute!" Lucy cried. "Whatever are we to do! Thrown out of our own home! It is unbearable, and I will *not* go to the workhouse, I will *not!*"

"It will never come to that," Robin Dalton said firmly. "No one is throwing you out of Woodside. It is yours, after all, left to you all equally by your father, so you may stay here as long as you wish, until you have decided how to proceed."

"What option do we have?" Annabelle said. "The house must be sold to pay the debts Papa left. Then we shall be homeless and penniless."

"You will have a home with us for as long as you want," Robin said. "Penniless does not mean friendless."

Annabelle softened at once. She had not much liked Robin when Rosamund had first married him. He was something of a dandy, who spent more time before his pier glass than was proper for a man, and far too grand for country girl Rosamund. But Annabelle had warmed to him when she had seen how happy he made his wife, and how solicitous of her comfort. And now he would willingly take her sisters under his wing, too.

"You are all goodness, Robin," Annabelle said, "but we cannot possibly impose on you. You could hardly squeeze all four of us into Holly Lodge."

"Then a small cottage in the village," he said. "With a couple of servants and your own good sense, you might live comfortably enough at very little expense to me."

"You have your own family to think of," Annabelle said.

"My wife's sisters are my family, too," he said mildly. "Besides, it is Rosamund's dowry which contributed to your father's ruinous financial state. We wondered greatly at the time where he had contrived to find twenty thousand pounds, but if I had known he had been obliged to mortgage the house to pay such a sum, I should never have agreed to it. Just because Mr Winterton promised it years ago, when he was better off, does not mean he was obliged to pay it when his circumstances had changed."

"And *why* did they change?" Lucy cried. "We were once very well off, I am sure we were."

"There was Mama's jewellery, too," Annabelle said. "Whatever happened to the famous Tilford sapphires?"

"I believe there were several pieces, not just the sapphires," Rosamund said thoughtfully. "They were supposed to provide our dowry, but Papa searched for them before I married Robin, and they were nowhere to be found. He was very upset."

"But he need not have mortgaged the house," Annabelle said.

"He had promised!" Fanny said. "It was a point of honour, and a gentleman must have honour, above all things."

"I should have said he must feed his family first," Lucy said.

Robin laughed. "That is important too, but I do not think the mortgage alone was so ruinous. Your father's gaming debts were considerable, from what I have heard. I do not think we need to look further for an explanation of how the estate came to be so encumbered."

"If Jeremy had lived—" Annabelle began tentatively.

"It would have made no difference," Robin said quietly. "Your father's affair with the dice began many years ago, long before your poor brother lost his life."

"But what are we to *do?*" Fanny cried, with a sob.

"Nothing at all, yet," Robin said crisply, "except to dry your tears, Fanny, and Lucy, too, and wait for Mr Plumphett to provide us with a full reckoning of the debts. Then we may begin to consider how to move forward. And you must come for dinner again today."

"Yes, of course," Rosamund said.

"You have been so kind to us, sister, brother," Annabelle said. "However, I believe it would be best for us to return to our usual routine, at least for as long as we can. Who knows what the future may bring? So let us enjoy Woodside while we can."

Rosamund hugged each of her sisters in turn, and then she and Robin departed for the short walk to their home at Holly Lodge.

"Well, if we are to dine here, I had better go and speak to Mrs Thompson," Annabelle said.

She found Havelock, the housekeeper, loitering in the passageway outside the kitchen.

"There now, Miss Annabelle, that's the worst over," she said.

If only that were true! Annabelle looked about her with new eyes, seeing, as if for the first time, the worn carpet, the faded paintwork, the chip taken out of the wooden panelling when the footman had dropped a whole tray of glasses. A footman... how many years was it since they had had a footman? Ten at least. The signs of increasing poverty had been clear for a long time, for those with eyes to see. But Annabelle had been beguiled by the comforting familiarity of her home. She loved its mellow stone, its odd wings of different ages and styles, its dusty, seldom-used corners and the passageways and stairs so well-known that she could find her way about blindfold. Her home.

She had been born at Woodside, they all had. Rosamund first, then Andrew who had died in infancy, then Annabelle, Lucy, Margaret and Fanny. Then poor Jeremy, sent away to sea at the age of twelve, to be made into a man worthy to inherit Woodside. But the sea had taken him from them on his first voyage, and there had been no more children after him, none that survived. Jeremy... the boy with the laughing eyes and the hair that always flopped across his forehead, no matter what he did to it. He would have been seventeen now, if he had lived. Almost a man. This mess would have been his responsibility, if he had lived.

This would never do! She must not get maudlin. What had happened had happened, and they must make the best of it.

"We shall be dining here today, Havelock," Annabelle said.

"Very good, Miss. Shall I give the orders to Mrs Thompson? You will not wish to be bothered with domestic matters today."

"Thank you, Havelock. She will know what to prepare. I cannot... cannot think about food at the moment."

"That's very natural, Miss, with the master only just buried and hearing the will, and all. But forgive me if I'm speaking out of turn, Miss, but... you look... I mean to say, it wasn't bad news, was it? The master didn't leave Woodside away from his own daughters?"

Annabelle gave a wry laugh. "Oh no, he did not do *that*. He left Woodside to us, equally, and he very generously left us all his debts, too. Tell me Havelock, have the servants been paid this quarter?"

The housekeeper shifted uncomfortably. "Well... no, Miss, not for a couple of years now, but it don't matter. Most of us have a bit put by, and we had a roof over our heads, and food on the table. We understood how it was."

Which was more than Annabelle had. No, that was not true. She had known perfectly well that there was less money than there had been, but she had assumed that Papa's income was being diverted to the gaming tables, leaving little for candles and coal. She had not suspected that the house was mortgaged. Rosamund had helped Papa with his accounts at one time, but whenever Annabelle had offered to do the same, he had bitten her head off, so she had never suspected the true state of affairs. They must have been living beyond their means for years.

She went back into the morning room. Lucy was alone there, still curled up in a miserable ball in the same chair. Annabelle took her usual seat on the other side of the fireplace.

"Where are Margaret and Fanny?"

"Probably in the attic, rearranging the furniture in the baby house."

Annabelle wished she had a comfort of that sort to turn to. Her books were her usual refuge, but today even that enticement held no charm for her.

"Whatever are we to do?" Lucy said. "Fanny would say we need a knight on a white charger to gallop to our rescue, but I do not know of any knights, do you? And even if one such should come, it would be useless, for you still pine for your lost love, I am far too dull to attract a knight and Margaret is too shy even to look at a man. But Fanny... could we find a knight to rescue Fanny? She has ineligible suitors a-plenty, but what about Mr Hawes? He is very eligible, and wrote poetry to her, so might he come up to scratch and whisk her away to Kellingborough?"

"I think not, for although he wrote an eloquent letter of condolence, he has not called at all. And he rides a black horse, not white," she added punctiliously.

Lucy did not smile. "It is not a matter for jest, sister. We are destitute, and I do not know what is to become of us," she ended tearfully, her voice rising in distress.

"Now, do not start crying again, dearest," Annabelle said. "Rosamund is a little... *sharp*, sometimes, but she is quite right — crying never made anything better. As to what is to become of us, we have only three choices... to find a husband, to live on the charity of our relations or to find employment. Since husbands are in short supply, and charity does not appeal to me, I shall find myself a post as a governess."

Lucy swung round to plant her feet squarely on the floor. "No!" she cried, leaning forward in her anxiety. "You must not, Belle, truly you must not! The role of a governess is of all things the most disagreeable, neither family nor servant. I do not remember ours, but I know that the Claremonts' Miss Lackey ate all her meals in her room, like a leper. *Most* disagreeable."

Annabelle laughed. "That was because she was young and pretty and made sheep's eyes at John and Rupert... *and* at Mr Claremont, and so Mrs Claremont banished her, and she was too proud to eat with the servants. I should not be so proud, I assure you. No, it will suit me very well to be a governess, Lucy, so do not repine upon it."

~~~~~

For a fortnight, they continued almost as if nothing had happened. Callers came to offer their condolences, letter after letter arrived expressing sorrow to varying degrees, and the sisters sat in their morning room each day sewing handkerchiefs and trimming bonnets almost as if their lives had not come unceremoniously to an end. Only the quantity of black crepe reminded them. But several times Mr Plumphett's gig creaked up the drive, and once the handsome tilbury of Mr Martin from Martin's Bank in Brinchester, and each visit reduced Annabelle's spirits a little more. There was no money in the bank, no investments secure in the three percents, there were debts everywhere, some astoundingly large, and half the tenant farms had already been sold off. The remaining holdings were worth no more than two or three hundred pounds a year.

Something needed to be done. The sisters met in their father's book room, together with Robin and Rosamund, to discuss their plight.

"We cannot survive on so little money," Annabelle said, looking at the reckoning Robin had made of their financial situation. "It would be a reasonable income if we had no other obligations, but these debts... Do they all need to be paid?"

"Unfortunately, I fear so," Robin said. "If you were to sell the house and remaining estate holdings, you might just clear all obligations of that nature. It would only be possible to stay on here on such a low income if one of you were to marry a man of substance. Do any of you have a lovelorn swain or two hidden away?"

Annabelle smiled, but shook her head.

"If I had ever been the type to attract rich, lovelorn swains," Lucy said, "I should never have taken poor Walter. Who marries a man of almost four score years except in desperation?" But she smiled as she spoke. "Dear Walter! Such a sweet man. I shall never find another like him."

"Then it seems that Woodside must be sold," Robin said sadly. "If you will give me the authority, I will engage to find an agent to manage the sale, and will myself undertake to settle with the tradesmen and pay the servants here."

"You are too good, Robin," Lucy said. "I do not know what we should have done without you." The others murmured their agreement.

"It is unfortunate that I do not have access to the income that will be mine one day," he said. "I could then have—"

Annabelle reached across to squeeze his arm. "Even if you had, it would not be prudent. The income to support us in a house such as Woodside is gone. It must be sold and that is an end to it. So we must look to what we shall do next. Robin, we are quite agreed that we cannot impose ourselves on you and Rosamund. One sister might have been useful to you, but four is too great a burden. Elsewhere, we have few relatives close enough for us to apply for aid, and none at all on Papa's side, but I have found some in Mama's family helpful. Aunt Letty and Aunt Pru can offer a home to one of us. Aunt Letty has recently suffered some ill-health and is almost bed-bound, and Aunt Pru writes that they would welcome a companion who could provide some company so that Aunt Pru is not tied to the sick room. They live very secluded, so perhaps that would suit Margaret. Do you think you could manage that, dear?"

Margaret nodded, her eyes huge in her pale face.

"Mama's only brother, Uncle Arthur, writes that he has twelve children now, poor man, so his house is quite full up. However, his sister-in-law is unwell and in need of someone to chaperon her two step-daughters about. He suggests that Lucy might be acceptable — a respectable young widow and so forth."

"Oh, yes!" Lucy said. "I should love to, although... I am in mourning. Would it be quite seemly? To attend balls?"

"Your mourning period for your husband has passed," Rosamund said. "For Papa, there is no reason not to go about after the first month or so. You will not dance, of course, but you may certainly act as chaperon. Do you not agree, Robin? I have seen widows even in deep mourning at entertainments in London, although nothing of a frivolous nature."

"Oh, certainly," Robin said. "For a husband, it could not be thought of, but while mourning for your father it is not necessary to keep secluded."

Lucy smiled happily. "Then I should be very glad to do it."

"Excellent," Annabelle. "So that leaves Fanny and me."

"As it happens, I might have some possibilities for you," Robin said, with just a hint of smugness. "Aunt Mary wrote to her friend Lady Harriet Hay, do you remember her? Lord Carrbridge's sister. Lady Harriet supports a charitable endeavour for women with no family to support them. They make fashionable gowns for ladies of lesser means, those not handy enough with a needle to make their own. She employs a number of women as seamstresses, and would like someone of a more elevated background to talk to the customers."

"It sounds charming, from Lady Harriet's description," Rosamund added. "The mamas bring their daughters to buy something special for an important ball, or to be married in."

"Oh, how romantic!" Fanny breathed.

"And you are so nimble with a needle, too," Rosamund said. "It would suit you admirably."

"Well, then," Annabelle said, with a sudden tremor. "It remains only for me to seek a post as a governess." After all the discussion and wondering and hoping and fearing, finally her family would be split asunder.

"Are you quite determined on such a course, sister?" Rosamund said. "I cannot bear to think of you in such a position. Governesses are hated by everyone — their employers, their charges, the servants. It will be miserable for you."

Annabelle was so tempted to answer with the stark truth. *I am miserable everywhere, so it hardly matters.* Instead, she said firmly, "My mind is made up, and I am well suited for the role, you must admit."

"Indeed, but... Well, no matter," Robin said. "If it does not answer, you may return to us and we will find room for you. For any of you, if you find your posts uncongenial. But if you are set on this, Annabelle, then there is a possibility. I asked Lady Carrbridge if she could help. Do you remember her? You will have met her in town."

"I remember her," Annabelle said. "I doubt she remembers me."

"She meets a great many people, it is true. Here, read her letter."

He passed across a sheet of paper covered in neat script. After the usual salutations, Annabelle read, *'There is an old friend of Lord Carrbridge's who might be in need of a governess. His wife died last year, leaving him with three young daughters to raise. The poor man is distraught and hardly knows what he is about, so he has not yet thought what he should do for them. Lord C has written to enquire of him if he would like a recommendation for a governess, but we have not yet heard from him. I will let you know if we hear word from him. In the meantime, do tell me a little more about your sister, so that I may know how best to describe her accomplishments. Constance Carrbridge.'*

"This came just today," Robin said, holding out another sheet.

*'So happy to tell you that Allan would be delighted to offer Miss W a post as governess. It had been on his mind that he should do something about the matter, but had not the least idea how to go about it. If she is all that you say, I am sure she will do very well there. His mother is in residence, so there will be not the least impropriety. He lives at Charslby, near Kenford in Cheshire, and is a very pleasant, amiable man. All the Skeltons are charming. I know his sisters quite well, and they are delightful. I am sure Miss W will be very happy there. Constance Carrbridge.'*

Happy. Annabelle could not imagine being happy ever again, but she was content to be unhappy at Charlsby. Robin wrote to accept Mr Skelton's offer, and to Charlsby she was to go to begin her life as a governess.

# 2: *Charlsby*

'Westerlea Park, Frickham, Brinshire. 15th January 18—. My dear Annabelle, Lucy, Margaret and Fanny, I cannot begin to tell you how grieved I am that you are all to quit the county entirely. Such a loss to us all! Your society will be sorely missed. I do believe you are right to refuse my nephew Robin's offers of assistance, for it would be galling indeed to remain at the scene of so many happy times, and yet in sadly reduced circumstances. In a new place, and amongst new friends, you may all find the happiness which presently eludes you, and renders your future so bleak. Such is my very earnest wish. Yours in great affection, Mary Dalton.'

~~~~~

Robin undertook to escort all the sisters to their destinations. Annabelle protested, but he said simply, "You must have a man to escort you, sister, and it will be a useful reminder to your new employer that you are not unprotected in the world."

Lucy and Margaret left first, both bound for Shropshire, although in such different locations that there was no expectation of meeting there. Then Fanny and Annabelle were be taken northwards. But two days before they were due to leave, Lady

Harriet herself arrived on her way home from Brighton, and whisked Fanny away to Yorkshire.

For two painful days and nights, Annabelle was alone in Woodside. The farewell calls from their acquaintances had been paid before Lucy, Margaret and Fanny had left, so there was no company to lighten the hours. Her tears had all been shed as she had watched her sisters driving away to the uncertainty and hardships of life as paid employees or poor relations. She spent the days walking slowly from room to room, gazing about her with eyes newly awakened to the pleasures of her home, fixing it all in her mind.

But at night in her room, listening to the familiar creaks and sighs of the house for the last time, Annabelle had never felt so alone. Once they had been a large, happy family, like thousands of others all over England. A contented Mama and Papa, a healthy son and heir, and five lively daughters to fill every corner of the old house with childish squeals and running feet and simple reels played with more enthusiasm than skill on the pianoforte. But Mama had died and then Jeremy, Rosamund had married and now Papa was dead too, and the remaining Miss Wintertons were scattered to the winds of capricious fortune. The house was all but silent, the bedrooms hollow and echoing without their familiar occupants. There was no one left to creep into bed with her and giggle over the new curate's lisp or Mr Claremont's flirting. And perhaps she would never see any of them again. It was a thought too appalling for tears. And beyond these sorrows, there was another, more personal, that would never leave her. So she curled up in her bed and tried very hard to sleep.

~~~~~

Robin was good company on the drive, pointing out features of interest and, when she lapsed into silence, talking more or less to himself. His valet, Brast, was not good company in the least, shivering and sniffling in martyred misery, while wrapped in a voluminous rug. However, Robin could not contemplate a night away from home without him, so his presence had to be borne, somehow.

They made good time, and were able to reach Kelford well before dark.

"This is excellent," Robin said. "We shall be able to make a leisurely breakfast and arrive at Charlsby before noon, and I shall be halfway home again before dark."

Having no maid, Annabelle called upon the services of one of the inn servants to help her dress for dinner. She was a well-rounded woman of middle years, who stroked the silk of the gown laid out ready on the bed, and then the fine cambric of the chemise with a sigh of pleasure.

"You going far, ma'am?" she said as she laced Annabelle's stays with more enthusiasm than was strictly necessary.

Annabelle would not normally reward the curiosity of an inn servant, but it occurred to her that they were so close to Charlsby now that the woman might know something of it.

"I am bound for Charlsby," she said. "I believe it is not far from here."

"Oh no, ma'am, not above ten miles or so. Less across the common. You stayin' there?"

That was too impertinent a question, so Annabelle said only, "My plans are not settled. Do you see much of the family here? I imagine this is the nearest town."

"Aye, but they don't come here much. The young ladies used to come to the assemblies sometimes, but they've married and gone away now."

"So it is just Mr Skelton and his mother who live there now?"

The lacing stopped abruptly. "Mr Skelton, ma'am?"

"The gentleman who owns Charlsby. His name is Skelton, is it not?"

"Oh, I see... the family is called Skelton, 'tis true, but he's Lord Brackenwood. He's an earl."

"An earl." The lacing resumed, and Annabelle began to laugh. "I did not realise that my employer is a peer of the realm."

The lacing came to another halt. "Employer?"

Annabelle sighed. "I am to be governess at Charlsby."

"Oh, those poor motherless girls," the woman said with a sentimental sigh. "I pity them, truly I do. I daresay they will be sad, pale little things, weeping for their mother all day long. A governess, eh — that'll be the very thing to cheer them up. Why, you'll be just like a mother to the poor chicks."

Annabelle smiled a little at this optimistic vision. If she could in time instil a little Italian into her charges, teach them an instrument and ensure they could curtsy without falling over, she would be satisfied. But perhaps they were too young for Italian? Perhaps they were only just learning their letters and numbers? She was shocked at how little she knew of her new role, how little curiosity she had felt. When her employment had been merely a nebulous, far-distant abstraction, it had not seemed very important to enquire into the details. The death of her father and the subsequent revelations had absorbed all her thoughts, and nothing else had seemed to matter very much. But her new life was now a mere ten miles away, and it was become a matter of some urgency to know exactly what faced her.

She waited patiently until Robin had made himself ready for the evening, dinner had been served and he had consumed his first glass of claret before she broached the subject.

"How is it, brother, that I was not aware that the gentleman who has engaged my services is an earl?" she said, in a teasing tone of voice. "I thought him a mere Mr Skelton of Charlsby, but the maid who attended me disabused me of such a notion. Imagine my surprise to discover I shall be entering the household of the Earl of Brackenwood. I am not sunk quite as low in the world as I had supposed, for the governess to an earl's daughters is a little out of the common way, I fancy."

Robin laughed. "Did you not know? I am sure it was mentioned... Rosamund knew, and we talked of it very freely between ourselves. But everything has been arranged in a scramble, and perhaps I forgot to mention it. You do not really care about such things, I wager."

"Not in the least, except that it will be a larger household than I had expected. A widower, his three daughters and his mother — that is what I anticipated, and servants to match, but an earl will have a much more imposing establishment."

"Oh, but he lives very quiet, apparently. He never goes to London or gads about, as some of these great men do. The house... well, I imagine it is quite large, and there will be a decent number of servants, but that is all to the good. You may have a servant of your own, you know. That is not uncommon in these great houses. But perhaps it may be no bigger than Westerlea Park."

Annabelle sipped her wine thoughtfully. "Do you know anything of him? Lord Brackenwood, I mean."

Robin shrugged. "Only what is to be found in Debrett's. He was the younger of two boys, but his brother died a few years ago, and the father not long after, so he inherited relatively young. He married a Miss Eloise Waterbury, who provided him with three daughters and died October last. I imagine he will be looking about him for a new countess." He hesitated, gazing into the depths of his wine glass as if it fascinated him. "He sounds as if he would make someone a good husband."

He spoke casually, but Annabelle was not fooled. "Someone who is looking for a husband, perhaps," she said. "Which I am not, Robin."

"Ah, Annabelle! You are too young to wear the willow for ever. Is it not time to live again, and open your heart to the possibility of love once more?"

"My heart is open to it, but it is difficult when one has once seen a man who encompasses everything that is good and amiable and generous. I must always hold him as my ideal, and no man has yet equalled him."

"He was not sufficiently amiable and generous as to marry you," Robin said acidly. "But this is past history, and perhaps in new surroundings with new faces about you, the gentleman may be left in the past where he belongs."

Her heart was too full to speak more on the subject. She had long since come to terms with her disappointment, but it still grieved her to hear the man she had once loved so dearly disparaged in any way.

"Tell me of the earl's daughters," she said, quickly turning the conversation. "Do you know their ages?"

"Debrett's informed me that the eldest is ten years of age, and there are twins of eight. Let me see... Dorothea... um, Florence and I forget the third."

"Excellent," she said. "I shall not then need to teach them their letters. That is good, for I have not the least idea how it may be done. I do not remember a time when I could not read, and spent most of my time in the schoolroom with my nose in a book, inattentive to what was being taught to the others. But if they are older — well, they can read what they need to learn in books, just as I did."

He laughed at that. "You may find a little more exertion is required than that, my dear Annabelle. Not all children absorb their lessons so readily."

"How else might they learn?" she said airily. "No one can pour knowledge and wisdom into ears unwilling to hear it. If they be receptive to learning, then they will read, and if not, there is nothing to be done for them."

"Nevertheless, you are being paid to teach them, whether they be willing or no. At the least, you must instil discipline into them, and turn them into ladies."

"Oh, stitchery, drawing and performance on the instrument." She shrugged. "There will be time enough for such work. They are very young yet."

"Annabelle—" He heaved a sigh, then reached for the bottle. "More claret, sister?"

"Thank you, Robin."

~~~~~

Charlsby was not quite as imposing as Annabelle had feared, in fact it was not much larger than Westerlea Park, and lacking the grandiose embellishments so frequently employed on great houses. There was no many-pillared portico, no domed roof fringed with statuary, no great sweep of steps to the entrance and no wings almost as large as the main house. It was a neat, elegant building with a pleasing symmetry, built of cool grey stone. The gardens were not imposing either, being laid out with simplicity after the fashionable manner designed to imitate nature. There were gently rolling hills, small streams and winding paths, with arbours and follies dotted here and there. Glimpses of water suggested a lake behind the house. Beyond the ha-ha, deer grazed placidly.

"How pleasant a vista to gaze upon," Robin said, and Annabelle could not but agree.

The butler and a footman emerged from the house as soon as the carriage arrived at the front door, followed at once by two grooms to help with the luggage and lead the coachman to the stables. Leaving Brast sniffling in the carriage, Annabelle and Robin followed the butler into the house. The entrance hall was a dark, echoing place, as cool as the ice house at the Park. Perhaps in summer there would be light filtering from high windows, but in January a pair of lamps on each wall did nothing to brighten it. Annabelle shivered.

"His lordship is expecting you," the butler said. "He is in the library."

That was better! A house with a library could not be a dismal place, for there would always be the means of escape conveniently to hand. One might open a book and find oneself in sun-drenched Sicily or the green slopes of Switzerland and forget entirely the dismal grey of an English winter.

The library was at the back of the house, and it was not at first sight an impressive room. It had the usual accoutrements of such rooms in the provision of shelves and ladders and, naturally, books, but the room was disappointingly small. Her father's book room was larger. However, there were tables scattered about, and every one was full to overflowing with books, and even more promisingly, book-shaped parcels yet to be unwrapped. Annabelle smiled.

There was no sign of the earl, just a line of dogs snoozing in front of the fire, but as they entered, the butler coughed and a face peered around the side of a huge wing chair in front of the fire.

"Mr Dalton and Miss Winterton, my lord," the butler announced.

"Thank you, Plessey." He unfolded himself from the chair and stood up, and again Annabelle was conscious of a twinge of disappointment. She had met a few of the nobility during her visits to London with Robin and Rosamund, and had a fair idea of what an earl should be. This man was nothing like it. He was not tall — shorter, in fact, than Robin, who was not himself above average height. He was rather solidly built, and although he wore the usual breeches, top boots, waistcoat and coat of any gentleman, they were chosen for comfort, with no style or effort at fashion, and his cravat was a mere knot. Beside Robin's impeccable appearance, Lord Brackenwood looked like a well-to-do farmer.

"Miss Winterton, welcome to Charlsby." He took her gloved hand and held it in both of his, while his eyes took in her black pelisse. "You are in mourning, just as I am. You have my sincere sympathy, for I know how much you must be suffering, and how difficult you must find it to leave your home and make a new life for yourself far away. It is my great wish that you will be happy here, as happy as I have been for many years, and will not feel the loss of your familiar surroundings to be unbearable. Whatever I may do for your comfort, you must ask and if it be in my power I shall provide it." His voice was warm and mellow, and she recognised the sincerity in his words.

"You are all kindness, Lord Brackenwood." She made her curtsy, but he was still holding her hand, gazing now at her face.

"The kindness is all on your side, I assure you, for I had not the least idea what to do for the best for my three ragamuffins. I hope they will not give you too much trouble."

Ragamuffins? Trouble? She was aware of a tremor of unease. "I am sure we shall get along charmingly," she said, with more confidence than she felt.

Lord Brackenwood then turned to Robin, and after that there were refreshments to be ordered and awaited. There was a small grouping of chairs at the far side of the room, with tables conveniently to hand. The earl shifted piled-up books to clear space for the tea and cake when it arrived, and the three of them talked industriously of the state of the roads and the weather and the quality of inns for some minutes.

He was not a handsome man, Annabelle decided, after some consideration. His face was pleasant enough, and his features were regular but undistinguished. His hair was an indeterminate shade of brown, like his eyes. Even his age was undistinguished, for he was neither young nor old. Somewhere between thirty and forty, she guessed. Again, she felt he could easily pass as a farmer or one of the better types of artisan. An artist, of some kind, perhaps, for he had long, delicate fingers, perfect for holding a brush. But his voice was gentle and well-modulated, and his manners were excellent.

For half an hour, they sat and chatted and ate and drank, like any gentry paying a duty call on a neighbour. And then Robin rose and said that he must take his leave, and the earl rang the bell to order the carriage brought round. And so they came to the moment of final separation. One by one, her family had left her, and now her last contact with her old life was leaving her and she would be quite alone. Friendless, homeless and penniless. But she smiled and shook Robin's hand and thanked him for his services in bringing her to Charlsby.

And then he was gone. She was alone.

# 3: The Governess

Annabelle stood uncertainly in the hall as the butler closed the door. Outside, the sounds of the carriage rattling down the drive dwindled into silence.

"Come, let me show you to your rooms," Lord Brackenwood said.

"Oh, but one of the servants—"

"Nonsense, pray allow me to be useful for a change. Besides, no one knows Charlsby as well as I do. Plessey has not been here above five years, and even Mrs Hale, the housekeeper, barely ten."

"Mrs Dawkins has been here longer than your lordship," Plessey said.

The earl turned to him, a smile lighting his features. "Ah yes, the cook! She was born here, as I was. And several of the outdoor staff also. Now, Miss Winterton, this is the music room in here, where Charlsby's ghost is reputed to appear, but only when the violin is played. My brother Duncan used to play, but he had to give it up, for the sake of the housemaids' nerves. Well, he *said* he gave it up on account of not wishing to raise the ghost, at any rate. Just beyond it is the dining room. We dine at six, winter and summer alike. My brother once put a basket of frogs under the table when guests were expected, but they all escaped too soon, and made their way all over the house. It took us a week to find them all. Through here is the morning room, my mother's domain. She keeps to her bedchamber just now, but you will meet her very soon. This is the Italian room, where my grandmother liked to receive callers. A funny thing happened here in my father's day..."

He had a story about every room, but almost all of them involved his father or his older brother, Duncan, who had been something of a scapegrace, it seemed, although the earl spoke of him with affection.

When they started up the stairs and the earl fell silent momentarily, Annabelle said, "When may I meet my pupils?"

"Oh... did I not mention it? They are away just now. We all went to my sister Mary for Christmas, and it seemed best to let the girls stay on with their cousins. This house is dreary for them without their mama. But I have written to tell them of your coming, and they will return as soon as Mary can arrange it. This floor is all bedrooms for the family and guests. If we go up again, I will show you the nursery and schoolroom, and your own apartment."

Her apartment consisted of a large sitting room with a fine view over the deer park, and a small bedroom. Two maids were engaged in unpacking her boxes, while another attended to the fires. There was also a spiral service stair behind a door, but the earl assured her it was never used now.

"I daresay the architect thought it a charming conceit, spiral stairs, but the chamber maids thought it less than charming, especially with buckets of coal to be carried."

"Oh, this is delightful!" she cried, looking around at the stylish furnishings, not at all the mismatched castoffs she had expected. "What pleasing rooms. I shall be most comfortable here."

He smiled again, and she was struck by how much younger and handsomer he looked. His habitual expression was serious, with a little frown above the eyes, but perhaps that was merely the weight of sorrow pressing down on him. Once he had grieved enough for his wife, he might be a different man altogether.

He indicated one of the maids. "Milly here will be your personal maid, since you brought none with you. I trust she will give you satisfaction."

Milly dipped a curtsy, with a mischievous grin that made Annabelle warm to her immediately.

"Thank you! You are all goodness, Lord Brackenwood," Annabelle said, with heartfelt sincerity, for she had not expected such solicitude for her comfort.

"I hope you will be happy here," he said. "This is your home now, and I wish you to treat it as such."

It was the second time he had expressed a desire for the governess to be happy, a wish that was surely unlikely to be fulfilled. How could anyone truly be happy who had lost home and family and a place in society, and become a paid employee? But she curtsied and said only, "Thank you. You are too kind."

With a few more words he was gone, and Annabelle was left with the maids, and the housekeeper, who arrived a few minutes later to ensure that all was as it should be. Her manner was perfectly correct, but there was neither the deference due to a guest, nor the welcoming smile that she might have afforded to a new servant. Annabelle would have to accustom herself to such coldness. She was neither family nor servant, and had no friends in this house.

An hour later, she was summoned to the dowager countess. It was not a request. *'Her ladyship the Countess of Brackenwood will see Miss Winterton now in the morning room.'*

She checked her appearance in the glass, glad she had changed her travelling gown for something a little more stylish, but not too stylish. She was only the governess, after all, and must not draw attention to herself.

Lady Brackenwood was as unlike her son as it was possible to be. Where he was unremarkable in every way, the countess was a striking woman in all senses. She sat, ramrod straight, on a gilded chair more like a throne than anything else. Even her gown of gold satin, trimmed with a vast amount of lace, made her look like a queen. From the still-blonde hair elaborately curled down to her embroidered slippers, she would draw every eye to her. She must have been above sixty, but her face was almost unlined and her beauty shone, pale and ethereal, like the moon. As Annabelle made her curtsy, she imagined the countess in her youth, turning every head in the room. How she must have been courted! The fifth earl must have been quite a man to have caught her.

And then she spoke. "You're the new governess, then." Her voice was harsh, almost croaking, and was the accent Welsh? And she was not from the top drawer, either. "Well, come closer, girl. Hmm. How old are you?"

"Three and twenty, Lady Brackenwood."

"Quite on the shelf." She sniffed disparagingly. "So your father left you penniless, then. Remiss of him. Your brother-in-law brought you, I understand? Seems an odd thing to let his wife's sister go for a governess, in that way. Why didn't he take you in himself?"

Annabelle bristled at such rudeness, but answered with composure. "There are four of us to provide for, and few men are generous enough or rich enough to fill their house with spinsters."

"What is his income?" the countess said in her strange, hoarse way.

Annabelle tried not to look startled at such an impertinent question. "I could not say."

"Come, come, you must have some idea. His father is a baron, is he not? There must be gossip about his income."

Annabelle enjoyed listening to gossip as much as the next person, but it offended all her sensibilities to repeat such things. But clearly the countess would not be satisfied until she had a number, so Annabelle plucked one at random. "It may be that Lord Westerlea's income exceeds three thousand pounds per year."

"A good sum," she said, nodding to herself. "Your other sisters have found employment, I take it? For they needn't come looking here. One destitute girl is quite enough."

"They are all settled, Lady Brackenwood."

"Good, good. But you mustn't call me Lady Brackenwood in that familiar way. Address me as *'my lady'*."

"I beg your pardon, my lady."

"That's better. You're a servant in this house, here to work, just the same as the scullery maid, so don't go putting on airs."

"No, my lady."

"Hmpf. You will take your meals in your room. You will keep the girls quiet at all times — I can't abide squealing children. I had enough of that with my own, and my nerves won't stand for it now. And one more thing, Miss Winterton. You will not, under any circumstances, set your sights on marrying my son. He must marry again, naturally, but it will not be the likes of you. Is that clearly understood?"

"Perfectly clear, my lady." Stung, she lifted her chin a little higher. "You need have no fears on that score. I have no intention of marrying."

The countess gave a bark of laughter. "Ha! Fine words, my girl, but I know your type. Ambitious as they come, I've no doubt."

"I am not in the least ambitious," Annabelle said proudly. "After two seasons in London, I could have married any number of earls, so *yours* is quite safe from me. I lost my heart a long time ago, and no title or wealth or property can tempt me now." She could have bitten her tongue in vexation for allowing herself to be provoked so, but she could not unsay the words.

"Hmm." The countess eyed her speculatively. Then, with an abrupt wave of one hand, she said, "Go now."

With a deep curtsy, Annabelle silently withdrew. She hoped her demeanour was calm, but inwardly she seethed. How dared she speak so! After her son's kindness, Lady Brackenwood's ill manners jarred painfully. So this was to be the way she was treated. Well, it was no more than she had expected, although expressed with brutal frankness. She withdrew to her rooms with what dignity she could muster, where Milly brought her tea and cakes and all the servants' hall gossip and made her laugh.

"Do you like working here, Milly?"

"Oh, yes, Miss! Well, her ladyship's a bit of a dragon, but nothing like as bad as—" She clamped a hand over her mouth. "Shouldn't speak ill of the dead, I suppose, but nobody liked her. The countess, I mean. When she died so sudden, like, the joke in the servants' hall was that his lordship had finally had enough of her and poisoned her."

"Good heavens!"

"Oh, he never would, Miss! Such a lovely man. Everyone likes *him*. But it *was* awful sudden. Just went to bed one night, and Lily found her stone cold the next morning. Dreadful day *that* was. Was your father like that, Miss? Sudden, like?"

"Not as quick as that, no. He had not been well for a long time, then he took a chill and was dead three days later. It felt sudden, but it was not unexpected." In fact, it was a wonder he had lasted so long, when he drank so much and ate so little, and spent his days, and quite a few nights too, huddled over the fire in his book room. Poor Papa! Her eyes filled with tears.

"Ah, there now, I've brought it all back," Milly said. "You have a good weep, Miss, you'll feel much better, so my ma always says. Have you finished with the tea things? I'll take them back downstairs then."

~~~~~

The first knock on the door barely registered. She had eaten her supper from the tray Milly had brought up from the kitchen, and had settled down with a glass of rather good claret and a book. No matter how dismal her mood, a book could transport her to a place where she could forget every humiliation. She was so engrossed that it took her a while to drag herself back from the dramatic tale she was reading.

The second knock was a little louder.

"Enter!" The door opened, but she did not look up from her book. "The tray is on the table over there. I have quite finished with it."

"I shall be sure to send someone to collect it," came the amused tones of the earl.

With a squeak, Annabelle jumped to her feet, sending the book crashing to the floor. "My lord, I beg your pardon!" He wore full evening dress, but somehow he still looked nothing like her idea of an earl. He was not dowdy, precisely, but his attire owed nothing to fashion. She curtsied hastily. "I had no idea—"

"How should you, indeed?" The smile faded, and his face settled into its customary seriousness. "But are you quite well, Miss Winterton? Your travels have overset you, perhaps?"

"No, my lord," she said, puzzled. "I am quite well."

"You did not come down to dinner so I thought—"

"Oh! Oh, I see. Lady Brackenwood expects me to eat in my room."

"Ah." He nodded thoughtfully. "And *I* expect you to eat with the family, Miss Winterton. After all, the chaplain sits at my table, and my secretary, so why not the governess too? We are not so grand as to render such an arrangement ineligible."

Annabelle thought quickly. It was a tricky problem, but surely honesty was best. "My lord, I do not wish to be caught up in a battle between you and your mother. Perhaps it would be better if I keep to this arrangement, which is quite the custom for those in my position."

"I am master in my own house, I hope," he said mildly. "I shall explain it to my mother. From tomorrow you will dine with us."

She curtsied again. "As you wish, my lord."

He frowned. "This *'my lord'* business... that is my mother, too, I daresay. Well, I do not like it. You are a gentleman's daughter, Miss Winterton, and you may address me by title, as all my acquaintances do. Although..." The smile broke out again, and his eyes glinted with humour. "...perhaps best to address *her* as *'my lady'*."

She could not help giving an answering smile. "I shall do so. Thank you, Lord Brackenwood."

He bent down to pick up her fallen book, and smoothed its pages before looking at the cover. "Ah, *'Belinda'*. A most enjoyable tale, although I believe I preferred *'Castle Rackrent'*. Miss Edgeworth is a most talented author."

"Yes, indeed! I had intended to finish reading her work on education, but I became distracted."

He laughed. "Who can blame you? Certainly not I, although there are a great many interesting ideas in *'A Practical Education'*. I look forward to discussing them with you when you have read it. Good night, Miss Winterton. I apologise for disturbing your solitude, and it is a relief that you are not, as I had feared, unwell."

He bowed, she curtsied and he quit the room, leaving her rather unsettled. The earl was all that was good and kind, but it remained to be seen how much mastery he had over his mother.

~~~~~

*'Dear Annabelle I have arrived safely Margaret'*

~~~~~

Annabelle slept surprisingly well, and was up and about well before Milly arrived, bearing her breakfast tray.

"Oh, am I banished to my room to eat again?" she said, with a laugh, trying not to be disappointed.

"Everyone has a breakfast tray, Miss," Milly said. "Even his lordship. He goes out for a long walk every morning first thing, then he breakfasts in his room and dresses properly. Like a gen'leman, I mean. For his walk he just throws on clothes anyhow."

Annabelle smiled, for that was exactly what she had thought of his appearance the day before. Clearly, that was just how he liked to look.

She spent the morning examining the schoolroom. It was a forbidding place, a big, empty room with three small desks in a row, and a larger desk facing them. There were a few books on a long shelf, but the Bible and Psalter were the only ones that looked well-used. There was a blackboard, a box of slates and chalks, and pens and ink, but not much else. No drawing materials, no instrument, no globes, although perhaps they had all been put away, behind the locked door in the corner.

Annabelle thought of her own education at home in the morning room, the five of them sitting around the big work table with Mama and Miss Perring, and later just Mama. Rosamund would be practising on the harp in one corner, and Margaret the pianoforte in another. Fanny was always sewing, and Lucy — well, Lucy never stopped talking, but she talked just as fluently in Italian, when required, so that was all right. And Annabelle herself had her books… there were books everywhere. No — she stopped herself. The books were gone now, and Woodside was empty. She had brought some with her, as many as she could fit into her boxes, but Robin had packed up everything else and taken it away to be stored in the cellars at Westerlea Park. "Just until you get settled," he had said, but when would that ever be?

She sat at one of the empty desks and wept quietly for a few minutes. Then she dried her eyes, and went back to her room. She would write to Margaret today, she decided.

~~~~~

Allan stared at his reflection in the mirror. Another dreary day gone by, the hours got through somehow. And now, another dreary evening ahead of him. It was Thursday, so the joint would be mutton. Then whist with his mother, Mr Penicuik and Mr Cross. Aunt Anne and Aunt Beth would play cribbage, squabbling gently over the points. And Great-uncle Jeremiah would drink too much, then snore in front of the fire, and have to be carried to his bed by the footmen. Dear God, how bleak his life was!

At least there would be a new face tonight. Miss Winterton, the governess. A pleasant woman, not at all forward, but then in her position she could not afford to be. He knew why his mother had not wanted her at table, of course. Poor Eloise had barely been cold in her grave before the hints had begun. She knew of a Miss This or a Lady That who had a great dowry... there was always a great dowry. Mother could not conceive that a man might marry for any other reason, or might not want to marry at all. How ironic that was, that she who had secured her husband by beauty alone, bringing not a penny piece to the marriage, should be so determined that he must marry wealth. And look where that had got him. If only...

But there was no point in regret. He had made his choice and that was an end to it. There's was no going back, and he could never have Marisa now.

For a moment, he toyed with the idea of leaving off the black. Was it not time? He had a blue coat that he was very fond of. But then he remembered Miss Winterton, also dressed in sombre black, both of them in mourning, she for her father and he for... not Eloise, but for what? His lost youth, perhaps. The lost opportunities, the time gone by that could never be recovered. He was four and thirty years old, and what had he done with his life? He had three daughters where sons were expected of him. He had hidden away in the country, when he should have taken his place in society, amongst his fellow nobles. He had repaired a few cottage roofs, instead of instituting the wholesale reforms of his land that so many were now undertaking. But nothing of note. When he breathed his last, the obituary writers would be hard-pressed to say more than, *'He was born. He lived. He died.'* No, while this dark mood gripped him, he would cling to his blacks, and at least Miss Winterton would not feel out of place.

He went down earlier than usual, and there she was, waiting in the saloon, gazing up at the portrait of his mother over the fireplace. Her hair was simply dressed, and she wore no jewellery at all, but her gown was fashionable and well made. It fitted her rounded form to perfection. How pleasant it was to see a woman with a little comfortable flesh about her, who was not all angles and sharpness.

"Good evening, Miss Winterton."

"Lord Brackenwood."

"It is a good likeness," he said, standing beside her and looking up at his mother in her triumphant youth.

"Yes, I can see that. But how awkward to wear a great wig like that, and that wide skirt. I am not sure I could walk in such a costume."

He laughed. "Do you know, I have seen that portrait every day of my life and never taken much notice of Mother's clothes. They are rather outlandish, to be sure."

"I am very glad that we wear simpler garments now."

He looked at her gown, with its pleats and tucks and tiny ruffles, a complex triumph of the seamstress's arts, and could only smile at her definition of simplicity. The others began to arrive just then, so he said, "Come, let me make you known to the rest of the household."

The aunts twittered over her like a pair of turtle doves. Mr Cross bowed in an exaggerated manner, kissed Miss Winterton's hand and then held on to it for far longer than politeness dictated. Mr Penicuik was polite but as restrained as always. He was not a man to be distracted by the arrival of a lovely young lady.

Was she lovely? An interesting question which had not occurred to Allan before. She was not a conventional beauty, certainly, but there was a serenity about her which was intriguing. A very composed woman, perfectly at her ease despite finding herself in a house full of strangers. She spoke demurely to the aunts, dealt briskly but firmly with Cross and spent some minutes chatting amiably to Penicuik, undeterred by his monosyllabic answers. A very well-bred lady indeed, which augured well for her training of the girls. And there was just a hint of mischief in her eyes sometimes. What did that mean, he wondered?

A voice boomed across the room, "Eloise? Eloise, my dear! How well you look."

"Ah, Great-uncle Jeremiah," Allan whispered in Miss Winterton's ear. "Pray take no notice. He is easily addled." Then, more loudly, "Uncle! Come and meet our newest resident. Miss Winterton, may I present to you my great-uncle, Mr Jeremiah Skelton. Uncle, this is Miss Winterton, come from Brinshire as governess to the girls. Do you remember? I told you all about it?"

"Of course I remember, m'boy! Not in my dotage yet. Where is that lazy fellow, Portman? I want my sherry. Ah, there you are, Portman, skulking behind the pillars as usual."

He took a glass and the decanter from the footman's tray and headed for his usual seat by the fire, near enough to be warm, but out of earshot of the aunts.

And finally, the double doors were thrown open and Plessey's stentorian tones announced, "The Right Honourable the Dowager Countess of Brackenwood."

Allan sighed. Poor Mother, always insisting on a proper announcement, even in her own house. She swept in regally, as always.

Then, not at all as always, she stopped dead, and glared at Miss Winterton. "What are *you* doing here, miss?"

# 4: A Misunderstanding

Allan rarely argued with his mother, for in general there was little point. She would have her way, and it made life easier to accept the inevitable without fuss. But there were limits, and even his easy-going nature could not be pushed beyond them. Miss Winterton was present at his express invitation, and he could not cravenly surrender the point to his mother without being abominably rude to a young lady who was already suffering the grievous loss of her father, her family and her home. He remembered her words — *'I do not wish to be caught up in a battle between you and your mother.'* Nor would she be.

There was always a price to be paid for rebellion, but he lifted his chin and spoke calmly, albeit louder than usual. "There was a misunderstanding yesterday, but from now on Miss Winterton will dine with us, Mother."

His mother's eyes flashed, and she looked more queenly than ever. She looked at him assessingly, then her eyes flicked over the silent onlookers — the chaplain wringing his hands, the secretary with a gleam of amusement in his eyes, the impassive footmen and butler, ready to relay the tale to every servant in the house.

Wisely, she decided to say nothing, but Allan knew he would be lectured about it later. Well, he knew how that would run. If he stood up to her, he was declared to be obstinate, like his father. If he surrendered, he was weak, also like his father. Whatever he did was a failing, in her eyes. Somehow, he was never perfect, like his brother. Poor, dead Duncan, so full of life, so much *fun*. Even after thirteen years, the pain still made him catch his breath.

When Plessey announced dinner, Allan led his mother in, as usual. Heaven forfend that they should do anything differently. Behind them, Mr Cross would escort Aunt Beth and Mr Penicuik Aunt Anne, as usual. Great-uncle Jeremiah would wobble in on his own, as usual, and flop into his usual chair.

But when Allan had settled his mother and had leisure to look around, he saw that Great-uncle Jeremiah, looking rather smug, had Miss Winterton on his arm. He led her straight to the seat beside Allan. "There you are, Eloise," he boomed, rendering the room silent, every eye turned towards them. The footman, his face a mask, held the seat for her, waiting for her to sit.

The countess rolled her eyes and sighed audibly. "Eloise is dead, you old fool."

"Dead?" he said, his voice suddenly querulous. Then, with sudden force, he added, "Ha! And who killed her? That is what I should like to know." He turned clouded eyes towards Miss Winterton. "Do sit down, my dear."

She smiled, and patted his arm, which she still held. "Thank you, sir, but I believe you have made a little mistake. This is not my seat."

The countess grunted, and nodded approvingly.

Allan frowned in irritation. Such rudeness to a stranger was beyond anything, especially when he had made it perfectly clear that Miss Winterton was to be treated as a member of the family. He could not permit it, even in his mother.

"This seat is yours tonight, Miss Winterton," he said. "You may tell me of your plans for my daughters' education."

Colouring slightly, she sat, Uncle Jeremiah took the seat beside her, and Aunt Beth and Mr Cross were relegated lower.

It was the oddest feeling to have an attractive young lady beside him at his own dinner table. Sometimes now when he dined out, there would be a daughter of the house or a niece sitting, blushing, beside him, the family watching hopefully, but when had such a thing last happened at home? He could not remember. Eloise had never been one for entertaining, so usually their dinners were quiet family affairs, and he ate with his mother on his left hand and his wife on his right. It was an unconventional arrangement, but his mother had decreed it and neither he nor Eloise had cared enough to object. Since the autumn, Aunt Beth and Aunt Anne had alternated the claim to his right hand.

Now, he delighted in the novelty of a dinner companion who was fresh and new, whose conversation he had not heard a hundred times before. Not that her words were particularly enlightening. She seemed delightfully vague as to how, precisely, she planned to take his three little terrors and turn them into young ladies who could be admitted to good society. Well, there was time enough for her to find a way, and he felt no anxiety for their futures. Well, Dorothea gave him some uneasiness, it was true. But the younger two bade fair to be pretty and he would give them all handsome dowries, so they would not want for suitors. After dinner, he had the pleasure of discovering that Miss Winterton was an accomplished performer on the pianoforte, and played a competent hand of whist. He could see that she would be an asset to their evenings.

When the card party broke up and Great-uncle Jeremiah had been carried to bed, Allan went to his room and poured himself a whisky. There were few traces of the family's Scotch ancestry left, apart from one ancient portrait in the attic of the first earl in his barbaric highland costume, now legal again, but thankfully not much worn. But a drop of whisky before bed always settled his stomach, somehow, after an evening of insipid conversation and dull play at the card table, or, as now, before a summons.

It was a relief to be alone again. His valet, who served double duty as the first footman, helped him dress before dinner and looked after his clothes but Allan needed no other assistance. He was perfectly capable of readying himself for bed and drawing his own bed-curtains. But tonight he did not undress. He sat, sipping his whisky, waiting.

He had not long to wait. A timid knock on the door revealed his mother's maid, almost as old as she was, although Denby had wrinkles enough for the two of them.

"Begging your pardon, my lord, but her ladyship would like a word."

He took his whisky with him. She would not offer him a seat, so he liked to have something to hold, a small but tangible barrier between them.

"Good evening, Mother."

She, too, was still fully dressed, sitting in one of her gilt chairs, her back straight, her face implacable. "It is not acceptable, Allan," she began, her rough voice even now commanding, with that regal tone that had made him tremble when he was a boy. He still trembled, truth be told, but he had learnt not to show it. "I will not have that chit at my dining table."

"I believe the dining table is mine," he said softly.

"Pfft, such quibbles are beneath you," she said, eyes flashing. "I will brook no argument over this, Allan. She will eat in her room, and there's an end to it. I won't have a chit like that stirring up trouble."

He sipped his whisky thoughtfully. It was futile to reason with Mother when she was in this mood, for she dismissed the validity of every argument. Yet he could not surrender the point. He had given his word to Miss Winterton, and it was a matter of honour as a gentleman for him to uphold his pledge. He could not reason with his mother, yet he must make her understand the position.

Pulling forward a matching chair, he sat and took another sip of whisky.

"I did not give you permission to sit!" she said, sitting up even straighter, if such a thing were possible. "You are discourteous to your own mother."

"Do you wish to talk about discourtesy?" he said in his mildest tones. "I do not advise it."

She flushed, but still she glared at him. "You're determined to allow the servants to pretend to be gentry, then? Soft — that's what you are. Just like your father. He would never listen to my advice, either." Her voice was even harsher than usual. She was tired, he suspected, yet she would never admit to it.

"Mother," he said, leaning forward and resting his elbows on his knees, "let us be rightly understood, and then we will not speak of this again. Miss Winterton is the daughter of a gentleman, and is entitled to a place at my table — *my* table, mind — by that fact alone. She has as much right to it as Mr Penicuik, and more than Mr

Cross, who may be an excellent secretary but whose ancestry would not bear close scrutiny. It is my will that each of these three be treated as guests in this house and not as servants, even though they each receive a salary at my hands. It is also my will that you treat each of them with the courtesy due to any guest under this roof."

She was silent, although her cheeks showed angry colour, and the knuckles gripping the arm of her chair were white.

He sat back in his chair with a smile. "Mother, I know that you are driven by a concern for my wellbeing, so perhaps you think that Miss Winterton is a fortune hunter, and will attempt to secure me as a husband. If so, let me reassure you. I have no intention of marrying again."

Her expression shifted, from outrage to something far less certain. "Of course you will marry again," she said, her tone bewildered. "You must have an heir."

"I already have an heir," he said.

"Pfft, that foolish peep-o-day boy! You need a son of your own."

"No," he said, rising. "I have made one match to please you, and I will not make another. Goodnight, Mother."

And in triumph, surprised by his own victory, he made for the door. But as he left, her bleak expression chilled him, and she looked shrunken, like an old woman.

~~~~~

*'18th January. My dear sister, I am delighted to hear that you are comfortable at Charlsby and are being treated well, for one hears such dreadful tales of governesses. Do you remember poor Miss Chambers who drowned herself? Or did she hang herself? It was*

*one of the two, and all because one of her pupils told her mother that she could not name the principal city of Persia. Miss Chambers could not name it, I mean, and the poor woman was so afraid that she would be turned off without a reference that she hanged herself. Or drowned herself. I am glad I am not to be a governess, for I have not the least idea what the principal city of Persia is. I am not very sure where Persia is, if I am to be honest about it. Is it in Africa? I am almost certain it is in Africa. Oh Annabelle, do you know the principal city of Persia? I am sure you must do for you read so many books, and proper improving books, not novels and such like, but if you do not, you had better look it up at once, for it seems like the sort of thing a governess would be expected to know. Where would one look up such a thing? Oh dear, it is a very good thing that I am not— Goodness, must rush. Lucy'*

~~~~~

Annabelle woke early, full of energy. Talking to the earl about her plans for the children's education had brought her to the realisation that, in point of fact, she had no plans at all, nor the least idea of how to formulate any. She scrambled into her clothes, and made her way eagerly to the schoolroom. Today she would determine a system of lessons for her pupils. She would make a list of subjects, and then she would make another list of those items she would need in order to teach them. An instrument, for one thing. Painting and drawing equipment. Deportment rings. Globes. And books... so many books.

Her own books had been brought through from her rooms and pushed, all higgledy-piggledy, onto the bookshelf. Her fingers itched to rearrange them... but no, she must make her lists first. She found some scraps of paper in a drawer and spent a little while preparing a pen and pouring ink into a pot. Only then could she begin.

How strange it was to sit at the teacher's desk. One day soon, when she looked up from her writing she would see three pairs of eyes watching her, three expectant faces waiting for her to pour knowledge and understanding into their unformed minds. What a great responsibility! She might never have children of her own to raise, but she could, perhaps, play a small part in the raising of these sorrowful girls, who must be so grief-stricken without their mother to comfort them and guide them gently towards the adult world. How wonderful to be of service to the poor dears! And if she were diligent in her stewardship, she might turn them into great ladies, worthy to marry a duke. That was an ambition to inspire her endeavours.

She bent her head to her task, and, with this glorious vision in her mind, worked steadily for an hour. After that, since it was not yet time for her breakfast tray, she decided to reward her industry by sorting out the books. This was, it had to be admitted, a task more suited to her temperament, for in her opinion there were few activities so enjoyable as those which involved books. So she sorted and shelved, kneeling before the low bookcase, and sang a little song as she worked.

"Good morning, Miss Winterton. You are happy in your exertions, I deduce."

"Oh!" She scrambled to her feet, smoothing her apron as best she could and wondering if her hair was dreadfully disordered. "Good morning, Lord Brackenwood." She dipped a curtsy to him, and he bowed, but he was smiling. How much better he looked when he smiled! That sad, worried look was quite vanished. "I was just sorting out the books." Which was a particularly stupid thing to say. He could see clearly what she was about.

He picked one up and flicked through the pages. She guessed he had just returned from his habitual morning walk, for he wore a disreputable old pair of boots beneath a moth-eaten greatcoat. Three dogs hung about his feet, tongues hanging out. He needed only a shotgun to complete the image of a gamekeeper.

"Do you have everything you need for your lessons?"

"Oh… no. I would prefer a big table to these desks — so formal! As for materials, there is not much here. I have a few books of my own, but—" She reached for a sheet of paper. "I have a list."

He frowned. "Globes? An instrument? We used to have such things here. Perhaps they are in the play room." He marched across the room to the locked door in the corner and rattled the handle. "Hmm… why would this be locked? Wait, let me fetch the keys."

He strode out of the room, and she heard him galloping down the stairs, the dogs lolloping after him. Several minutes later, he came back into the room jingling a big ring of keys, a boyish grin on his face, as the dogs panted enthusiastically around his feet. "Right, let us see if we can break into the play room."

It was the seventh or eighth key before the lock turned with a satisfying clunk. He pushed open the door and Annabelle followed him into the room. She had expected a dusty store room of toys, but instead she saw a neatly appointed bedroom. The furnishings were surprisingly luxurious, the bed hangings the sheerest gauze, and the dressing table and wardrobe made of finely polished wood. Apart from a desk under the window, it was every inch a lady's bedroom, the brushes and pots of cream still in place before the looking glass.

"I had forgotten about this," the earl said, staring at the bed with an unreadable expression on his face. "When I was a boy, this was the play room, where the toys were kept, but Eloise… my wife liked to sleep up here sometimes. She had a proper bedroom downstairs, much larger and grander, but this room was quieter, she said, and more conducive to her repose, and cooler in summer, on this side of the house. She was never well after her last confinement — a boy, born dead. No, no, say nothing of it, for it is a sorrow much softened by time, and I have never cared as much about the need for an heir as my mother has. I have a perfectly fine heir in my second cousin, who is a splendid young man and will make an excellent earl. Far better than I," he added, almost inaudibly.

"What is behind these two doors?" she said hastily, for his face had fallen into its sad mask again.

One led to another of the spiral service stairs, but the other was locked. Annabelle could guess the size and shape of the room beyond it, however.

While the earl fumbled with keys, Annabelle said, "This arrangement is the mirror image of my own rooms. Does every corner room have a small room within it, and service stairs?"

"Yes," he said absently, his attention on the keys. "A dressing room, or maid's room."

"The governess's room, perhaps," she said, amused. She was delighted with her spacious suite, but it was excessively generous for her station. She had expected an attic room, too hot in summer and too cold in winter.

He smiled, but shook his head. "We never use these small rooms as bedrooms. The library has been rearranged somewhat to make a larger inner study, where I keep my paperwork and deal with business with Mr Cross's assistance. The library is smaller as a result, but that is only my retreat, so I need nothing bigger. The others are all as they were. As for the stairs, they are closed off at the lowest level, for the servants never use them now, but the upper ones are still in occasional use. Mine connects my bedroom with the library, which is very useful if I need a fresh book in the middle of the night. Ah, there we are."

He swung the door open, and there were the toys and books and globes, a rocking horse, an elderly pianoforte and even a baby house. Several large boxes promised hours of enjoyable exploration to come.

"Wonderful," she said. "Thank you, Lord Brackenwood. I am sure I shall find everything I need in here."

"Good." He took her hand, held it palm up and dropped the keys into it. "There. If you need anything else, just let me know. And of course, my library is at your disposal, whether for teaching purposes or... how did you describe it? Distraction!"

She laughed, but before she could reply, a voice called out, "Miss? Are you in here, Miss? Do you want your tray here?"

Milly's face was a picture when the two of them emerged from the play room, and Annabelle imagined that juicy piece of gossip whispered around the servants' hall. *'In her ladyship's bedchamber, all alone! Just fancy!'*

"What an excellent idea," Lord Brackenwood said cheerfully. "Let us take breakfast together, Miss Winterton, for I am minded for company this morning. Milly, tell Portman to bring my tray here, and then you will stay with us while we eat, for propriety."

It was a little late to consider the propriety of being alone together, Annabelle thought in amusement, and eating together would no doubt spark even more gossip, but she could hardly object to the earl's expressed wish.

For the first time, she realised how precarious her position was as a paid employee in his house. Today he ordered her to take breakfast with him. What orders might he give tomorrow? And what would happen if she refused? But she smiled and took the tray from Milly's hands, reminding herself that the earl was a gentleman and would deal with her honourably. Or so she must hope.

# 5: *Pupils*

Allan found himself walking with a spring in his step all day. His good humour was not, he told himself sternly, because Miss Winterton was young and pretty and embodied his ideal of the feminine form. No, it was her novelty, and the freshness of her manner which inspired him to break out of his boring rut.

Taking his breakfast in the schoolroom took him back more than twenty years — almost thirty, perhaps. There had been a square table at one end of the room where they had eaten their meals, the four of them. Duncan, always laughing and full of mischief. Mary and Lizzie, their heads together, giggling. And himself, the youngest of them and the most timid. There had been a governess then, too, or rather, a succession of them, plain, harassed women who never stayed long. Then Duncan had gone to school, and the light had gone out of their lives for weeks on end until he came home for the holidays. Christmas, Easter, the long summer days — those were the good times. By the time Allan was sent away to Eton, Duncan had moved on to Oxford. Not that he stayed there long. Then everyone went off to London — Papa, Mother, Duncan, Mary and Lizzie. Two marriages in rapid succession and then...

But he would not think about that, not today. He had been gloomy for too long. Today, he was not in the least gloomy. In the chapel, he joined in the responses with unusual energy. His hour with Mr Cross passed without the usual wearisome debate about the pasture at Hillend Farm or the not-so-subtle invitations to visit families who just happened to have marriageable daughters. Then he went to the stables to clear his mind after the lowering effect of business. An hour's ride and then home, to spend the afternoon in his chair in the library. Or perhaps he might call on Sir Henry, and invite the old man to dinner. Yes, he would do that.

No sooner had he settled on this plan than the sound of a carriage could be heard on the drive. A caller. Probably for his mother, but still, he hesitated. There were days when he was not in the least minded for company, but this was not such a day. He could surprise his mother by appearing in her morning room without being summoned, for a change.

He spun on his heel and strode through the house to the hall.

"Papa! *Papa!*" Two small figures bounded up the steps and through the door Portman was holding open. They screeched to a halt, then curtsied demurely, before peeping up at him mischievously. "Is she here? Is she?"

"She is. You will find her—" But they were already gone, hurtling up the stairs with two nurse maids in pursuit.

One, slightly taller, figure remained. "I suppose she's hideous."

"Not in the least hideous," he said, with a smile. "But go and see for yourself. She will be in the schoolroom, I daresay."

"Perhaps later," Dorothea said coolly. "Or tomorrow. If I feel like it." She lifted her chin and glared at him defiantly.

Such a troublesome child! Eloise had complained of her constantly, and poor Miss Winterton was likely to have a difficult time of it. He said firmly, "Certainly tomorrow, Dorothea, and you will be in the schoolroom every day thereafter, except Sundays. Just as with your mother."

She set her lips in a thin line, but dared not defy him further. Bobbing a quick curtsy, she stalked away up the stairs, head high.

~~~~~

*'Dearest Annabelle, I hope you are well, and settled into your teaching routine now. We are all well, except for Robin's father, who cannot seem to shake off this heavy chest that has plagued him all winter. We have had word that Robin's cousin Charity is to return from Italy with Lord Ramsey very soon, but certainly in time for the season. Or so they say, but they have changed their minds before. Never has a honeymoon lasted so long! How are you getting on with Lord Brackenwood and the Dowager? You have not mentioned them, but perhaps your paths do not often cross. It is sometimes so in these great houses. Are you confined to the schoolroom and your own apartment? Or do you occasionally spend an hour in the drawing room with your pupils? Do let me know if the fashions are much different there. I hope you are not too lonely. Your loving sister, Rosamund.'*

~~~~~

Annabelle spent the evening fending off the attentions of Mr Cross, the secretary. He engaged her in conversation before dinner, sat beside her during the meal, and then tried to arrange a card game that would include her. She resolutely refused to play, however. In this scheme she was aided by Lady Brackenwood.

"Sit down, Cross. You may partner me tonight."

"Whist, my lady?"

"Yes, of course whist. We always play whist."

"Shall we not play loo for a change, my lady? That's an amusing game, and Miss Winterton may play also. Or she may take my place and I'll watch, don't you know."

"No, indeed," Annabelle said. "I have no intention of playing. Pray do not change your arrangements on my account."

"But—"

"Whist," Lady Brackenwood said with asperity. "Sit, Cross, and shuffle."

Annabelle settled herself with her sewing, but there were not sufficient candles to enable her to move far from the card tables. Two minutes later, Mr Cross called out, "I have an excellent hand, Miss Winterton. I shall do very well, I fancy."

"I am glad to hear it, sir," she replied.

Five minutes after that, he again called across to her, "I was not so lucky after all, Miss Winterton, but I am certain the next hand will be to my advantage."

"You would play better if you paid more attention to the game," Lady Brackenwood said with asperity.

Annabelle agreed, and decided it would be advisable not to encourage him by replying further.

They proceeded in silence for some time, but then Cross burst out again, "Miss Winterton, I have just enjoyed the most magnificent hand. I led with the king first, but then his lordship countered with the ace, and so I thought it was all up for me. But no, because Penicuik made the mistake of playing his queen, and so I was able to—"

"*Will* you stop talking, Cross?" her ladyship said. "I never knew such a rattle."

"Beg pardon, my lady. I did not mean—"

"Tomorrow I shall ask Anne to play, and you may play cribbage with Beth, for I am sure you are the most irritating man I have ever encountered."

"I humbly apologise, my—"

"Will you shuffle, or must I do everything myself?"

Lord Brackenwood looked across at Annabelle for the first time. "Have you enough light to work by, Miss Winterton? Portman, bring some more candles and set them on the table beneath the mirror over there." He smiled at her, that warm smile that lit his whole face. "That will be easier on your eyes for such delicate work, and the sofa will be a more comfortable seat for you."

"Thank you, my lord," she said, dipping a curtsy and scuttling away to the far side of the room, safe at last from Mr Cross's attentions, although he still threw long glances her way, and occasionally waved to her. As she stitched, she had leisure to wonder what his interest in her was — simple pleasure in a new face, a light flirtation or... something more? He was only a secretary, so could he afford to take a wife? Or had he something more sinister in mind?

She went early to her bed, exhausted by Mr Cross's attentions and the prospect of a full day with her pupils tomorrow. She had met them only briefly, for she had been out walking in the gardens when they arrived home, and was only permitted a quick visit to the nursery. The two younger girls had smiled and looked friendly. The older girl had glowered. She would have her hands full with that one, she could see. Well, she would have to be firm with her, and assert her authority.

Still, she arose in a cheerful mood. The schoolroom, she discovered, had been transformed. The line of formal desks had gone, replaced by a rectangular table. The teacher's desk now sat in front of one window, although there was little enough light there, for it faced north and the January sky was ominously heavy. She set out several books on the table ready for her pupils, then settled at the desk to write a list of subjects upon which to test them — reading, numbers, knowledge of the world, deportment, French... she had determined from Lord Brackenwood that he preferred them to learn French, not Italian.

"It is the old alliance," he had said, eyes brimming with amusement. "The Skeltons are of Scotch origins, you see, and the Scotch have always aligned with the French against the English. Indeed, there is French blood in the family."

"We are all one nation now, Scotland and England," she had said, raising an eyebrow.

"That is what we want you to think," he had said gravely, making her laugh.

So, French it was to be. There were only a few sheets of paper in the desk drawer, and she had found no other supply. Perhaps there were more in the play room. She went through to the odd bedroom, so well appointed, and looked about the room. She could not remember seeing any supplies of paper in the smaller room with the toys, but the desk bore a writing set, so there must be paper in one of the drawers. She sat down and began to search.

The first drawer contained no paper. Instead it was filled with bottle after bottle of medicines, tonics and sleeping draughts and several that she could not identify. She hesitated, not liking to touch the late countess's effects, yet reluctant to leave such things here, so close to the schoolroom. She could lock the door, but if she came in and out to retrieve equipment from the small room, sooner or later the door would be left unlocked.

Then she remembered that one of the big storage boxes in the small room had contained several inner drawers, each with a key. That would be a safe place for all her ladyship's medicine bottles and pill boxes. She cleared out everything in the drawer, and then searched meticulously through every other drawer and cupboard in the room until she was sure that everything had been safely locked away. Only after that did she go back to the desk.

The other drawers were crammed with notebooks. Lots and lots of notebooks, all filled with a single hand, small, rounded, very regular. Every page bore a date, and the lessons set for that day. *'Clark's Guide To England, copy 1 page, 1 hour. Numbers, adding, 1 hour. Breakfast, 1 hour. Exercise, walking round the room, 1 hour. Bible, copy 1 page, New Testament only, 1 hour. Sewing, 1 hour."* Then, at the bottom of each page, a chilling number of additional comments. *'D very rude, no breakfast.' 'D's work very poor, to be repeated instead of exercise.' 'D would not sit still, had to lash her to the desk, and she made so much noise Fl and Fr cried.' 'D rebellious, had to beat her three times before she would work.'*

Annabelle cried out as she read these words. Lashed to the desk? Beaten three times? It was unimaginably cruel.

And yet, between the pages of the books, pressed flat, she found several dried flowers, all of the same delicate type, with tiny petals that had once been pink and leaves with distinctively crinkled edges. She had never seen any plant with such a flower, or such leaves, but she wondered a little at a woman who could treat her own daughter with such cruelty, and yet admire the beauty of a simple flower.

Noises in the schoolroom alerted her to the arrival of her pupils. Her hands trembled as she stowed the notebooks safely away again. Blinking back tears, she went through to the schoolroom to greet them. Only the two younger girls awaited her, gazing in surprise at the new arrangement.

"Good morning, Lady Florence. Good morning, Lady Frederica. How are you both this morning?" They turned moon faces towards her, wordless. "Have you seen how dark the sky is? We shall have snow soon, I fancy."

It was fortunate that they were not at all alike. One was fair, the other dark. One had blue eyes, the other brown. One had long, slender fingers, the other stumpy ones. But they were both small and thin.

They curtsied uncertainly, then said, "Good morning, Miss Winterton," not quite in unison, so their words sounded like an echo. "Shall we write the lessons on the board?" Florence said.

"You do not yet know what today's lessons are to be," Annabelle said.

They looked at each other. "It is Saturday," Florence said, puzzled.

Annabelle smiled. "I daresay your mama had got into a routine, but I do not know you well enough yet." The door opened with a crash. "Ah, Lady Dorothea. Good morning."

Dorothea glowered at her. "I don't want to be here. I don't want to learn, and you can't make me. You're not my mother, so you can't make me."

Looking at her angry face, Annabelle could think only of the poor child being beaten or tied to her desk. All her intentions of firmness and asserting her authority flew away, and she could feel only compassion.

"No, I cannot make you learn," she said gently. "No one can make you learn except yourself. It is your father's wish that you spend your days in the schoolroom, and there is learning to be had here for those who are willing, but I shall never force you." Dorothea's eyes widened. "But consider this — I do not want to be here, either. My father lost all his money and left me destitute. Fortunately, I chose to learn when I was a girl, and so I was able to find a position as a governess. Had I not learnt when learning was to be had, I should be in the work house now. So think about that when you decide whether you want to learn or not."

Dorothea nodded thoughtfully. "Papa has not lost all his money, though, and when I am grown up I shall have a large dowry and make a very good match. So I don't need to be educated."

"And what man of sense will want an ill-educated wife? A gentleman looks to his wife to raise his children properly, and if she herself is ill-mannered and ignorant, with a poorly-controlled temper, he will look elsewhere, no matter how pretty she is or how large her dowry."

Dorothea tossed her head, and stormed off to the window seat. Annabelle ignored her. She would either come round in the end or she would not, but there was no point in trying to force the child to do anything against her will. If beatings had caused no improvement, then she would see what kindness might achieve.

"Now, where shall we sit?" Annabelle said briskly to Florence and Frederica.

After some astonishment at being asked, they decided that they would sit on one side of the table and she on the other, and they began the tasks she had settled on to determine their capabilities. Within half an hour, she had lost any respect for the late Lady Brackenwood's skills as a teacher. The girls could read, although haltingly, as if they were unaccustomed to reciting, and could write very well, if copying or writing their own names. When asked to describe their own garden, they were completely flummoxed.

"But you can see the garden, Miss," Florence said.

"Why would anyone want to write down what it looks like?" Frederica said.

In numbering, they could add and subtract, but had never tackled money. When their breakfast arrived, they displayed their poor table manners. Their knowledge of the world was limited to what they had copied from Clark's Guide to England, although they knew something of Scotland and France. They knew the King's name, and all the royal princes. They could manage a curtsy, although they had no idea how to adjust for the different ranks, or how they would address a duke or a marquess, or, for that matter, the King himself. They had no notion of French or drawing or music.

"Mother said we should start such subjects when we were twelve, if we were very good," Florence said.

"It is never too soon to begin," Annabelle said. "We will start French lessons first thing on Monday morning, and drawing as soon as I have obtained enough paper and found pencils. Or charcoal, perhaps. The pianoforte will need to be tuned before we can begin on that, but I can teach you a few unexceptional songs that you might learn by rote."

"You are not our mother," Dorothea said, from her perch on the window seat. "You have no right to change everything."

"I have every right," Annabelle said. "Your father has charged me with the task of educating you, and I must do that in my own way."

"Look!" Frederica said. "It is snowing!"

"May we go to the window and look?" Florence said.

"Should you like to go outside? There is nothing so magical as snowflakes falling onto one's face, as soft as can be."

"Yes! Yes, *please*!" they both cried.

"Go and fetch your cloaks, then — and gloves, mind!" Dorothea jumped down from the window seat and started after them. "Not you, Lady Dorothea," Annabelle said. "Your sisters have worked hard this morning, and have earned a reward for their endeavours. You have not — yet."

"I can read!" she said fiercely. "I can read better than *they* can, and write better, too, and not just copying."

"Oh, I should like to see that very much," Annabelle said.

Dorothea hesitated, and Annabelle held her breath. But then the girl said, "No, you'd just laugh. Go out without me, I don't care."

And with a huff, she stalked back to her window seat. But later, when Annabelle and the twins had stood on the front steps until they were blue with cold, and come back blowing into their hands, and then tried to think of all the ways they might describe the sensation of soft snowflakes descending silently around them and on them, Dorothea leaned forward intently to listen. Annabelle was optimistic.

~~~~~

Allan liked Sundays. No callers, no tedious business to deal with, a goose or turkey for dinner — he was very fond of turkey — no cards in the evening, and he could sit in his library all day, pretending to read sermons. The only small snag in this otherwise perfect scheme was the two hours spent in the chapel.

The service was held at noon, in deference to his mother's late rising. Mr Penicuik's sermon was a bore, like the man himself, but still, there was pleasure in seeing the chapel full. It was the only occasion guaranteed to find all the family in attendance, even Great-uncle Jeremiah, sober for once, and the rows of servants with their shining faces and smartest uniforms. And his daughters, of course.

His daughters. Dorothea, Florence and Frederica. They frightened him a bit. He never quite knew what to say to them. Dorothea was so sour-faced, without an ounce of charm, and how she was ever to find a husband he could not imagine, even with a good dowry. Would she suddenly blossom, as some girls did? His sister Mary had been a gangly hoyden, and even her own mother had described her as *'well enough, if there be not too many candles'*, but suddenly one day she was grown up and a beauty and all the local bachelors were loitering about the house. Whereas Lizzie had been a pretty child, yet made rather a plain woman. Still, what a match she had made! She had become rather a fine duchess, he thought.

Now, Florence and Frederica had more potential than their sister. They were subdued around their father, but he heard them chattering and laughing sometimes as they went from one room to another. A little liveliness went a long way. A man liked some vivacity in a wife... No, he should not follow that train of thought.

And then, for some unfathomable reason, his eyes strayed to Miss Winterton, sitting demurely reading her psalter. So prim she seemed, and yet he had observed a sparkle in her eyes that spoke of hidden depths. He would like to explore those hidden depths... No, no, no, this would never do! She was a governess, after all, and therefore quite out of his reach — too gently born to be his mistress, and too lowly now to make his wife. Not that he wished her to be either of those things, naturally.

But still, he liked to observe her undetected like this, watching the rise and fall of her chest as she breathed, and the smooth line of her cheek, and her gently rounded form. How he admired her gently rounded form! She would fill his arms admirably, if only... He sighed audibly, and his mother turned to him with a disapproving frown.

Mr Penicuik brought his sermon to a resounding conclusion at that moment, and, upon reflection, Allan was glad of it. Miss Winterton was filling his thoughts all too often, but it would not do. He must put her entirely out of head.

# 6: The Heir (February to April)

*'30th January 18— Sagborough, Yorkshire. My dearest Annabelle, I am so happy to hear what you have to tell me of Charlsby. It sounds very agreeable and I am sure your young pupils will be amiable and eager to learn. You do not say much about Lord Brackenwood, but how sad he must be to have lost his wife when he has such young daughters to raise. How relieved he must be to leave them in your capable hands, for who better to teach them than you? And perhaps he will be so grateful to you that he will come to regard you as something more to him than a governess. Indeed, who could blame him, and if he is as amiable as you say, he cannot fail to do so, for you are so charming and clever and would make a perfect Countess. Your loving sister, Fanny.'*

~~~~~

Annabelle was ready early on Monday morning, sitting in the empty schoolroom awaiting her pupils. At such moments, with nothing else to occupy her thoughts, she could not prevent her loneliness seeping into her mind. All her life, she had been surrounded by her family — her sisters, in particular. Rosamund, always so sensible and grown up. Lucy, the chatterbox. Margaret, the quiet one. Sweet, gentle Fanny, with her romantic ideas. They had always been there. And Mama and Papa and Jeremy, too, but her sisters had filled her life with their hopes and fears and laughter. Now they were all gone, and the pain was almost too much to bear. If only—

The door from the nursery shot open, and Florence and Frederica bounded into the room, then stopped dead.

"A house!" Florence cried.

"May we play with it?" Frederica said, hopping with excitement.

There on the table was the baby house. One of the housemaids had spent a whole day cleaning it, carefully dusting and polishing and replacing every tiny chair in the dining room, and the gleaming copper pans on the miniature kitchen range, and the collection of tiny dolls who inhabited it.

Annabelle pointed to the girls' chairs.

"*Bonjour, mes enfants. Aujourd'hui, nous parlons en français.*" They gazed at her in bewilderment. Behind them, Dorothea crept into the room. "*Asseyez-vous, s'il vous please.*" Again she pointed to the chairs, and the two girls slunk into their seats. "*Très bon. Regardez, voici une maison. C'est une très petite maison. La porte est verte. Il y a—*"

"Miss, I cannot understand you," Florence wailed, tears sparkling on her lashes.

"*Francais,*" Dorothea said. "It's in French, silly."

"*Oui. Merci, Mademoiselle Dorothea. Nous parlons en francais,*" Annabelle said, smiling. "*Répète après moi... nous parlons en francais. Nous parlons en francais.*"

Florence and Frederica exchanged glances, but Dorothea huffed impatiently. "Just listen, you'll pick it up. Say it again, Miss."

"*Nous parlons en francais,*" Annabelle said, very slowly.

*"Nous parl... parlons en francais,"* Dorothea said. She pulled another chair to the table and sat down, turning to her sisters. "Go on, try it."

"Noo parlon fronsay," Florence said.

*"Oui! Très bon, Mademoiselle Florence! Regardez, voici une maison. C'est une très petite maison. La porte est verte. Il y a une fenêtre ici et une autre fenêtre ici. Le toit est rouge et il y a beaucoup de cheminées."*

"Chimney!" Frederica cried, and they all laughed.

*"Oui, mais parlez en français, s'il vous plaît."*

*"Cheminées,"* Dorothea said.

"Oh, it is almost the same," Florence breathed, awed. *"Cheminées. Cheminées."*

*"Une cheminée, deux cheminées, trois cheminées... beaucoup de cheminées."*

*"Beaucoup de cheminées,"* Florence said happily.

~~~~~

### FEBRUARY TO APRIL

Allan could see the change in his daughters as the weeks passed. Not so much in Florence and Frederica, but Dorothea smiled more, and was less inclined to flounce away. But perhaps it was the greater contact that made them more used to his company, and he to theirs. Instead of a strained half hour after chapel on Sundays, they now came regularly to the saloon before dinner, and twice Dorothea had been permitted to eat with the family. All Miss Winterton's idea, and the biggest change was her doing too.

"Your daughters would very much like to spend more time with you, Lord Brackenwood," she had said one day. "They see you so rarely, and seldom in circumstances where they have your undivided attention. May I bring them to you in the library one afternoon?"

"Whatever should we talk about?" he had said. "I have not the least idea what to say to them."

"You could read to them," she said. "Or teach them to play whist."

"Whist? Are they not too young for such games? They are supposed to be learning the globes and French, not becoming dissipated."

"It is possible to play whist while speaking French," she said gravely. "One is not constrained to one activity at a time. That is what we do in the schoolroom — while we sew, we converse in French, or we recite poetry while walking in the garden."

"I should like to help, but I still do not see what I can contribute to this pleasant scheme."

"Lord Brackenwood... I can teach your daughters a great deal, but there is much that they can only learn from you. Their place in society, for instance, your view of the world and your expectations for them. The better they know you, the more comfortable they will be in whatever role you envisage for them."

"They will marry, of course," he said. "My sisters will bring them out and take care of all that."

"Yes, but do you expect them to marry to please you, or may they choose for themselves, within reason, of course?"

"I— Miss Winterton, I cannot imagine discussing such subjects with girls of ten and eight while playing cards."

She laughed. "No, of course not. *'My trick, I believe, and oh, by the way, be sure to marry a man with at least ten thousand a year.'* It is absurd. But the more time you spend together, the better they will get to know you and the better they will understand your mind and the principles which guide you. And then, when they are grown, you will not have to explain such matters to them, for they will know exactly how to go on, with your example before them."

He ran a hand tiredly across his forehead. "My wife would have taken care of all this. She spent all day with them—" He broke off, seeing a strange look cross Miss Winterton's face, and he remembered the numerous times when Eloise had gone out for the day. Sometimes, he had found her in the saloon, composedly reading, telling him airily that she had set the girls their work for the day and the nursery maid would keep an eye on them. "I suppose she was not well," he said, half to himself.

So he agreed to see the girls every day at four, if he had no visitors and had not himself gone out calling. He read to them, from books which Miss Winterton supplied, and some of his own, and then they discussed what they had read. Mostly, he and Miss Winterton carried the discussion between them, but the girls asked intelligent questions and in time grew bold enough to venture their own opinions.

He enjoyed it, that was the surprise. It made him feel like a father for the first time. He had admired his daughters when they were born, he had taken pleasure in watching them grow, he had loved them, but from a distance. Now he knew that Florence and Frederica still sucked their thumbs occasionally, that Dorothea sat straight-backed in her chair, just like her grandmama, and that the twins were so close that they invariably thought alike, and sometimes even finished each other's sentences. Or rather, Frederica finished Florence's sentences, for Florence was very much the leader. No wonder Dorothea was a little cross sometimes, being the eldest and yet somehow excluded from that perfect pairing.

Easter brought his heir, George Skelton, to Charlsby. George was Allan's cousin, a lively young man who was so enthusiastic about life that he made Allan feel a hundred years older than him, instead of a mere ten. George both played and sang, he flirted outrageously with Aunt Anne and Aunt Beth and even managed to keep Great-uncle Jeremiah awake for most of the first evening. And he displayed an obvious admiration for Miss Winterton.

"Where did you find her, cousin?" George said, lounging in the matching wing chair to Allan's in the library the next day. "She would be a tasty armful, do you not agree? And she has roguish eyes. I think she likes me."

Allan very much agreed that the lady would be a tasty armful, but he could hardly say so. "I do not notice the roguish eyes, and nor should you, if you are sensible. Her sister has some connection to the Marfords — the Marquess of Carrbridge's family."

"I know who the Marfords are, dear cousin. I have been on the town for three years now, after all. Not that I aspire to such circles, you understand. Far above my touch, the Marfords. Fearfully grand. They condescend to acknowledge me, because of your friendship with the marquess, but that is all. So you do not want me to chase the governess then... fancy her for yourself, do you?"

And he grinned at Allan so impishly that it was impossible to be cross with him. "Of course not, but you can look much higher for a wife, as a future earl, George. Do you want me to increase your allowance, so that you can make more of a splash in town? You could have the pick of the debutantes. I should not say so, for you have too good an opinion of yourself already, but you have a certain charm that appeals to the ladies."

George laughed good-humouredly. "Cousin, making a splash is not one of my ambitions, and you are far too generous already. Besides, I have no wish to accustom myself to high living, for there is no danger of the title ever coming to me. You are young enough to sire a whole stable full of lusty sons yet. I know, I know, it is too soon to be thought of. But in a year or two you will find yourself a sweet young thing, and then you will cut me out, and I shall be making do on the modest competence Papa left me, and looking for a wife who knows her way about the kitchen. So you see, the comely Miss Winterton would do very well for me."

Allan was too honest to deny the logic of it.

His mother was not about to let him wait a year or two, and seemingly planned to fill the summer months with a parade of sweet young things for him to choose from. A Miss Lorrimer arrived from Chester, no fewer than three Miss Waltons from Lancashire, and Miss Hunt and her friend Miss Barnett from Liverpool, all of them, Lady Brackenwood told him complacently, equipped with large dowries.

When Allan had gently queried the necessity for so many guests invading the house, she had said airily, "Oh, but it will be company for George, you see. Charlsby is very dull for him, when everyone is older than he is. We must entertain him."

Allan agreed that Charlsby was very dull, but George must be well used to it by now, and if he felt the need for entertainment, he was perfectly capable of creating his own. However, there was no point in objecting to anything his mother planned. He had insisted on having Miss Winterton at the dinner table, and now he must pay the price for his wilfulness by submitting to his mother's schemes. So he dutifully paid attention to each young lady in turn, however painful. Miss Barnett had an accent that made Allan wince. Miss

Hunt had not a thought in her head beyond balls and gowns and the money she so obviously enjoyed spending. The Miss Waltons giggled constantly, and went about arm in arm, inseparable. And Miss Lorrimer, whose gown and manners at least proclaimed her to be a lady, was too shy to utter a word in his presence, but blushed and blushed again.

At least he had more sensible company in their chaperons, or rather, their husbands. Mr Lorrimer and Mr Walton were not from the upper echelons of society, but they were easy conversationalists, and Captain Hunt was a sensible man of some intelligence, who made no pretence regarding the suitability of his niece or her friend.

On his first evening at Charlsby, as the gentlemen enjoyed their port in the absence of the ladies, Hunt said, "Lord Brackenwood, I would have you understand that I disapprove of my wife's plan to throw my niece at your head. Bella's a silly girl and I cannot recommend her to any man, least of all a member of the nobility. She will improve, I think, but she is not ready for marriage yet. And as for Daisy Barnett... very pretty, and so forth, but the family! They are accepted into society in Liverpool, but there is some unorthodoxy there, if you take my meaning."

"I do not, unfortunately," Allan said.

"The girl's a bastard," Mr Walton said in his brusque way. "No one speaks of it, because they have enough money to pass muster, but it's well known."

"Yes, she is the natural daughter of a gentleman from Brinshire, who left a great deal of money to her mother and brother," Captain Hunt said. "The elder Miss Barnett disgraced herself, so they hope to do better with the younger."

"Your warning is well-given," Allan said. "However, I am not minded to remarry, so you need not fear that I will be drawn in."

"May I enquire as to the origins of your Miss Winterton?" the Captain said. "Is she connected, perhaps, with the Wintertons of Brinshire?"

"Indeed she is," Allan said. "Her father died recently, leaving the daughters in straitened circumstances. You are acquainted with the family, Captain?"

"No, not at all, except for a son who passed through Liverpool some years ago. A sad case, for the sea took him on his very first voyage. I only met him briefly, but the case was so tragic that the name stuck with me. Jeremy Winterton. Would it distress the lady if I mention the matter to her, do you suppose?"

"I cannot say. She may be glad to meet someone who remembers the boy. Shall we re-join the ladies?"

~~~~~

*'My dear, dear sister, How are you? Is it very miserable being a governess? At least Lord Brackenwood seems to be a kindly man who does not sequester you away in the schoolroom, and does not object when you argue points with him. He sounds charming, quite delightful, but even though you eat dinner with the family and sit with them in the evening, it is not the same as being recognised as a part of normal society, and you cannot go to balls or receive invitations to any evening engagements, and I know how you love to dance, my dear Annabelle. I at least go out a little and move in society and it feels more normal whereas you must stay at Charlsby and never go anywhere ever again. How dreadful it must be. Do write and let me know how you are, truly I mean, for you always sound so cheerful and I am sure you cannot be, situated as you are. Your worried sister, Lucy.'*

~~~~~

Annabelle was glad when the house began to fill with visitors, for it distracted Lady Brackenwood's baleful glare away from her, and also relieved her of the ever persistent attentions of Mr Cross. Mostly he was kept in check by the presence of his employer, but when the earl and the dowager countess were invited to dine with one or other of the neighbouring families, Mr Cross became annoyingly attentive, and no amount of rebuff or coldness deterred him. But the arrival of other, younger and prettier, targets drew him away from Annabelle.

After the gaggle of young ladies with their parents and chaperons came a series of dashing young men. But she was surprised to find that none were of the level in society she might have expected, given Lord Brackenwood's rank. Having seen the circles that Lord Westerlea and Robin moved in, with only a barony, she had supposed an earl might call upon rather grander acquaintances than these. Captain and Mrs Hunt were respectable enough but the others had a certain air about them that made her suspect trade.

The evenings were lively now, with music and dancing and a great deal of laughter. Even the earl smiled occasionally. Annabelle was not, naturally, a part of this, sitting quietly in a corner with her sewing, or playing for the dancers when required, but her lowly status and her mourning both rendered her ineligible to participate. She had left off her blacks now, but the half-mourning colours of grey and lavender were perfectly suitable for a governess.

She liked George Skelton very much. He was sufficiently well-bred to make the effort to have some conversation with her every night, without making her feel that he was merely doing his duty or that he had some nefarious intent. He would plop down on the sofa beside her, stretch out his long legs and fold his arms, and say companionably, "Well, Miss W, and what do you make of it so far? Who will win our eligible earl, do you suppose? For myself, I fancy that Miss Barnett is a touch ahead just now. She has a certain... *je ne sai quoi*, do you not agree?"

She laughed. "She is rather pretty, and such lovely blue eyes. I had a wooden doll once with eyes just that astonishing shade of blue."

"And what happened to her? I do hope you did not lose her, or let the dogs bite off her arms?"

"Nothing so tragic. She was much loved by me, and then by Lucy and Margaret, and eventually by Fanny, who loved her so greatly that all the paint came off her face and her hair fell out."

"Ah, that is the fate that befalls us all," he said in such a mournful tone that she could not help laughing again. "And what of you?" he said, suddenly serious. "What is your fate, Miss Winterton? For you are wasted as a governess, I vow. Shall you throw your cap into the ring against Miss Barnett and the other young ladies, for I do not scruple to tell you that I would not wager against you in such a contest, dowry or no."

She flushed, but answered as composedly as she could. "I have no ambition to be a countess, Mr Skelton, none whatsoever. Indeed, I do not want to be a wife of any sort."

"Bravely spoken," he said. "Even so, who can say when the delights of love may strike?"

"They will not strike me."

"Yet how can you tell, if you have never yet experienced that magical delirium?"

"I did not say I had not experienced it," she said tartly. "Only that I shall not experience it in the future. Forgive me, Mr Skelton, but I must not keep you from the other guests. Miss Barnett, I believe, is all alone at this moment."

He rose and bowed politely, not at all discomfited by her rebuke, and made his way to Miss Barnett's side with his ready smile. She was not to be left to her needlework for long, however, for Captain Hunt sought her out not long after.

He made some general comments, before saying, "Miss Winterton, I hope you will forgive my impertinence, but I have reason to believe that I have a most unusual connection to your family."

"Indeed, sir?"

"You had a brother, I understand, who was lost at sea?"

"Jeremy, yes. He was the youngest of us, so he would have been seventeen now. You know something of him, Captain?"

"I do. In fact, it is my belief that I may have been one of the last people to see him alive."

"Oh!" She clapped her hands in excitement. "You *met* him... in Liverpool, of course. Oh, pray tell me everything!"

"Thank goodness," he said, with a smile. "I was so afraid that my words would distress you. But let me tell you how it came about. I had just been promoted to Captain and was awaiting my ship, so I was at rather a loose end, and making myself useful to the Rear-Admiral. He was a kindly soul, so he liked to have me meet the new midshipmen, those of a genteel nature, and ensure they were prepared for the rigours of their new life. Essentially, I took them off for tea and cakes, chatted to them for an hour or so, and then delivered them to the appropriate vessel in time for dinner. Generally I never heard of them again, but in your brother's case the ship foundered less than a sennight later in a storm in the Irish Sea. I thought of him often — such a pleasant boy, and so enthusiastic for his new life."

"Enthusiastic?" she said, bewildered, trying to reconcile this image with the Jeremy she remembered, terrified and protesting loudly that he would do *anything* rather than go to sea.

"Oh, very! Most are ambivalent, but he was keen as mustard and knew a great deal about it, too. I daresay he had read up about ships, for he knew all the terms, you know. No danger of him mistaking port for starboard. He would have done well, had he lived, despite his small stature."

"Small stature? Captain Hunt, are you sure you have not mixed up my brother with some other boy, because Jeremy was unusually well-grown for his age, everyone said so."

He frowned, thinking, then said, "I believe not. The memory is very clear in my mind, despite the distance in time, because of the loss of the ship so soon after."

"And did he look like me?"

"That is impossible for me to say. His colouring... his hair... that was not unlike yours, but I do not recall the colour of his eyes. Miss Winterton, forgive me but... sometimes fondness makes a child seem more advanced than average, whereas a stranger may see the true situation without the lens of affection."

"It must be so, in this case," she said, subdued.

She said nothing more, merely thanking the captain for the information, but it was unsettling, all the same. Still, there was no point worrying over whether he remembered her brother or not, for Jeremy was drowned and nothing could alter that.

And then all thought of Jeremy flew out of her head, for the door opened and Plessey announced, "Mr Charles Keeling, my lady."

# 7: The Suitor

Allan happened to be standing not far from Miss Winterton when Mr Keeling was announced, and heard her cry of... what? Surprise, certainly, but what else? Not fear... When he moved slightly, the better to see her face, her complexion was ashen but the wide eyes, the lips slightly apart, the admiration in her gaze told their own story. She lowered her eyes, and scrabbled about to recover the needlework which had slid off her knee. Then she bent industriously over her stitchery, but her hands trembled violently. The captain murmured something to her, too low for Allan to hear, but she shook her head, still lowered.

Mr Keeling was a fine fellow indeed, and just the sort of man to draw the eye of any young lady. He dressed well but without flamboyance, his manner as he crossed the room to make his obeisance to his hostess was confident without arrogance, and his bow was all that was proper. His smiling features betokened an amiable nature, and Allan begrudgingly allowed that he might be considered handsome, if one was not irritated by constant smiling.

His mother summoned Allan to meet the new arrival with a crook of one bony finger. He responded with greater willingness than usual, for he had a lively curiosity to know more of a man who could affect Miss Winterton so profoundly, she who was always so composed.

"Allan, may I make known to you Mr Keeling from Brinshire. Mr Keeling, my only surviving son, the Earl of Brackenwood."

They exchanged bows, and again Keeling's was precisely correct. He responded to Allan's polite greetings in a suitably proper manner, neither too deferential nor too friendly.

"Do come and meet the next Earl of Brackenwood," Allan said, for he had no wish to loiter by his mother's side any longer than necessary. "I have no sons, but my cousin makes an admirable heir. George, may I present Mr Keeling from Brinshire. My cousin, Mr George Skelton."

They were much of an age, the two of them. Keeling was the taller, perhaps, but George had broader shoulders, and it was clear that they liked each other on sight. And George, with his open nature, had within moments asked the question that filled Allan's thoughts, too.

"You are from Brinshire? Why then you must know Miss Winterton! Where is she? Ah, over there, lurking in the shadows. She is governess to my cousin's daughters, so she never puts herself forward, but she is quite charming. You must know her, I feel certain."

Keeling started violently at the name, then looked where George indicated. He was, if anything, as pale as she was, and just as startled.

"Miss Winterton? I do know the Miss Wintertons, it is true. But... a *governess!* I had no idea of *that*. Then the rumours are true... the father has left them penniless. But I assumed... her sister is married, so..."

"With four unmarried sisters to consider, the brother-in-law could hardly support them all," Allan said.

"I suppose not. He played his part in giving Annabelle— Miss Winterton two seasons in London, and he would have done the same for the others, had they wished it. But still... a governess."

He had not taken his eyes off her, but now she happened to look up and in his direction. Hastily, he turned away, and Allan imputed that to the best of motives, that he was nervous and unprepared to meet her just yet, and not that he intended to ignore her. And indeed, in a few minutes more, he excused himself and made his way to her side, where she sat alone, Captain Hunt having moved away.

Even from the other side of the room, Allan could see the awkwardness of the encounter, she with her cheeks aflame, her eyes demurely lowered, and he with his ready smile slipping somewhat. He stayed only a few minutes, making his way back to Allan and George with a request to meet the other guests, and George whisked him away to the aunts. Allan was left to watch Miss Winterton try to recover her composure.

After a little while, he crept round the room to where she sat, and settled himself on the sofa beside her.

"Do you wish me to get rid of him?" he said conversationally. "One word in his ear, and he would be gone and trouble you no more."

She looked up at him, startled, and he thought she looked like a deer, wide-eyed and innocent, and a little frightened. He was swept with the urge to protect her from the hurts of the world. She had suffered so much already, and he wished with all his heart that it was within his power to soothe her wounds and make her truly happy.

She did not pretend to misunderstand him.

"Oh... you are so kind!" she whispered. "But no. He is here as a guest of Lady Brackenwood, and it would be discourteous to send him away. It was a shock to see him again, I confess, but now that the first meeting is past, we shall be easy again. Besides, I shall see very little of him, just at dinner and no one will notice if I slip away afterwards."

"I shall notice," he said, before he could stop himself. "You and I... we have an affinity, Miss Winterton. We are the only two still in mourning. My mother has little compassion for my feelings with this parade of eligible young ladies."

"Eligible?" she said, with a half smile. "Rich, perhaps, but is any one of them qualified to be a helpmeet for an earl? It is not easy to imagine."

"Your words are apt," he said. "But what qualities should such a person have, do you suppose?"

"Steadiness of character," she said at once. "That is the most important — the ability to take everything as it comes. A well-rounded education. The ability to talk to anyone of any level, from the King down to the scullery maid. And she must not be timid. So many young women are so modest and retiring, one wonders how they will ever manage to run a household or raise their children, still less stand up to—"

"Yes?" he said, amused, for he guessed what she had been about to say. "Stand up to their husbands, perhaps?"

"No," she confessed, a flush covering her cheeks. "I was going to mention mothers-in-law, but that is impolite. Forgive me."

He gave a bark of laughter. "My mother is intimidating, it is true. Any woman who can stand up to her will be a creature worthy of my unparalleled admiration. Naturally, I should offer for her immediately."

She laughed at the absurdity of it.

It was just as well that Plessey announced dinner just then, for Allan began to feel the impropriety of showing too much attention towards the governess, especially on the subject of marriage.

He led his mother through to the dining room, and the rest followed in rank order. He settled his mother, then looked around for a lady to invite to sit on his other side. He was forestalled. George had Miss Winterton on his arm, and was towing her, despite her resistance, directly towards him. He sat her down beside Allan, and then waved Captain Hunt into the seat beyond her.

"Very likely the lower end will get rowdy tonight," he said. "Miss Winterton is much better off out of it." Then he skipped away to find a seat lower down.

Allan understood it. George was protecting Miss Winterton from any contact with the man whose presence so distressed her. It would have been an effective scheme, if it had not been for his mother. Eyes narrowed, she glared at Miss Winterton. When Great-uncle Jeremiah made to sit beside the dowager, she said sharply, "Not you, you old fool. Mr Keeling? Mr Keeling! Do come and sit beside me."

And Allan was helpless to prevent the two from sitting almost opposite each other. It was almost as if his mother was intentionally trying to embarrass them. Allan determined, therefore, to devote himself so completely to the comfort and entertainment of Miss Winterton, that she might forget entirely the face opposite her. He had never exerted himself so much as he did that evening, although it hardly felt like exertion. She was such easy company, once the initial embarrassment was got over, that it was not the least trouble in the world to talk to her, and he was quite astonished when the ladies rose to leave.

"So soon?" he murmured, quite bemused. From the other end of the table, George grinned at him.

As the gentlemen moved into a closer group and resumed their seats after the ladies had left, Allan had Mr Keeling at his left hand.

"Your efforts to distract Miss Winterton are greatly appreciated, Lord Brackenwood. I fear my presence makes her uncomfortable, and I would not for the world have her distressed. At the risk of offending Lady Brackenwood, I fear I must remove myself from the house at the earliest opportunity."

"Your feelings do you credit, sir," Allan said. "I am sure my mother will understand."

"You must believe me when I say that nothing would have induced me to accept Lady Brackenwood's kind invitation had I known that Miss Winterton was in the house. It is the greatest mystery to me why her ladyship invited me, for I was not previously in her society, and my acquaintance with her friends in Brinshire is very slight. If my nature were of a suspicious bent, then— But no, it is impossible. Her ladyship could not have known the distress her generosity would cause to Miss Winterton and myself."

Allan had not previously considered this aspect of the matter. Had his mother known of Mr Keeling's existence? As he had pointed out, she had friends in Brinshire and if the nature of their previous acquaintance had been such as to cause gossip... And what precisely was the nature of their acquaintance? He was desperate to know, yet propriety forbade him from asking directly. Fortunately, Mr Keeling revealed it himself.

"You must be wondering what has occurred between Miss Winterton and me." Allan demurred politely, but Keeling went on, "It is no secret that I would have married her, if I had had a free choice. My father had no objection to the match, the lady herself was tolerably encouraging, but there was the question of money. I had no expectation then of more than the twelve hundred pounds a year that was my father's, and so I approached Mr Winterton to enquire about a dowry. He refused even to discuss the matter, and on the third attempt, he told me not to come near his daughter again. It was a grievous blow, but I could not disobey such a clear instruction."

"No, indeed you could not," Allan said, yet wondering why twelve hundred pounds a year was not sufficient to keep a family in tolerable comfort, with care. "And yet his reasons are now clear — he did not have the money to pay a dowry."

"So it appears. I wish he might have said so plainly. Honesty is the greatest virtue in such cases. I went away believing myself rejected because of some defect in my character. You cannot imagine how tormented I have been as a consequence. If I had known it was a mere question of money, I should have been a great deal easier. Ah, money! How it dominates our lives, does not it?"

Allan raised an eyebrow. "Does it?"

Keeling smiled good-humouredly. "Not for your lordship, I daresay. Those who have plenty think nothing of it, but those of us less well endowed must consider every expense, and count every penny with care, and marry prudently or not at all. It is very difficult." He sighed.

"We must all of us live within our means, Mr Keeling," Allan said, "and choose a wife with a due regard for our respective stations in life. We are both constrained to marry prudently, where we marry at all."

"It is the duty of every man to marry, if he can," Keeling said. "I certainly mean to do so, and as soon as I find another such as Miss Winterton with fifty thousand or so, I shall pursue her relentlessly, you may be sure." He laughed. "This is excellent port, Lord Brackenwood. You must give me the name of your vintner, for I declare I can get nothing half so good."

"I take no credit for it, since it was probably laid down by my father," Allan murmured.

"Ah, yes. When I have my own cellar, I shall begin to lay down the best wines for the future."

~~~~~

*'Friday. My dearest Annabelle, I cannot believe that Charles Keeling has the effrontery to show his face again, after the way he treated you. Why is he even there? I never heard that he was acquainted with anyone in Cheshire, still less an earl. If he had a shred of decency he would take himself away at once and not plague you any more. It is bad enough to raise your hopes and then dash them in the most painful way, without turning up here, there and everywhere, just as if nothing had ever happened. May he rot in the fires of Hell, the horrid, deceitful man. Yours in anger, Lucy.'*

~~~~~

Annabelle had hoped to creep away after dinner, but she was called upon to play a duet with Miss Lorrimer, and then to turn the pages for the youngest Miss Walton, and then, as the gentlemen returned and drew the young ladies' attention, to play herself while the rest of the company enjoyed cards or flirting or both. But her solitude in the corner helped to compose her mind, and her position hidden behind the instrument kept her from notice.

Charles here! It was the last thing she had expected, here in Cheshire, where the family lived so quietly as a rule. She had never heard that Charles had any acquaintances in the county. But she guessed how it was. She had herself told Lady Brackenwood that there had been a great love in her life, and her ladyship had gone to the trouble of tracking him down and inviting him to Charlsby. But for what purpose? Not merely to discomfit Annabelle, surely, for the countess could not be so vindictive. More likely she hoped to distract Annabelle from any thought of the earl.

But that had not worked! He was too gentlemanly not to notice her distress, and had made it his business to distract her at dinner, and to great effect. She had always had a good opinion of him, but his unparalleled kindness tonight had rendered him the best of men in her eyes. His behaviour must even bear comparison with Charles...

Here her heart misgave her. Charles had not, in fact, behaved as he should. His attentions to her in the past had been so marked as to attract an uncomfortable degree of comment, and then that night at Willowbye when he had kissed her and whispered love into her ears... And yet nothing had come of it. Without any explanation, his attentions had diminished and finally vanished altogether, leaving her broken-hearted and, which was perhaps worse, exposed to the ridicule of the world. And even now, she wondered if one word from him would bring her back to loving him just as desperately.

Eventually, when it was clear there would be no dancing and she would not, therefore, be needed, she crept out of the saloon and made her way to the stairs. She was half way up when a voice called up.

"Annabelle!"

She stopped and turned, although she knew his voice. No other could make her tremble so, and set her heart fluttering. "Mr Keeling."

He leapt up the stairs two at a time, and placed himself in front of her on the half-landing, so that she could not move up or down without difficulty. "We have had no opportunity to talk," he said, his face alight with warmth. "When we spoke before, I was so shocked to find you here and in such a position, that I scarce know what I said. Will you not come back to the saloon and talk with me? May I not make such a claim on you, as an old friend? I should very much like to hear all your news, and how your sisters go on, which I did not think to ask about before. As soon as I can, I shall quit this place and leave you in peace, but for this one night, it would give me the greatest pleasure to sit and chat, as we used to."

It was on the tip of her tongue to point out that he could have had the pleasure of sitting and chatting at any time these last three years, had he wished to. It was not as if they had never met, after all. They moved in much the same society, although he lived far enough distant from her that their meetings were not frequent. But his request was so reasonable, and his manner so eager and yet respectful that she could not refuse him. Nothing could possibly come of it, she knew that, but where was the harm in talking?

So she went back into the saloon with him, and brought out her needlework again, so that she need not look at him too often. They talked at first of her family, and the dramatic change in circumstance that had befallen the four youngest sisters.

"It surprises me that your brother-in-law takes no better care of you than this," he said. "You were not born to be a governess, Annabelle."

"Who is?" she said lightly. "Besides, we have no claim on the Daltons, and with four of us—"

"Nonsense! With the twenty thousand your sister brought him, and the expectation of six thousand a year from his father, he could very well support all four of you." Annabelle raised her eyebrows at this frank discussion of her family's finances, but Charles seemed not to notice for he went on, "I am sure he is a good sort of man, but it is shabby, all the same. *I* should not act so, in his position."

"You must not speak so ill of him. He offered to house us but we had no wish to be a burden to him, and we have all found congenial employment."

"I beg your pardon," he said at once. "I did not mean to disparage him, but it was such a shock to see you thus reduced in circumstances. I allowed my anger to overwhelm me. Forgive me."

As they talked, it was almost as if they had never separated, and he had never given her three years of unhappiness, and the prospect of many more. The friendship between them was almost as strong as it had once been — almost, but not quite. For she could not forget — she would *never* forget — the pain he had caused her. The days when she had waited in vain for him to call, the balls where he had not come near her until she had every dance already spoken for, the months of agonised wondering and then, eventually, the dreadful acceptance of the truth. Nothing could wipe out the evil memories, or the tears she had poured into her pillow each night.

"Tell me about your sisters," he said.

"Lucy is a chaperon to the step-daughters of an aunt-in-law, Margaret is companion to two elderly aunts and Fanny is working as a seamstress for Lady Harriet Hay in the wilds of Yorkshire. There is still snow on the high moors, Fanny says."

"A seamstress! Great heavens! Lady Harriet Hay... hmm. *That* is a good connection. Who is she the daughter of? Duke? Marquess? Earl?"

"The Marquess of Carrbridge."

"Oh, excellent! Is he married? Or has a son of marriageable age? That would be a splendid match, if she could manage it."

"Fanny is not hanging out for a match, splendid or otherwise," Annabelle said acidly.

But he laughed, not at all put out. "Of course not, but if it should happen, just think how glorious it would be, and a marquess could take care of any number of unmarried sisters, you know. Why, his income must be fifteen or twenty thousand." He paused, a beatific expression on his face at the prospect. He sighed. "Just imagine it! It makes my father's twelve hundred quite paltry by comparison, although..." He lowered his voice, but when he spoke there was a tremor of excitement. "It may be that he will soon have a great deal more. Do you remember me speaking of my Uncle Albert? His entire fortune now rests with a very sickly boy of five, and if— Well, let us not even think of the dreadful possibility."

But he smirked as he spoke, and lounged against the padding of the seat, his arms stretched out along the back.

Annabelle bent her head to her needlework, shocked, and wondered just when he had become so obsessed with money. Had he always been so, and she had never noticed it before? But her regret at his loss was curtailed as she saw this new aspect of his character.

# 8: *An Arrival*

Allan watched with growing anger as Keeling conversed with Miss Winterton. He had said he would leave, he had expressed with great feeling his wish not to distress her, yet there he was, engaging her in conversation as if there were nothing between them. It was not kind in him, not in the least kind! Her expression, normally so composed, registered her discomfort, her cheeks flushed, eyes averted. Yet she was too polite to deter him.

The next day, Allan expected the fellow to act decently and take himself away from Charlsby, but he was disappointed. And as each subsequent day arrived, it became clear that, whatever Mr Keeling had said, he had no intention of leaving.

When an opportunity arose, he spoke to his secretary. "Do you have acquaintances in Brinshire, Cross?"

"A few, my lord."

"See what you can find out about this Keeling fellow, will you? I know nothing about him, and it seems to me that I should know something of my own guests."

"I would be delighted, my lord." Cross grinned at him conspiratorially. Perhaps he guessed Allan's motive for asking, but he was too annoyed to care.

Three days later, Allan was reading to Dorothea, Florence and Frederica in the library, when the nursery maid came to take the girls away to change for their riding lesson.

Allan said, "Miss Winterton, please stay for a moment. We will leave the door open, and Portman is directly outside, so do not be concerned. I wish you to know that I am delighted with my daughters' progress. They have come on wonderfully under your tutelage."

"Why, I thank you for the compliment, but most of the improvement comes from their own efforts. I have not forced them to learn, indeed, I do not know how I could do so. And perhaps you are seeing more in them because you are spending more time with them than before."

"That is true, and it has given me greater pleasure than I had anticipated. That too is of your doing, so I am afraid you must take some of the credit, you know. It cannot be avoided."

She laughed and agreed to it.

"There is one other matter... please, will you sit down?" She sat, for she could not refuse, but he could see the discomfort on her face. She must guess the subject of his discourse. "You may consider my words unwarranted interference, and perhaps they are, but they are driven by a very sincere wish for your happiness, now and in the future. I have no right to advise you, but you have no father or brother to watch over you, and so I shamelessly take that role upon myself. It is unpardonable, but I trust you will impute it to the best of motives and not think too ill of me."

She hung her head, but said in a low voice, "You wish to put me on my guard against Mr Keeling, I presume."

"It is of that gentleman I wish to speak, yes. He has made no secret of his former attachment to you, and it is proper that he should inform me of such matters, as your employer. But he has also made known to my cousin George some details which gave him some concern. George has the happy knack of inducing confidences, and so it has proved with Mr Keeling. George related the whole to me, and left it to me to decide whether to convey this information to you. I thought it a matter which ought to be laid before you, but if you do not wish it, or if you are on terms of such intimacy with Mr Keeling that there are no secrets between you, then—"

Her head shot up. "I am not on such terms," she said proudly, eyes flashing, and for a moment his breath caught in his throat. How beautiful she was when she was provoked! And why had he never noticed it before? But then she was hard to provoke, the so-composed Miss Winterton. "If you have aught to tell me of Mr Keeling, good or bad, I would hear it, Lord Brackenwood. I am objective enough, I hope, to admit that he is not without fault. I would know all there is to be known of him."

"Very well then. He spoke to George of the time three years ago when he was first attached to you, and wished that attachment to become— No, let me not prevaricate. He wished to marry you, but he felt he could not afford to do so without a substantial dowry. He knew that your older sister had had twenty thousand pounds, and so he felt justified in asking your father for the sum of ten thousand pounds."

"Papa had not ten *pounds* for any of us at that time, let alone ten thousand," Miss Winterton said, her eyes widening in shock.

"Indeed, although he seems not to have confessed as much. So Keeling, undeterred, went again and this time asked for five thousand. And yet again, this time asking only two thousand, and was most aggrieved to be refused. Your father seems to have tired of him by this time, for he told him not to come near you again."

"Well, he obliged him in *that!*" she cried. "At least the question is now answered as to why he never offered for me. How mortifying that all his professed love for me was not sufficient inducement. But now he knows that Papa had not a penny piece left after Rosamund's dowry was paid, and he mortgaged the house to find so much. So why—?"

"Indeed," Allan said softly. "Why does he pay court to you even now? For I cannot describe his attentions in any other way. He spends every evening by your side. Although I have to tell you that during the day, when you are busy in the schoolroom, he is just as attentive to Miss Lorrimer and her twenty thousand pounds."

"So I have heard," she said, her face lighting up with a sudden smile. "I have never been ashamed to listen to the servants' gossip, Lord Brackenwood, for it is astonishing how much may be learnt thus. I know all about Miss Lorrimer, and I do not think he will succeed there. Her parents are not at all encouraging. But I cannot understand why he pays any attention to me. Given our previous situation, he must surely see the danger of raising expectations in my breast that he might be called upon, as a gentleman, to honour."

Allan was silent for a long time, wondering just how to express the fears that George had laid before him. But Miss Winterton was no fool, and she reached the obvious conclusion before he could get his thoughts in order.

"Oh!" she cried, leaping to her feet, so that he was obliged to stand too. "He would *not* honour them! He sees me penniless and friendless, reduced to the position of governess, and with an attachment that he might easily rekindle, is that it? This is what you wished to warn me of?"

"That is my fear, yes, and George's too, although if it is of any comfort to you, I believe from my own observation that his regard for you is genuine. His heart would be yours, even were you his mistress."

"It is *not* any comfort," she said, her face dark with anger. "Lord Brackenwood, I cannot thank you enough for your kindness in bringing this to my notice. It need not be said, I trust, that he should never succeed in such a dishonourable objective."

"No one who knows you could believe it possible," he said with a bow. "My only desire in relating these facts is to set you on your guard against him and perhaps spare you some of the unhappiness you must feel when he is lost to you again. I myself know the misery of a love that can never end in the perfect felicity of a marriage of equals, so if I can protect you from some small part of that grief, I must do so."

"You are too kind," she said, and with a very few more words, she quit the room.

This exchange both relieved the worst of his anxieties for her wellbeing, and also unsettled him in some unfathomable way. She was, as ever, sensible and worldly. He had feared tears or hysterics, or, perhaps worse, complete disbelief, but she had accepted it all calmly. And yet... what was the matter with him? He was almost light-headed, and that was something more than mere concern for an employee.

But of course she was far more to him than an employee. Right from the start he had seen her as a friend, someone he could talk to as he could never talk to his mother, his aunts or uncle, Mr Cross or Mr Penicuik. Or to Eloise. He and his wife had lived in the same house and eaten at the same table and passed long evenings together for years, and he would never have called her a friend. Now, her sister, Marisa — there was someone who could, perhaps, have become a friend if...

No, he would not start down the path of *'if only'* again. The past was dead and gone, and must be forgotten. Just as Miss Winterton must forget Mr Keeling, so Allan must forget Marisa, for she was quite beyond his reach now. He must live in the present, and enjoy the new friend that chance had brought him. Miss Winterton. Annabelle. He rolled the name around in his mind, savouring the secretive pleasure of it.

There had been other secret pleasures, too. His bedroom lay beneath hers, so sometimes he heard the floorboards creak above him as she moved about, and he imagined her dressing for the day, or sitting at her writing desk penning one of her endless stream of letters to her sisters. From his library, he often heard her taking his daughters out for a walk around the estate, and sometimes, if he observed the group pass by his window, he would feel the urge for some exercise himself, and would hastily don his greatcoat and stride after them. Then he would come upon them in the woods, or the lane that bordered the deer park, and common politeness forced him to accompany them for a spell.

Dorothea, already leaving childhood behind, stayed with the two adults as they walked, while the twins raced hither and thither, bringing leaves and berries and twigs to Miss Winterton for identification. The berries intrigued them the most. "Are these edible?" they would say, and Miss Winterton would answer gravely, "Unless Portman serves them to you in a dish with sauce, they are not edible." Mushrooms and toadstools she would not allow them to touch at all. "Some varieties are so poisonous that even the juice on your fingers might be sufficient to poison you beyond any hope of recovery."

"That type growing on the trunk of the tree is very tasty," Allan murmured to her one day. "Chicken of the woods, the locals call it. I am very fond of it."

"I like it too, but if it is growing on yew, it is poisonous," she said. "It is better for children not to risk it. With their smaller, more fragile bodies, they are less well able to tolerate even mild forms of poison. Let those who know every variety intimately decide what to pick and what to leave alone. One cannot be too careful, in my opinion."

He could not fault her for her caution.

That afternoon his books held little charm for him. Although he sat in his massive wing chair before the fire, book open on his knee and Madeira to hand, he was not reading. His thoughts were all on a certain young lady, in love with a worthless young man. One day soon, Keeling would leave Charlsby without making her the respectable offer of marriage she deserved, and she would suffer greatly. Allan could only hope his words today would help to mitigate her suffering to some small degree, when that time came. Poor Miss Winterton! One could not help who one fell in love with, and sometimes love caused nothing but pain.

Late in the afternoon, when he was beginning to think about his dinner — it was the day for beef, of which he was very fond — a carriage was heard on the drive, and then the doorbell jangled distantly. It was an odd time for callers, but perhaps it was one of the many visitors who had been out for the afternoon and was now returning. Or perhaps it was Dr Wilcox attending his mother. He often came at odd hours.

Some minutes later, Plessey entered. "A lady to see you, my lord." He proffered a card on a silver salver.

Allan took the card and read it without much interest, then jumped to his feet with a yelp of astonishment. "Please show her in at once, Plessey. And send Mrs Hale to me. She will need to prepare a room."

He bowed and withdrew, returning moments later. "Mrs Jacob Pargeter, my lord."

She bounced in, as full of life as ever. She was a little plumper than he remembered, and considerably better dressed, but the sparkling eyes and wide smile were just as he recalled.

"Marisa," he said, bowing over her hand. "What a delightful surprise, and so unexpected. I hope there is nothing wrong to bring you here?"

"Nothing in the world. This visit is driven only by a wish to see my brother-in-law after all this time. We have both lost a spouse in the last year, and I a sister also. We have so much in common that I have thought of you a great deal lately. Who better to lighten your sorrow than one who also suffers it?"

"I am glad to hear there is no darker cause behind your arrival. Sister, you are very welcome."

"Thank you! But Allan, how are you? You look thinner than I remembered. Whereas I, you see, am very much wider. That is what having children will do for a woman. Or perhaps it is my fondness for cake, who can say?"

"What an excellent idea," he said. "Plessey, send in some cake, and tea. Or would you prefer coffee, Marisa?"

"I'll have what you are having... Madeira is it? But cake would be lovely. Lord, Allan, how many years is it?" She plopped herself down in the wing chair opposite his, and began to untie the ribbons of her bonnet.

"Twelve," he said promptly. "Much has happened since then. I was so very sorry to hear about Mr Pargeter, Marisa. He was not a young man, but still it must have been a dreadful shock for you."

"It was a shock, yes. He had not been well — there were some irregularities in the beating of his heart. Even so, his physician was pleased with him and felt he could live for many more years yet, but it was not to be. Still, he left me very well provided for, and now that I am out of mourning, it seemed like the perfect opportunity to travel about a bit and decide where I want to settle in my widowhood."

"What about your children? You had two sons and two daughters, unless my memory is faulty."

"You are quite right, and I have left them in Devonshire, at least for the moment. Jacob's son from his first marriage is there, and he is lately married to a very good sort of girl who quite dotes on them. They are best left where they are for now, to grow up amongst their Pargeter relations. When the girls are older, I may take more notice of them, but they are too young to be interesting. Whereas yours are just reaching the age when they need a mother. How they must miss Eloise! I should dearly love to see them, and perhaps I may be able to help them with their lessons, you know, for I daresay they are greatly idle without their mother's watchful eye."

"They have a governess now, and are not idle at all," he said, with a smile.

"A governess, eh," she said, eyeing him thoughtfully. Then she dimpled and said, "A pretty young thing, I make no doubt, and *so* very grateful to you for giving her a place, thanking you prettily with innocent eyes. You are too wily to be taken in by such schemes, I am sure, Allan."

He laughed at this image of Miss Winterton, and said, "And she is too much a lady for such stratagems. She has no ambition to become a countess, I assure you."

She looked disbelieving, but Plessey came in just then, followed by the footman carrying the tea things, and Mrs Hale, the housekeeper.

"Ah, Mrs Hale, pray prepare a room for Mrs Pargeter, if you please."

"Beg pardon, my lord, but, with so many visitors in the house, all the guest rooms are taken. The only room not used is her ladyship's room."

"Oh, do not concern yourself, Allan," Marisa said. "I am sure I can find an inn—"

"Nonsense," he said. "Naturally you will stay here, but shall you mind being in Eloise's room? It has not been altered at all since her death, and I daresay her gowns are still hanging in the wardrobe. But if you find the prospect too morbid, then you must take my room, and I shall sleep in one of the attic rooms."

"I would not countenance such a plan," she said, with her wide smile. "I have never been of a morbid nature, Allan. My sister's room will suit me very well, just as it is. There is a rightness to it, do you not agree? Yes, I shall very much enjoy sleeping in Eloise's bed."

# 9: Friends (May)

*'Dear Annabelle. Thank you for your letters. I am quite well. Aunt Letty is a little better. Aunt Pru is quite well. Yesterday I walked to church by myself. Aunt Letty's son is to visit. I hope you are well. Margaret.'*

~~~~~

### MAY

Lady Brackenwood wished to invite a new batch of hopeful candidates from which her son might choose a new wife, and so the earliest visitors began to depart. The Miss Waltons went back to Lancashire, Miss Hunt and Miss Barnett returned to Liverpool and Miss Lorrimer went home to Chester. Even George Skelton had gone off to London to enliven the capital and enjoy the delights of the season.

A day later, Mr Keeling also departed, and Annabelle could guess his destination. Milly confirmed that he had enquired about the best inns and hotels in Chester before he left.

"He will not have any better luck there than he did here," Annabelle said, not sure whether to be amused at his persistence, or offended by the thick skin which enabled him not to acknowledge the obvious disapproval emanating from Miss Lorrimer's parents.

"Betty said Miss Lorrimer wants to see him at a ball," Milly said. Betty was the chambermaid, and an even bigger gossip than Milly. "She wants to waltz with him, and then she will decide whether to encourage him or not."

"If she agrees to waltz with him, he will take that as very strong encouragement," Annabelle said. "The whole world would be in daily anticipation of an announcement. Her mama will surely not let her dance the waltz in public with a man she is neither married to nor betrothed to."

"Ooh, is it so very scandalous, the waltz?" Milly said. "I've seen it done once or twice — when Timothy the groom was married last year, there was some waltzing at the wedding feast, and I never saw so many couples clutching each other tight and twirling round till they fell over. That was wild, to be sure. But I thought the quality would be... well, more genteel, like."

"It is... very intimate, compared to a cotillion or a country dance," Annabelle said. "I have never attempted it myself, although I know the steps. It is a very elegant dance, and I love to watch it being performed. My sister and her husband are a pleasure to watch. But one must know a gentleman very well, I should think, before one would stand up with him for the waltz. Or so it is in Brinshire. Perhaps Chester is more open-minded, who knows? Waltz or no, I wish her joy of Mr Keeling, if he has been so fortunate as to win her regard."

"There are those who thought his tastes ran a different way," Milly said archly.

Annabelle smiled sorrowfully, but did not pretend to misunderstand. "You are a romantic, Milly, if you imagine that he could ever have married a lowly governess. A young man of modest fortune must make very sure that his tastes lie with rich young ladies."

"That's a sad view of things, Miss."

"Yet it is the way of the world, Milly."

Annabelle was glad he was gone. Not merely relieved, but happy to be rid of him. He had not, in the end, made any improper suggestion to her, but perhaps it would have come to that, if she had not already been aware of the possibility.

He had come upon her once in the schoolroom when she was alone, busy at the desk writing her notes for the day, and preparing for the next day's lessons.

"Miss Winterton? I am come to view you in your domain — may I come in?"

She jumped to her feet. "Of course, Mr Keeling, but as you see, lessons are over for the day. Lady Dorothea, Lady Florence and Lady Frederica have gone for their riding lesson." She began tidying away her papers and books.

"Ah. But you will show me around, I am sure."

"Forgive me, but some other time, when my pupils are here, perhaps."

"You were not always so… inhospitable," he said, but softening the words with his easy smile.

Oh yes, she had been very hospitable once… when she had believed he had marriage in mind. Now, she would not dream of allowing him to kiss her.

"I was not always a governess," she said acidly. "That is my station now, however, and even a lowly employee may still have a reputation to maintain, Mr Keeling. We are quite alone here, for even the nursery next door is empty. It is not proper."

She straightened her pile of papers, and slid them into the desk drawer, then turned for the door. With several quick steps, he placed himself in front of her.

"Annabelle! It cuts me to the quick to be treated with such distance, such distrust, such... *disdain*. We were the best of friends once... can we not be so again? Do not go! Stay and talk to me, I beg you!"

There was such sincerity in his manner that she was almost convinced. But not quite.

"Mr Keeling—"

"Charles, please! Do not call me Mr Keeling in that cold way."

"Mr Keeling," she said firmly, "friendship is founded on respect, and without that there can be nothing."

"But I do respect you! Of course I do!"

"If that were true, sir, you would not be here now, trying to persuade me to linger alone in this room with you."

For a moment a flash of irritation crossed his face, but he schooled his expression and continued more quietly, "I beg your pardon if I have misunderstood you. You do not scruple to be alone in the library with Lord Brackenwood, so I imagined you might offer the same courtesy to an old friend."

"My employer has a need to discuss his daughters' progress in privacy. Besides—" She stopped, tired of trying to explain it to a man who ought to see the distinction, but clearly could not. The earl had never given her a moment's unease, and had always left the door open, whereas she had no confidence that Charles would behave in a gentlemanly fashion towards her. Even if he had made an incorrect assumption, he should have withdrawn the instant she had expressed her disquiet, and the fact that he had not told her everything she needed to know about him.

She stepped around him and he made no move to prevent her leaving the room. She went directly to her own apartment, hurled herself onto the bed and wept for an hour.

~~~~~

Allan watched Keeling's modest carriage rolling down the drive. Annabelle was well rid of him, although undoubtedly she did not see things that way, not yet. His heart ached for her. One day she would be heart-free again and would think no more of this man who was so unworthy of her, of that he was utterly confident.

He could speak with some authority on the matter, for had he not himself suffered the grief of a love that could never be? And yet now he was free of it, and the keys to release him had been given to him by the lady herself. Twelve years ago he had fallen deeply in love with a young lady who was everything he admired — pretty, well-rounded, engaging and with a lively wit. And then he had obediently married her older sister, whose great virtue was her dowry. For twelve long years he had chafed at his lifeless and loveless marriage, remembering the prettier, livelier sister.

Until Marisa herself had arrived on his doorstep. Meeting her again and comparing the older Marisa with the younger version lodged indelibly in his memory was like being doused in cold water. Her prettiness had lost its bloom, the well-rounded form verged on fat and her wit... There was a coarseness to her language sometimes that he could not like. On her first evening, he had asked politely if her room was to her satisfaction, and she had laughed throatily, and tapped him playfully on the arm with her fan.

"It is very much to my satisfaction, and since it was your wife's room and adjoins yours, I must hope that you do not walk in your sleep or else it might be to *your* satisfaction, also."

He was too shocked to answer her. That night when he retired, he made certain that the connecting door was still locked before he went to bed.

Within three days, her shameless behaviour and the irritating way she rested her hand on his arm in a proprietorial manner whenever she spoke to him had served to make him question what he had ever thought attractive about her. And as the days drifted past, he found himself comparing Marisa more and more with the one person in the house whose behaviour had never given him the smallest concern, who was unfailingly a lady.

Annabelle.

Yet she had never looked at him. Her affection was all for the undeserving Keeling, who had once again raised her expectations and dashed them, leaving her bereft by his departure.

Perhaps he could distract her from her sorrow for once. One afternoon, he bounded up the stairs two at a time, then up again to the nursery floor. He knocked tentatively on the schoolroom door.

"*Entrez!*"

He went in, and then laughed out loud at the sight before him. "The old baby house! I have not seen that for years."

"*En français s'il vous plaît, Papa,*" Dorothea said primly.

"*Mais oui, bien sûr, madame... um, Dame Dorothea?* What am I to call them?" he said helplessly to Miss Winterton. "'*Lady*' does not translate comfortably."

Miss Winterton smiled but said nothing, nodding her head towards Dorothea.

*"En Angleterre, je suis Lady Dorothea, mais en français, je suis Mademoiselle Dorothea."*

*"Eh bien. Pouvez-vous me montrer la petite maison, mesdemoiselles?"*

So they showed him the house and all its inhabitants, a ducal family, the twins insisted, and their tiny beds and chairs and plates and the portraits on the walls, every word in French, and although the sentences were not always correct, Miss Winterton would merely repeat the words as they should be and the girls would nod sagely and carry on talking. It was a game to them, but they were becoming fluent in French as they played.

After an hour or so, the nursery maid came in to take them away to be bathed and fed and readied for bed. They disappeared still talking in French.

"So how did I do?" he said with a smile to Miss Winterton, as he began replacing the little dolls in the house. "My French is a little rusty, but I did not make too many mistakes, I believe."

She shook her head solemnly. "I am disappointed in one who professes to have French blood in him. Your grasp of tenses is tenuous at best, my lord, your verbs are ramshackle and the less said about your use of male and female pronouns the better. But your vocabulary is adequate."

He laughed out loud. "Adequate! I thank you for the compliment, madam. I must practise more, must I not? Where does this little lady go? Oh, she is wearing her tiara, so I will put her in the ballroom. There!"

"I think you did not come here to play with dolls, Lord Brackenwood," Miss Winterton said.

"No, and if you had asked me if I wished to do so, I should have thought you mad, but that was the most astonishing fun. Although I am very sorry about the duchess's leg. I hope her grace will forgive me. I did not realise she was quite so fragile."

She laughed. "Mr Hamlyn will be able to glue her back together. At least it was not one of the dogs. There would have been a riot if any harm had come to the dogs. The people are of far less interest to the girls. Where are your dogs, by the way?"

"Confined to the library, sadly. They make Miss Wotherspoon sneeze."

"Oh dear." She bit her lip, and he could see her trying not to laugh.

"I know, I know. It did not seem possible that my mother's second choice of guests could be any worse than the first, but I truly think she has outdone herself."

"Oh but Miss Wotherspoon is the granddaughter of a duke, and the Miss Simkins are—"

"—second cousins once removed from Sir Rupert Hardy's wife Susan, yes, I know. They tell us of the fact almost hourly. And then there is Lady Alice Fortescue, who is older than I am, and more interested in the house than in me. I keep finding her tapping the walls in the search for secret passages. Why my mother imagines I would marry one of these ladies is beyond my comprehension, but there it is. However, there is one great asset amongst our guests — Mrs Simkins likes to perform on the pianoforte, and she has put herself forward to play for the dancing in the evenings. Are you minded to dance, Miss Winterton?"

"I? Certainly not! A governess dancing — how irregular. Her ladyship would be horrified."

"But I would not be. Will you not take pity on a poor earl who has not a single other soul in the house with whom to have a sensible conversation?"

She looked at him askance. "Surely Mrs Pargeter—"

"*Not* Mrs Pargeter," he said firmly. "I will dance with her if I must, and also with Miss Wotherspoon and both the Miss Simkins and with Lady Alice, if she wishes it, but I should like to dance with *you* as well. Will you oblige me in this, Miss Winterton?"

She was silent, gazing at him uncertainly. He understood her concern, for her position in the household was a difficult one, neither family nor servant. He had no wish to expose her to gossip, but he had such an irresistible urge to dance with her.

He took one of her hands in his. "Miss Winterton, your life now is one of toil and worry and poverty such as you are not accustomed to. You were not born to sit in dim corners with your needlework, excluded from society. I should like to bring you out into the light for once, so that you may be Miss Winterton of Woodside again for a short time. I should like to see you dance and enjoy yourself and *smile*. Will you not allow me that pleasure, just this once? I promise you I have no other motive in view."

And even as he spoke the words, he wondered if that were true. This was not the disinterested care of an employer looking after his governess. There was, for him, more to it. He wanted Annabelle to come out of her corner so that he could get to know her as an equal, not as a governess. And perhaps then... but he would not put the nebulous thought into words, not yet. For now, he merely wished to know her better.

"Well, if you wish it, then it shall be so," she said, gently withdrawing her hand. "However, I shall accept no responsibility if

Lady Brackenwood should be sent into spasms by the sight of me joining the dance."

The prospect made him smile all afternoon. He may even have startled Portman by whistling while he bathed. He startled him even more by asking for his blue coat instead of the black, and wearing pale satin knee breeches for the first time since Eloise had died. It was more than six months, after all, and for a man there was no fast rule about the wearing of black or the length of time to do so. He had mourned his poor wife for long enough.

His mother smiled when she saw him, taking his new brighter attire as a sign that he was finally turning his thoughts in the proper direction to secure the succession. And perhaps he was, although not perhaps in a direction his mother would approve. He took care not to pay too much attention to Annabelle before dinner, but he noticed that she had finally left off her black gloves, and that was a good sign. He sat beside Lady Alice during the meal, and when the dancing began, she was his first partner, as her rank dictated. But then he looked across the saloon to Annabelle's dark corner. She was watching him, a little smile on her lips, her sewing laid aside for once.

He made his way across the room, never taking his eyes off her.

"Miss Winterton, may I have the honour?"

"Thank you, my lord, I should be delighted."

He was aware of conversations suspended as he led her towards the small area set aside for the dancing, but he looked neither to right nor to left, and therefore could only imagine the displeasure on his mother's face. He was not perturbed by the thought. He was four and thirty years of age, of sound mind and tolerable intelligence, and could decide for himself with whom to dance in his own house. He wished to dance with Miss Winterton, and if she were willing, he could not see what it had to do with his mother. Even had he wished to marry Miss Winterton, he need consult only his own wishes in the matter.

Only Marisa dared to speak as they passed her by. "The governess dancing — how unusual!" she murmured, but with her customary wide smile to soften the reproof. Allan ignored her, too.

Annabelle danced well, of course. That did not surprise him in the least. She was excellent company, and again it was no surprise. That, after all, was why he had chosen her, as a friend, someone capable of conducting a rational conversation with some wit. No, what surprised him most was how the exercise heightened her colour and improved her looks. He had always thought her a handsome woman, but very pale, which, when combined with her habitual composure, gave her an air of coldness. Now, with her cheeks flushed and her eyes sparkling, a wide smile enhancing her mouth, she was entirely beautiful.

Watching her, he was entranced. He was enraptured. He was in love.

# 10: *Impropriety*

The dance ended all too soon, but Allan had no need to return Annabelle to her secluded corner, for Mr Cross eagerly claimed her hand, and several of the other young men, seeing that the earl had distinguished her and that she had no objection to dancing, were watching her with interest. Allan returned to his duties as host, and accompanied Miss Simkins onto the floor, then her sister and finally, between bouts of sneezing, Miss Wotherspoon. Duty done, he rewarded himself with a rest.

It was one of those May days that give promise of the summer to come, and the doors to the terrace stood open to the evening air. He stepped outside to cool himself after the exertions of the dance, and leaned against the balustrade, gazing out into the garden. Sweet scents drifted up from the flowerbed below him. There was still a hint of colour in the western sky, and the birds were hard at work in the trees, singing their tiny hearts out.

He felt like singing himself, for suddenly the future was full of hope. There had been a time when he had been young and optimistic, when the future had been some glorious unknown, yet to reveal itself, but, whatever it might be, he knew it would be wonderful. But the early death of his brother and his father, and his too-hasty marriage had taken that away from him. So many dull years wasted, but no longer. Now at last he was in control of his own future and his own happiness. He could not rush into it too quickly, of course. She needed to be given time—

"Allan, what are you doing hiding out here?"

Marisa. He sighed, but turned to her with a forced smile. "Just taking the air."

"You will not mind if I join you." It was not a question so he made no answer. "I too weary of the dance."

"I am not weary of it, merely a trifle overheated, and the cooler air out here has refreshed me perfectly. Should you care to dance, Marisa?"

"Let us enjoy the solitude here for a few moments more," she said. "There is no impropriety in that, is there?"

"Not the least in the world," he said, although he was wary of being alone with her. He no longer trusted her to behave in a seemly manner.

"There, you see, do we not always agree? We are of one mind in all things, and it was always so, was it not? You and I were ever in perfect attunement."

He thought it best to make no reply to this.

"It once seemed as though—" she began, but then bit her lip, and stopped, hanging her head. She sighed heavily. "But it was not to be, not then. But now, it is almost as if the fates are conspiring to throw us together again," she said, with a tinkling laugh. "First Jacob went to his maker, and then Eloise... it is almost like destiny, both of us being free at the same time."

Unbelievable as it was, he could not mistake her meaning, but such a line of thought had to be stopped at once, and without any possibility of misunderstanding. "I do not know what might be in your mind, Marisa, but if you are thinking that we are free to marry each other, then you would be quite wrong."

He hoped — oh, how he hoped! — that she would be shocked by the very idea, would deny it instantly. If so, he could at least salvage some shred of respect for her. But she did not.

"Oh, you are smitten by the governess, is that it? There is no thought now for your poor Marisa."

"This has nothing whatsoever to do with Miss Winterton or any other person. This is a family matter. You are the sister of my late wife, and the church forbids such a union."

"Pooh, no one takes any notice of that! I know any number of cases, and there are plenty of clergymen willing to marry such couples."

He turned to look her full in the face, horrified. "My dear Marisa, you cannot be serious!"

"It is done all the time, Allan. There is nothing really wrong about it. Such marriages go on happily for years, just like any other."

"They go on happily until someone lodges an objection, at which point the marriage becomes void and all the children bastards," he said sharply. "I am a peer of the realm, Marisa, with a title and estates entailed on my legitimate male heirs. I cannot in all conscience throw my entire line into confusion by allowing any possibility of doubt in the matter of inheritance. There are few duties imposed on me so clear as this one. If you had any idea of such a marriage, you must give it up entirely."

"I thought you loved me," she whispered, tears shimmering on her lashes. "I see now I was quite mistaken."

And so saying she turned and ran along the terrace and down the steps into the garden. Allan watched her until she was swallowed by the darkness.

He should have pitied her, perhaps, but he could not. He paced up and down the terrace for a long time, trying to bring his anger under control, but failing. He wondered now if this was her whole objective in coming to Charlsby. For twelve years, she had not come near him, even though she could have visited her sister at any time. Eloise had invited her to come many times, but she had not, nor had she invited them to Devonshire. Yet now, as soon as Eloise was dead— No, that was wrong. Eloise had been dead for months. It was because Marisa's own period of mourning had come to an end, that was why she had arrived at Charlsby now, and why she had made that strange remark about sleeping in Eloise's bed. She had meant that in more than the literal sense.

Good God, what a dreadful woman! As if he could ever consider marrying anyone so selfish and insensible of honour!

From inside the saloon, the sound of the pianoforte wafted out, Mrs Simkins' fingers being quite tireless in pursuit of her daughters' enjoyment. Amongst the voices drifting through the open window, Lady Brackenwood's was the most strident. Could Allan return to the room and smile and dance as if nothing had happened? He could not. But where could he escape to?

Two voices were closer to hand, standing just inside the open door.

"Do come outside! The cooler air is most refreshing, I assure you." The wheedling tones of Mr Cross.

"I should not. Mama—" One of the Miss Simkins.

"Your mama will never know."

"Just for a moment, then."

Not wishing to be discovered, Allan ran down the steps to the garden and hid in the shrubbery that edged the terrace. He could still hear their voices, however, and not wishing to overhear, he made for the path that circled the house and began to walk. There was enough light still in the sky and emanating from the windows to guide his steps around the corner and out of sight.

And there he made an interesting discovery — the window to the library stood wide open, and there was a stone bench conveniently placed beneath it. He could regain the house without either walking through the saloon, disturbing the servants below stairs or, humiliatingly, knocking on his own front door.

He climbed up onto the bench, whereupon he discovered that it was not as easy as he had supposed to break into his own house. The window was high, for one thing, the whole ground floor raised by the need for the basement to have windows. Then the casement would not stay open and kept flapping into his face or, as he climbed, poking him painfully in the back. As if that were not enough, there was a rose tree set against the wall which was determined to get in the way. But eventually, scratched, bruised and torn, he gained entry to the library and half scrambled and half fell to the floor.

There he lay, laughing, for some minutes, and rather wishing his mother could see her son lying on the floor in such a state. The thought of her indignation only made him laugh the more. But eventually he pushed himself upright. He was in the corner beside the drinks cabinet, and this seemed like rather a good idea under the circumstances. He stretched up for the decanter and a glass, placing them beside him on the floor, poured himself a large measure, then settled back in his corner, leaning against the wall with his legs stretched out in front of him.

The decanter was full of rum. It was not his usual drink, but he could not summon the energy to move, so he drank it and found it rather good. He poured himself another glass. And perhaps there was another after that, he could not say for sure, for his eyes were unaccountably heavy. At some point, he woke to find Portman moving about the room, dousing the candles, humming as he worked. The door clicked and there was silence. There was still enough light from the fire to see the decanter, so Allan poured himself another drink.

~~~~~

Annabelle had to confess that she had enjoyed herself enormously. After the earl, she had danced with Mr Cross, then with Mr Knight, Mr James Knight and Mr Smythe, the latter puffing and wheezing so much that she was rather afraid that he might expire on the spot. To save him the embarrassment, she proclaimed herself exhausted by the dance and let him lead her to a seat. He would have deposited her in her usual corner, but Lady Brackenwood crooked a finger at her and so she had no option but to smile and take a seat beside her ladyship, leaving Mr Smythe to be snapped up by the card players.

"You are enjoying yourself, Miss Winterton?" Lady Brackenwood said in her strange hoarse voice. Unaccountably she was smiling.

"I am, thank you, although I am quite worn out from the unaccustomed exercise."

"My son has such a kind and generous nature, to take pity on you in that way. He was always so, and such a sweet-natured child, although nothing to his brother. Ah, poor Duncan! We miss him still. But Allan does well enough in his way, although he lacks judgement. Why, at times I think he forgets that you are merely a governess, and treats you quite as one of the family, as he did tonight. I don't suppose his generosity will be repeated, however, for naturally he can't be seen to give consequence to those far below his own elevated position in society. Sometimes he forgets he's an earl now, and can't give way to every charitable impulse."

"Lord Brackenwood has all my gratitude."

"Now Mr Smythe is a different matter. No connections, no position in society but he has seven thousand a year free of all encumbrances, and is very much in want of a wife, one who is not too high but knows how to go on. I am sure you take my meaning, Miss Winterton."

"I believe I do, my lady."

"There now, you're a good girl, I'm sure, despite all this French and horse riding you have the girls doing. Ladies are too delicate for such a physical activity as riding."

"Lord Brackenwood gave his approval, my lady."

"Indeed. As I said, he lacks judgement. Where is he, do you know? He seems to have vanished."

"I have not seen him for some time," Annabelle said.

"Well, the dancing is finished for the night, it seems, so you may go to bed, Miss Winterton. You are not needed for cards."

Thus dismissed, she retreated to her room, although smiling at Lady Brackenwood's high-handedness. The Dowager Countess was determined to keep the lowly governess away from her son, and to that end she had tried first Charles, and then, when that had not answered, the rich Mr Smythe. Well, that would not answer either, but Annabelle could not believe that the earl had any thoughts in her direction. There had been admiration in his eyes as they danced, certainly — she had been out for long enough to recognise that! But the leap from admiration to matrimony was a large one, especially given the disparity in rank. What sort of earl would so far forget himself as to marry the governess? And Lord Brackenwood did not seem like a man who strayed very far from the path expected of him. He was a dutiful man, and before too long would dutifully marry some suitable young lady and then dutifully set about cutting Mr George Skelton out of the inheritance.

Somehow that made her rather sad.

Annabelle was far too lively for sleep. The dancing had absorbed her energy, but it had not quieted her mind. Fortunately, there were advantages to living in the household of an earl. The library was one of them, as the neat pile of books on her bedside table attested. Another was never-ending supplies of good coal and the best beeswax candles, even in the governess's room. After she had readied herself for bed, she brought the fire to a good blaze, then lit several candles on the table beside her reading chair and settled down happily with a volume.

She had read for some time, and her eyes were beginning to grow heavy, when she became aware of noises emanating from an unusual quarter — the service staircase. Someone, it seemed, was ascending the stairs from below, someone singing and occasionally missing a step with a cheerful, "Oops-a-daisy!" followed by a chuckle.

Annabelle jumped up to lock the door, but there was no key — why had she never thought about this possibility before? But even while she was frantically scrabbling through drawers looking for a key, the door burst open and the earl half fell through it.

"Oops!" he said again, and laughed. In one hand he held a nearly empty decanter, and in the other a glass, fortunately empty, for it drooped upside down in his hand. "Made it!" he yelled, beaming at his own cleverness in climbing the stairs unaided. But then considering how drunk he was, Annabelle thought it was indeed an achievement. "Jus'... have... l'il nightcap," he said, trying and failing to rest the decanter on a cabinet.

"I believe you have had enough," Annabelle said, deftly lifting the decanter from his hand and whisking it into a cupboard.

"Hey!" he cried indignantly. "My *rum!* Where'sh my *rum?*"

"Is that what it is? No wonder you are bosky. A very little of that goes a long way. There now, give me the glass too."

"Ann'belle? Mish Wint— Mish Winner— Wha' you doin' in my room? You come to gimme a kish, eh?"

She could not help laughing at his hopeful face. The sad, dutiful earl had vanished, replaced by this smiling, amusingly befuddled fellow.

"No kisses for you, my lord," she said briskly. "You are in the wrong room. Off you go, back downstairs to your own bed and sleep off your excess of rum." She turned him round and pushed him towards the open door, but he simply spun round again and held his arms wide.

"C'mon, Ann'belle, gimme a kish, eh?"

"Not the slightest chance," she said, laughing. "Good lord, you are as drunk as a wheelbarrow, and I never kiss men who are foxed, you know, as a matter of principle. Go on with you, go back to your own room."

Again she pushed him towards the stairs, and again he turned round and set out to claim his kiss. Seeing that a different stratagem was required, she backed away across the room, through the door into her bedroom and towards the bed. Happily he followed her, and when he was alongside the bed she gave him a good shove so that he collapsed onto it. For an instant his face was a ludicrous expression of confusion. He thrashed about, trying to regain his feet, but when he failed, he lay back against the covers and closed his eyes. Swiftly she lifted his feet onto the bed, and before two minutes had passed by, he was snoring loudly.

"Well, you had better stay there, my lord," she murmured, "for I am sure that I cannot lift you and you will not want me to rouse the footmen at this hour to carry you from my bedroom to your own. That *would* set tongues wagging."

She extinguished all but one candle and then, having checked that no one else was about, she crept out of her room and across the night-darkened landing to the schoolroom, and the safety of the late Lady Brackenwood's little room, where at least there was a lock with a working key to protect her from drunken earls with amorous intentions. She climbed into the slightly fusty bed, and closed her eyes. Yet she lay awake for some time, smiling in the dark, and wondering what it would have been like to kiss the earl, even with the smell of rum on his breath.

~~~~~

Allan woke with a groan, his head thick, his mouth dry as dust and something strangling him. His neckcloth. Why on earth was he still fully dressed? Only when he tentatively opened his eyes, groaning again at the brightness, did he begin to realise that there was something more fundamentally wrong than the fact that he still wore his evening clothes.

This was not his bedroom.

He swung himself upright, and instantly regretted it. The room spun violently and whatever was in his stomach seemed to have an urgent need to leave it. He groaned again, closed his eyes and tried not to cast up his accounts. Gradually, the room and his stomach settled into a more peaceable state.

Opening his eyes again, he realised with a bolt of horror where he was. Dear heaven, this must be Annabelle's room! Whatever had he done? There was no sign of her in the small bedroom. Gingerly he stood up, waited again for the room to stop revolving, and crept towards the door. The sitting room was empty too. Thank God! And perhaps if he were lucky, he could regain his own room before Portman arrived with his morning chocolate and washing water.

It was not his day for luck. Portman was pretending to rearrange neckcloths in a drawer while studiously ignoring the pristine state of the bed.

"Ah, Portman..." The footman could not possibly be unaware that Allan had arrived from the bedchamber above his own.

"Good morning, my lord. I trust—"

"Portman, if you are about to ask me if I slept well, I shall wring your neck. And if you breathe a word of this to a soul, you will be turned off instantly without a reference, do you hear?"

"My lips are sealed, my lord. Might I suggest that if your lordship is feeling a trifle knocked-up this morning, a little brandy might be just the thing?"

"Hair of the dog, eh? Oh, very well, very well."

After the brandy, followed by a wash, a leisurely shave and dressing in his comfortable old clothes, he had to admit that he felt a little better. His usual walk before breakfast cleared his head somewhat, and by the time he had returned to his room and nibbled without enthusiasm at some toast, he felt able to don his morning attire and face the world with nothing worse afflicting him than a slight headache.

And a guilty conscience. He could not forget that.

Mr Cross awaited him in the library. "Good morning, my lord. I have brought the accounts for your inspection, and there is a letter—"

Wincing, Allan waved him to silence. "Not today, Cross. Leave everything on my desk for now. I may look at it later, but you need not stay. Would you be so good as to go up to the schoolroom and ask Miss Winterton if she would favour me with her presence in the library as soon as it may be convenient?"

"Very good, my lord."

But moments after he had departed on this errand, there was a knock on the door. She had come to him! To upbraid him, no doubt. And what on earth was he to say to her?

*"Entrez!"* he called out.

But it was not Annabelle who came through the door.

"Marisa? What do you want?"

She looked at him, puzzled. "Why, Allan, to talk to you, of course."

"Is it urgent? I can spare you five minutes, that is all."

She pouted at his brusqueness, but after her behaviour the previous night — *that* at least he remembered in full — he could not bring himself to offer her much courtesy.

"It will not take so long. I have come to give you this." She proffered a sheet of paper, half covered in writing. "It is a letter written by Eloise last year, in which she speaks of her innermost fears. My poor sister was terrified, Allan."

"Whatever could she have to fear?"

"She suspected someone was trying to kill her."

# 11: An Unsent Letter

"Where did you get this?" Allan said, staring unseeingly at the letter in his hand.

"I found it in her escritoire when I was looking for paper yesterday," Marisa said. "It is not directed at anyone in particular, so I cannot tell whether she intended to send it to someone — me, for instance — or whether she merely hoped it would be found after her death. The date is barely a month before her death, do you see that? And she died so suddenly, Allan, one cannot help but wonder…"

"Wilcox saw nothing untoward about it. He examined her thoroughly and found nothing to alarm him, for you may be sure I asked him very particularly."

"Oh, but perhaps he merely thought it expedient to say nothing. Or perhaps he had a hand in it."

"Good heavens, Marisa, what are you suggesting? That Dr Wilcox murdered my wife? Why would he do such a thing? Why would anyone do such a thing?"

"Who can say?" she said archly. "It is not for me to speculate. I have done my duty, and now it is for you to decide what must be done about it. There, you see — I have not taken up so very much of your valuable time, have I?"

And so saying, she swept out of the room.

Almost at once, Portman entered. "Miss Winterton is here to see you, my lord."

"Oh... oh, of course. Show her in." All his humiliation swept back in an instant. Whatever was he to say to her? He laid Marisa's paper aside to think about when he was less distracted.

She curtsied very demurely, but there was a knowing twinkle in her eyes.

As soon as Portman had left the room, Allan shut the door firmly behind him. He wanted no witnesses to this conversation.

"Miss Winterton... I cannot begin to express my regret for my behaviour last night. I dare not even beg your forgiveness, for it was quite unpardonable. The worst of it is, my memory is utterly blank. Did I... did I hurt you?"

"Not in the least. You were amusingly drunk, that is all."

Relief washed through him. He had not injured her! That was something, at least. "Amusingly! You are more magnanimous than I deserve, Miss Winterton."

"Oh, I am used to it. My father ended the day foxed more often than not."

"Is that where you learnt such expressions?"

"Foxed, you mean? Oh, yes! Whenever anyone suggested, no matter how gently, that perhaps he might be better off to go to bed and drink no more that night, he would yell at the top of his lungs, '*I am not foxed!*' Or bosky or disguised or jug-bitten or fuddled or in his cups or... well, you get the idea. He was less entertaining than you, I must admit. You were very good-humoured."

"Was I? But why was I in your bed? I feared the worst."

But she only laughed. "You really remember nothing? It seems that after you disappeared from the saloon, you found the rum and decided you liked the taste of it very well. I assume you were in the library and set off up the service stairs to your room above, but missed your own door and ended up in my room instead. Finding me already in possession, and the rum filling your mind with nonsensical ideas, you expressed a wish to kiss me and attempted to accomplish the same."

"Oh," he said faintly.

"In this endeavour you were unsuccessful, but I managed to persuade you to the bed, where you promptly fell asleep. I then slept in the late Lady Brackenwood's room off the schoolroom."

"Ah," he said.

"So you see, there is no harm done, and your sore head will be better soon, depend upon it."

"It is not my sore head that concerns me. Miss Winterton, Portman knows where I spent the night."

"And the maids will know where I spent it. They will draw the obvious conclusion, that you were drunk and I chose to sleep elsewhere."

"But—"

"Lord Brackenwood, you refine too much upon it. No harm has come to me, and I was not in the least distressed by your antics, I assure you. I have seen my father in far worse case, so let us speak no more of it."

"You are all goodness, Miss Winterton, but you must see that this cannot be the end of the matter. I have compromised your reputation and must make it right."

"No, no, no!" she cried. "Say no more, I beg you! No man should be bound by his foolishness when in his cups. I am going now."

She spun round and would have quit the room, but Allan moved swiftly to prevent her. Taking her hand in his, he said, "The foolishness of drink may reveal a deeper truth. You assume that rum made me want to kiss you last night, but I am as sober as a judge this morning and I still want to kiss you. Marry me, Annabelle, please!"

She raised a finger to his lips. "Hush now. You are an honourable man, and I respect and admire you for that, but there is no question of marriage. When time has soothed your conscience a little, you will be glad that one of us has retained a shred of common sense. I am going back to my pupils now, and you will go back to your usual morning occupation, and we will never speak of this again. And tonight at dinner, we will meet again as earl and governess, and no one will ever suspect what has happened."

~~~~~

Annabelle did not, in fact, go directly back to the schoolroom. She had left the girls reading about Henry VII, under the supervision of one of the nursery maids, so there was no need for her to hurry back and her nerves were too overset to think about the Tudors. She went instead to her own room, and paced up and down her sitting room for fully half an hour.

She had refused the earl by instinct, for a marriage between a peer and a governess was so far beyond the pale that he could not be serious. Only his conscience made him offer to marry her. And yet... he had said he wanted to kiss her, and he was not a man to invent such a thing. Her father had once said, after an overwrought suitor had snatched a kiss from Fanny, to her outrage, that every man desired to kiss every pretty woman he meets, that there was something badly amiss with him if he did not and that it was a compliment to her beauty. But Lord Brackenwood was not every man, nor was he given to flirting, so if he said he wanted to kiss her, it suggested something more than normal male desire.

Oh, how tempting it was! Even had she still been Miss Winterton of Woodside she would have been attracted to the idea of being a countess, but how much more enticing was the prospect from her present lowly position. Marriage, respectability, a position in society and no worries about money ever again... what bliss it would be. And the earl was a lovely man, so gentlemanly and respectful, when he was sober, which he almost always was. Last night had been an aberration, unlikely to be repeated.

But she was not in love with him. Did that matter? The man she loved... or rather, the man she had once loved, was out of her reach, whereas the earl... No, that was a foolish way of thinking. She had been right to turn him down, and once he considered the matter in a proper light, he would understand that and be thankful for his narrow escape.

Still, she could not help wondering a little wistfully what her life would have been like, if she had said yes.

Eventually, she was composed enough to return to the schoolroom, and distract herself with some work on the globes, and then some French. They were just beginning their work on irregular verbs when Portman came in with a note for her.

*'Miss Winterton, I should very much like to discuss with you a family matter of the utmost secrecy, entirely unrelated to our discussion this morning. If you would be willing to favour me with your counsel, please meet me in the Grecian Temple at 4 o'clock. Be not alarmed — I promise to keep well away from the rum*

*beforehand. However, if you do not feel it to be proper, I will
endeavour to find some other way to discuss the matter with you
privily. Brackenwood.'*

Although she laughed out loud at his promise to avoid rum,
she wondered greatly at his wish to discuss a private family matter
with her. Could it be appropriate to involve an outsider? Yet the
earl, who knew the circumstances, must be the best judge of that.
Curiosity won out and so at the appointed hour she left the girls
working on their samplers, fetched her cloak and set out in the rain
to meet the earl. Circumspection led her to approach by a
roundabout route, heading first across the park to the woods and
then some distance under the trees before circling back to the lake,
where the Grecian Temple sat on a small hill overlooking the water.

When she arrived, he was sitting on the marble bench which
ran around the interior wall. Jumping up with a pleased expression,
he came towards her with hands outstretched, before
remembering himself and bowing instead. She curtsied and he
waved her to sit down, seating himself a little distance away.

"Thank you, thank you! I was so afraid—" he began eagerly,
then huffed a breath, and spoke more calmly. "Your forbearance is
unparalleled, Miss Winterton. It is the greatest relief to me to have
someone to turn to who is neither family nor outsider, yet whose
opinion may be entirely trusted."

"It gives me pleasure to be of service to you and your family,
Lord Brackenwood, although I cannot imagine how I may advise
you on a family matter."

"It concerns my wife's death. Would you be so good as to read
this? Mrs Pargeter found it in my wife's desk."

Her curiosity now even greater, she took the paper and began
to read.

*'25th September 18— Charlsby. Unpleasant as this duty is, I am compelled to record some circumstances which give rise to the greatest alarm in my breast. It is no longer possible to deny that someone in this house wishes me dead. First there was the fish which was said to be bad, yet no one but I was laid low by it. Then there was the incident with Alan's curricle, which could have been an accident, perhaps, were it not for everything else. And only two weeks ago, as I was walking beside the lower lake and stopped to admire the swans, for the cygnets are so well-grown now and beautiful to behold, I felt a hand at my back and the next moment I was in the water. I pretended I had merely slipped, but in truth I am not so careless. And now I wonder what next will happen to me? For it may be that the next attempt will succeed. I am so afraid.'*

Annabelle looked at the earl in dismay. "You believe your wife wrote this?"

"It is her hand, yes."

"So she was ill after eating some fish, there was an accident in the curricle, she fell in the lake and then she died very suddenly in the night. Is that the sum of it?" He nodded. "Tell me about the fish."

"There was a fish dish — I cannot even remember what it was, now. Eloise was violently ill within an hour of eating it. The cook said it was probably off, for the weather had been very hot. The curricle... the axle broke, and I cannot see how anyone might have contrived that. Besides, Eloise was not injured in any way, was not even thrown from the vehicle. The lake incident I barely remember, except that she was late for dinner one day and the reason she gave was that she had fallen in the lake. But she laughed at herself about it, and called herself a widgeon, as I recall. As for her death, Dr Wilcox himself said he saw nothing alarming in the circumstances.

She had not been well for some years, and was taking a number of different tonics and pills and so forth. That her heart should give out suddenly was tragic, perhaps, but not unexpected. There is nothing here that seems in the least suspicious to me, beyond the lurid fancies born of long illness. Miss Winterton, what should I do? I cannot bear the thought of reviving old memories, just when I feel I may begin to look to the future again, yet if there is anything untoward in Eloise's death, it must be uncovered. What if some vile person has indeed murdered her, yet is now living free and comfortable and unafraid of being discovered?"

Annabelle read the letter again, more carefully, then laid it down, frowning. "It is curious that this was never discovered before."

"Not really," he said. "After her death, the room was closed up and no one went in there, except the servants to dust occasionally. Everything is exactly as she left it. No one slept in the room, until Marisa arrived. She found this in the escritoire when she was looking for paper. If I had had the room emptied, as I should have done, it would have been found months ago."

"How do you spell your name?" Annabelle said.

"My name? Brackenwood?"

She laughed. "No, your Christian name. Allan has two L's, does it not? The inscription on your portrait in the hall is spelt so. Yet here it is written with only one L."

He shrugged, not much interested. "I daresay she wrote in haste and made a mistake."

"Yes, it must be a mistake, for your wife would know how to spell her husband's name. But I do not think the letter was written in haste, for the hand is very regular, each letter carefully inscribed. I wonder who the intended recipient was? You, perhaps?"

"Marisa thinks it was intended for her."

"Yet it is not directed so, and there is no salutation at the start, or room for any. No attempt was made to send it. Perhaps it was meant to be left in the escritoire, to be found only after her death. And yet, to leave it in such a place... If the room were in regular use, then Mrs Hale would replenish the supplies of paper from time to time, and there was a good likelihood that she would find it."

"But perhaps Eloise kept it hidden somewhere safer, and then put it in the escritoire— But no, for she could not have known she was to die that night." He sighed. "Your questions are good ones, but I do not understand the letter, that is the long and the short of it. But that is immaterial, for the only question is what must be done with it."

"You have three choices," she said crisply. "You could decide that there is no truth in the fancies of a sick woman, and burn it. Or you could try to uncover the truth behind these allegations yourself. Or—" She stopped, knowing that she was stepping onto thin ice.

"Or?" he said, smiling at her. "Do not hesitate to speak your mind, Miss Winterton. That, after all, is why I took you into my confidence in this irregular way, because I value your opinion. You may speak freely, without the least fear of censure or disapprobation."

She took a deep breath. "Very well, then. The third option is to lay the whole before the constables and leave them to investigate in whatever manner seems good to them. Or perhaps they will feel, as you do, that this is nought but the fancy of a woman who was suffering much illness, and perhaps dwelt too much upon trivial events."

He leaned back against the marble wall of the temple, folding his arms, considering. "I cannot simply burn this and pretend it never existed. If poor Eloise believed someone was trying to kill her, then the least I can do is to take her fears seriously. Yet it goes against the grain to involve outsiders in our family trouble. Therefore it seems to me that I must investigate it myself. What do you think? You look serious, Miss Winterton. Do you disagree with my reasoning?"

Her heart was thundering in her chest. Here was the point of no return, and she could not in all conscience prevaricate. She must say what needed to be said, no matter the consequences. "There is an aspect of this that perhaps you have not yet considered, my lord."

"Which is?"

"That if there was indeed an intention by some person to end Lady Brackenwood's life, then that person must have had a reason to do so."

"Yes, of course. So?"

"And the reason must have been a strong one to make that person consider murder."

"I cannot fault your logic, Miss Winterton," he said smiling.

"In other words, that person must have stood to gain something of great value by Lady Brackenwood's death."

"Again, I agree with you," he said, the smile faltering. "Yet I do not see who stood to gain anything by Eloise's death. Her dowry is settled on her daughters, her jewellery is theirs too, and her other bequests were small — gifts of money to the servants and such like. But this is not what you mean, I think, and since you will not look me in the eye, I must look elsewhere for—" His intake of breath was audible. "You mean that *I* stood to gain, of course. Because I had no son, and no likelihood of one, so, growing impatient, I murdered my own wife, is that what you believe?" His voice was harsh suddenly.

"No, no, no!" she cried. "I believe nothing of the sort! You are incapable of such evil. But do you not see, it is what will be said of you, if once the idea of murder gets about. Who gained the most by her death? Why, her husband, who is now free to marry again and provide himself with an heir of his own body. Do you see? If murder is to be talked of, then you are the most obvious, indeed the *only* suspect!"

# 12: A Musical Soirée (June)

He was silent for so long, his features so dark, that Annabelle feared she had insulted him beyond reconciliation. Here at last was the point at which their friendship foundered. She had as good as suggested that he had murdered his own wife, and although she believed no such thing, she could understand that he would eschew her company in future. There could be no confidence subsisting between them with such a suspicion in the air.

But then he smiled, indeed, he even laughed. "This is what I like about you, Annabelle," he said, his lips still quirked upwards. "You say exactly what you think. You are no simpering sycophant. If the idea of murder gets about, then I am the obvious suspect. Who else stood to benefit from my wife's death? No one! So if she was murdered, then I must be the guilty man. But I understand your meaning. If this business is to be investigated, then it must not be I who does so."

"Exactly, because if you do so, and you decide that there was no murder, there will always be those who say that you swept your own evil deeds out of sight."

He nodded, and his lightened expression reassured her. He was not angry with her, and the relief she felt was overwhelming. She exhaled sharply, her pulse beginning to settle.

"But I must take issue with you in one particular," he said.

"Oh?" She felt a stab of fear, but he was smiling, so surely it could not be anything bad?

"You gave me three options, but I believe there is a fourth. I could lay the whole before some disinterested third party — *not* the constables, who are— how shall I put this? — not always sympathetic to the peculiar requirements of the peerage. Some other party, the family lawyers, perhaps, who could investigate the matter without dragging the whole into the public arena. I should very much like this to be dealt with discreetly, and not be the subject of gossip in every tavern in Cheshire."

"That sounds eminently prudent," she said. "You believe, then, that it should be investigated further?"

"I can do no other," he said. "I owe that much to poor Eloise. But Annabelle... I beg your pardon, Miss Winterton... will you stand my friend in this? May I come to you to unburden myself? For I cannot talk to my mother about it, or Marisa, and there is no one I trust more."

"I should be honoured by your confidence," she said, trying not to blush and failing.

He heaved a deep sigh, his eyes twinkling in the most unsettling way. "And I *still* want to kiss you."

But she dared not encourage him in that line of thought. "Then I suggest you ensure that there is plenty of mistletoe about the house at Christmastide," she said tartly.

~~~~~

143

### *JUNE*

Allan explained as much as he dared to his mother. She thought it all nonsense, as he did himself.

"Eloise always had a nervous disposition. Such a silly girl, in many ways. Take no notice of this letter, Allan. Who knows what she meant by it? For all we know, Dr Wilcox had given her laudanum and she was allowing her imagination to run riot. She was prone to silly fancies. She thought her maid was stealing from her, do you remember?"

"Well, she *was* stealing from her. Mrs Hale caught her with the coins in her hand. She gave some explanation for it, but Eloise was about to turn her off without a reference. As it was, with Eloise dead, she was allowed to leave without a blemish on her character. Mother, I am going to London to speak to the lawyers. I daresay I shall be gone for ten days or so, but when I get back there must be a thorough investigation. Will you oblige me by clearing the house of all your guests as soon as may be? I do not want this business talked about everywhere. There will inevitably be some disturbance while this is going on, and it will be better if there is no one here apart from the family."

"What about the governess? Shall I clear *her* out of the house, too?" She looked at him archly.

He clicked his tongue in irritation. "Miss Winterton is here to teach the girls, Mother. If she leaves, I shall only have to get another governess, and think of the inconvenience of finding someone suitable, and the disruption to the girls."

"Ack, you're a fool, Allan, but you won't be told. Bed her if you must, I shan't object to that, but if you have any consideration for my feelings, don't marry a nobody like that."

"Hardly a nobody, Mother," he said. "She is a gentleman's daughter. As Eloise was. As you were. And if you want me to look higher than the gentry for a wife, then find me someone a little more likely than Lady Alice Fortescue. For all your efforts to fill the house with marriage prospects for me, Miss Winterton is by far the most appealing young lady I have seen for some time, and you could hardly blame me if I were to marry her."

So saying, trying not to smile at the look of horror on his mother's face, he swept out of the room and went to organise his packing.

Allan rather enjoyed travelling. His coach was comfortable, the roads were tolerable and the inns, with rooms secured by the efficient Mr Cross in advance, were as comfortable as could be expected. Best of all, there was no one demanding his attention, no dutiful mornings confined to the study with Mr Cross, or riding about the estate with Mr Pratchett, the land agent, and no long, dull evenings trying not to be ensnared by ambitious young ladies and their mamas, or playing whist with his mother.

And no distracting governess. The urge to take her in his arms and kiss her for a very long time was ever-present, and he could not decide whether he was truly in love with her, as he had thought when he danced with her, or merely drawn to the only woman for miles around who was both marriageable and sensible. Nor was he certain whether he was relieved that she had turned him down or not, but a week or two out of her company would settle his mind one way or the other.

Allan had never liked the family's London house, a monstrosity of a place that he associated with gloom, death and lawyers, having been summoned there after the deaths of his grandmother, his brother and then his father. After his marriage, he had brought Eloise to London so that he could take his seat in the House of Lords and she could be presented at court. They had quickly agreed that London did not suit them, so the family house had been rented out and Allan had taken a modest suite of rooms for his infrequent visits to town, which now also served as a pied-à-terre for George.

It was to this residence on a quiet street that his coach deposited him. He was expected, the industrious Mr Cross having notified the housekeeper of his plans, and it was no more than an hour before he had changed out of his dusty travel clothes, and settled down with tea and freshly baked buns in the tiny study to write letters notifying various people of his arrival.

This was where he was tracked down by George, who bounded in with a wide grin. "Cousin! How charming this is. Are you here for the delights of the season? It is the Bucknells' ball tonight, which I am sure my credit is good enough to get you into, and the Marfords' have theirs the day after tomorrow, but I am not sure I can procure you vouchers for Almack's..."

Allan laughed. "George, you never fail to amuse me. How grand you are, talking about the Bucknells and the Marfords as if you are the best of friends. *I* introduced *you* to the Marquess of Carrbridge, after all. But I am not here to put myself about. Something has occurred which needs a lawyer's mind." Briefly Allan told George of the letter that Marisa had found, and what he proposed to do about it.

"Well, that is all poppycock, cousin," George said. "Who on earth would want to murder Cousin Eloise?"

"The obvious suspect would have to be me," Allan said wryly.

George burst out laughing. "Oh, for heaven's sake! I would more easily believe that the dowager killed her. She was the one obsessed with you getting a proper heir, after all."

"I have a proper heir," Allan said in amusement. "No son could be better."

"Oh..." George breathed. "You do pay a fellow splendid compliments, cousin. But who else could it be? A thwarted lover, perhaps, who wants to marry you and removes the only obstacle. Or a servant with a grudge. Or someone getting revenge on you... No, for you have no enemies, do you?" He sighed. "The very idea is ridiculous. I can see no reason for murder."

"Nor I, but the suggestion cannot be left to fester. For my part, I am inclined to think her death was an accident. That quack of hers gave her so many different tonics and potions and remedies, the day was bound to come when she mixed them up and took too much of something. She was not so ill that her death was hourly expected. But enough of such tedious matters. Tell me what you have been up to."

"Oh, the usual, you know. White's, Tattersall's, the Daffy Club, Hyde Park, Jackson's Saloon. Nothing special. But what news from Charlsby? How is the delectable Miss Winterton? And is the place still stuffed with hopeful would-be countesses?"

They talked round and about for some time, but Allan said nothing of Annabelle and George said nothing very much of his own affairs, although Allan thought him a little subdued.

The following morning, Allan spent two hours closeted with his lawyers. Then, after visiting his tailor, shirt maker and bootmaker, and ordering supplies of clothing identical to those previously bought, he ventured off in a different direction, to Carloway House, the London home of Mr and Mrs Robin Dalton.

Dalton was at home, and so Allan was admitted to a pleasant study where he was invited to look into the eyepiece of a microscope and admire some beetle or other. He made polite noises which he hoped sounded suitably admiring.

But eventually he was led to a chair beside the unlit fire, with a glass of Madeira to hand.

"And how is my sister-in-law?" Dalton asked. "My wife receives regular letters from Annabelle, but one never gets quite the same information from a letter, do you not find? She was well when you left Cheshire?"

"Perfectly well, yes, but it is about those letters that I am come, so that you do not mistake certain events. I am ashamed to admit that I got abominably drunk one evening and attempted to kiss Miss Winterton. I was not successful in my efforts, but nevertheless I felt it only proper to offer her the protection of my name subsequently."

Dalton raised immaculately shaped eyebrows a fraction. He was one of those men who always made Allan feel inadequately attired. He had left his rooms wearing his finest town garments, and yet beside Dalton's elegant form he felt like a country bumpkin, his boots lacking polish, his coat poorly fitted and his neckcloth deficient. It was dispiriting.

His host brushed an imaginary speck of dust from his perfectly-fitted breeches. "And how did Annabelle respond?"

"She turned me down. I think she felt I was not in earnest, but I *was*," he said, aware that he sounded petulant. "I wish you to know, Dalton, that my intentions towards her have never been less than perfectly honourable. Whatever Annabelle may say of me, I am *not* flirting with her, nor do I mean her the least harm. It would be troubling if you were to take a wrong impression of me from any report that your wife receives from her sister. I want you to hear the truth of it directly from me, since you are her nearest male relative."

Dalton's lips quirked in a half smile. "Are you seeking my permission to pay your addresses, Brackenwood? You do not need it, as I am sure you are aware. If you want my blessing, then you have it, certainly, for it would be an excellent match for her. I am well aware of her many admirable qualities, which render her perfectly able to grace any position, even that of countess. Between ourselves, however, you surprise me, I confess. You are an earl in full possession of both title and fortune, and still young enough to be a very desirable match for any young lady. You could aim a little higher than your governess."

"I do not see her as my governess," Allan said, a little affronted on her behalf. "She is Miss Winterton of Woodside, and every inch a lady, who would grace any position. But the devil of it is that she *is* a governess, and my employee, and it would not be honourable to court her openly. It might give rise to unpleasant gossip. I do not even know if I wish to court her, only that she intrigues me and I should like to get to know her better and I have no idea how to do it."

"Then turn her off," Dalton said easily. "Send her here to me, and you may court her freely. If you decide against it, or she will not have you, then this is also the best place to find her another position."

Allan's stomach flip-flopped painfully. Not have him? Find another position? Lose her once and for all? It was unthinkable. He decided on the spot that he would do everything in his power to keep her at Charlsby. Was that love? Did he truly want to marry her? He had no idea, only sure of one thing — that he wanted her to be a part of his life. He turned the subject, therefore, and they talked on indifferent matters for the remainder of his visit.

As he rose to leave and they moved out into the hall, the sounds of the harp drifted down from an upstairs room.

"Ah, the harp! Such a beautiful instrument," Allan said. "Your wife plays?"

"Rather expertly," he said with a smug smile. "Mrs Dalton is a talented musician. We are to hold a musical soirée here tonight. Should you like to attend? Your cousin is to be here."

"George? A musical soirée?" It seemed rather unlikely, knowing George's proclivities.

"Oh yes, he comes regularly to our little evenings. Do come — it is very informal. An hour or two of music and a light supper."

And Allan set off to walk home with the puzzle of George's sudden interest in music filling his head.

The instant he walked into the Daltons' music room that evening, he understood. She must have been eighteen or nineteen, as pretty as paint, with dark hair that curled about her face, and huge blue eyes the colour of cornflowers. George's intake of breath was audible as he caught sight of her. Yet Allan knew at a glance that she was far, far out of George's reach. Her gown was shimmering silk with a spangled overtunic and the hand of an expert *modiste* in every tuck and stitch and delicately embroidered flower on the bodice and sleeves. There were diamonds at her throat, about her wrists and even in her hair. Her assured manner, and her obvious intimacy with the high-ranking ladies surrounding her made it plain that she was noble born. Poor George! He would need more than the distant possibility of an earldom to secure such a catch.

As Allan made his greetings to Mr and Mrs Dalton, he asked his host quietly, "Who is she, the beauty in the ice-blue gown?"

"Ah! Lady Grace Bucknell, youngest daughter of the Duke of Camberley. Thirty thousand at least," he added in a whisper. "You could not do better, Brackenwood. Very eligible."

Allan laughed, and made no attempt to explain that his interest was not on his own behalf. But his heart sank when he saw the young lady's face light up when she saw George crossing the room towards her. If George were to suffer the pangs of unrequited love, it would do him no harm at all, but if the lady returned his regard, he foresaw nothing but trouble.

Most musical soirées during the season were no more than an elegant attempt at matchmaking without the expense of a ball, but this one was of a higher standard than most. Mrs Dalton opened with a delightful performance on the harp, then Lady Grace on the pianoforte, then a succession of others, all chosen for their ability rather than their marriageability. Lady Grace was the only single lady to perform, although there were several in the audience. Allan was amused to note how many of these turned their eyes rather often in George's direction. He, however, had eyes only for one person.

As they walked home through the quiet streets later, they were both silent for most of the way, but eventually a heavier than usual sigh from George prompted Allan to say, "She is quite above your touch, I am afraid."

"Oh, I know it," he said, not pretending to misunderstand. "Nothing can come of it. Well... that is, unless you should be so obliging as to drop down dead soon, and frankly I prefer you alive."

"Thank you for that!"

"Well, it is true!" George said indignantly. "I would not for the world have anything happen to you, and the sooner you marry again and produce a son to supplant me, the better for my peace of mind. No, I dare not even think of Lady Grace. But she is such a darling, and she likes me, too, I flatter myself."

Allan grunted. "In which case, the honourable course is to withdraw from her society."

"I know it," he said, and the heaviness of his tone tore at Allan's heart. "I met her briefly last year, and she hardly noticed me in the crowds thronging around her. But we met again in Bath over the winter, and there were so few acquaintances of our own age that we were thrown together somewhat and she... she seemed to take pleasure in my company. And then, when we met again last month... but I did nothing to encourage her, I swear. I never danced with her more than once, or invited her to drive out in my curricle or anything so particular. But it will not do, and I must leave town, for her sake, if not for my own. May I travel back with you, when you go?"

"Of course. I shall be glad of your company, although sorry for the circumstances. And I apologise profoundly for my continued good health. I would not for the world deprive you of your delightful young lady by my protracted existence, but I cannot help it, you know."

George burst out laughing. "That is what I like about you, cousin — you are not stuffy, and nothing offends you."

"I should point out that Mr Dalton described Lady Grace as a suitable match for me. He informed me with great directness that she has thirty thousand pounds at least, and he thinks me not too decrepit to be a desirable match. But be not alarmed, cousin, for I am not minded to cut you out."

"No, for you are in love with Miss Winterton," George said smugly.

"Am I?"

"You can see at once how I feel, can you not? You see the way I look at Lady Grace. Well, that is how you look at Miss Winterton."

"Is it, now?" Allan said pensively. "And I thought I was being so discreet."

Oddly, this conversation settled Allan's mind wonderfully. If George could see love in his eyes when he looked at Annabelle, then love it must be. It was not the tongue-tying, stomach-churning calf-love he had once endured for Marisa, it was more a gentle happiness whenever he looked at Annabelle, or thought of her, or enjoyed her company. She was so much the sort of woman he liked, or perhaps he should say, she was very far from the sort of woman he strongly disliked. She was not a head-turning beauty or a cutting wit or an interfering manipulator. She was a sensible woman who would make him an admirable countess, and he would be happy for the rest of his life if he could have her by his side. But the tricky question, the one he could not answer no matter how much he wrestled with it, was whether he could ever make her forget Mr Keeling and be happy too.

# 13: The Lawyer

Allan accompanied George to the ball given by the Marquess and Marchioness of Carrbridge at Marford House the following evening. He was not an enthusiast for such events, but it was the easiest way of meeting the few people he felt obliged to see while he was in town. He had no invitation, but he was an old school friend of Lord Carrbridge's and the butler recognised him on sight. He was greeted with easy familiarity by the host and his wife, and moved into the body of the room. He was unfashionably early, so the room was still pleasantly uncrowded and fresh. He procured a glass of champagne from a footman passing with a tray, and took up a position beside a pillar to watch the dancing.

George knew everybody, was on friendly terms with everyone and headed straight for the wallflowers' bench to rescue some poor girl from humiliation. He was soon dancing energetically, while regaling his partner with some story that kept her in fits of laughter. Lucky George, Allan thought, to be so charming and amusing and flirtatious in the lightest possible way. He was so like Duncan, yet without Duncan's darker side, that left ruined housemaids and disappointed debutantes in his wake.

"Allan! How like you to turn up here, quite the thing, when I waited in all morning for you."

His sister Mary, in a strikingly fashionable ensemble, apart from an appallingly tasteless pearl choker.

"Did you so? Then I am sorry for it, but I never said that I would call at any particular time, you know, only that I had arrived in town and would see you before I left. Which I am now doing."

"How disappointingly logical you are, but it is just as Mal thought. *'Depend upon it,'* he said when your letter was delivered, *'he will want his hair cut before anything, for they have no barbers worth the mention in Cheshire. Therefore you need not stay in on his account.'* Did you have your hair cut?"

"No, I was replenishing my supply of neckcloths."

She laughed out loud at that. "Oh, Allan, how mortifying to be considered lower in importance than neckcloths. But you look very well." She smoothed the sleeve of his coat. "Yes, you look remarkably well. I like to see you in your London finery, like the nobleman you are. Although do not stand anywhere near the exquisite Mr Brummell, for the comparison would not be favourable to you."

"I have no ambition whatsoever to stand comparison with Mr Brummell," he said. "Is Lizzie here too?"

"No, Matlock is ill again, and she will not leave him, so you will have to call upon her. She is increasing again, did you know?"

"Good heavens, has she not done her duty by him in that regard? Three sons already, and I know not how many daughters."

"Four. But Mother tells me that your thoughts are turning in that direction. Well, you look conscious, so I will not tease you about it, although I am dying to know more, for there are mysterious hints about the governess — you know what Mother is like! But I am sure it cannot be true."

"Is Mal in the card room?"

"Yes, but I am not going to let you escape so easily. Let me at least have the pleasure of seeing you dance, brother dear. There is a young lady that I should like you to meet…"

Meekly, Allan let her lead him round the room, and introduce him to a Miss Cantwell, who was not a day above sixteen, timid as a mouse, and, he soon discovered, somewhat muddled as to the matter of left and right, a strong handicap in the dance. Allan was not the man to mind a partner who bumped into him or trod on his feet, however, so he kept up a stream of trivial conversation and after a while she began to settle down.

"I am so sorry, my lord," she said as he took her back to her party. "I am not very good at remembering the movements yet."

"You will get the hang of it soon enough," he said. "We have all had to endure the pain of learning the steps."

"Oh, you are so obliging to say such things! I was so nervous, because you are an earl, you see," she said, smiling artlessly up at him. "But you are so kind to me."

"When you have been out in society a little longer, Miss Cantwell, you will discover that earls are just men like any other."

"Oh, *no!* That cannot be so! You are *noble.*"

"I am only noble because some scapegrace ancestor served Henry IV with ale at a timely moment, and was made a baron for it. One can only suppose that His Majesty was excessively thirsty at the time. The baron's sons and grandsons managed to keep their noses clean long enough to be made up to viscount and then earl. The King may hold the throne by the grace of God, but the peers hold their places by the grace of the King, and have no greater claim to virtue than any other man. I certainly do not."

She looked up at him with wide eyes, and he sighed. His tolerance for innocent ingenues was somewhat limited.

After that, there was another young lady and then a third, after which he begged to be relieved of his role as dance partner and was allowed to escape to the card room. There he found Mary's husband, Mal. Viscount Falkness was the sort of large, blustering man who made Allan feel inadequate. Despite his widening girth and features coarsened by over-indulgence, Falkness was effortlessly stylish. He was too well-built for elegance, but his neckcloth was tied in some complicated manner that made Allan's carefully contrived knot look positively rustic.

"Brackenwood! Dear boy, so glad to see you. Shall I cut you in on the game? Waterbury and Latheron will not mind." His two companions murmured their agreement.

"Thank you, gentlemen, but no. I am only here to give you this." He handed the viscount the letter he had written earlier. "It explains some family business that Mary needs to know about. No cause for alarm, but it will come best from you. And if you would be so good as to show it to Matlock, so that he may tell Lizzie."

"Very well, dear boy. But what is this I hear about you eyeing up the governess, eh? Is she tasty? We had one once who was the meekest little creature imaginable by day, but at night—"

"There is nothing of that sort going on," Allan put in quickly. "Nor will there be."

"Aye, that is just like you, Brackenwood," Falkness said, with a laugh. "Never knew a more straight-laced fellow. If ever you bedded the wench, you would likely feel obliged to marry her at once." The three men laughed at the absurdity of the idea, but then

Falkness raised his eyebrows and poked Allan in the chest. "Aha! You look conscious! I shall tell Mary to expect an announcement then, shall I?"

"Shouldn't marry the governess, Brackenwood," Latheron said. "Not done. Not done at all. Marry some dull stick of a duke's daughter, and keep the governess for sport, that's the way to do it."

"I thank you for your advice," Allan said, bowing stiffly. "You will excuse me, gentlemen. I will not keep you from your play any longer."

And, seething, he made his way back to the ballroom, and before too long made his escape.

~~~~~

Two days later, Allan was at breakfast when the housekeeper came in. "Beg pardon, my lord, but there are three gentlemen to see you, sent by the lawyers, they say. I've put them in the study, for now."

Allan read the letter of introduction and then, puzzled, the cards, before making his way to the tiny room designated as his study. It was barely big enough for the four of them, containing only a desk and chair, a single bookcase and a sofa squeezed against one wall.

"Gentlemen, I am Lord Brackenwood."

A man of around thirty, ostentatiously attired in the style favoured by pinks of the *ton,* stepped forwards a little. "My lord, I am Pettigrew Willerton-Forbes, from the chambers of Markham, Willerton-Forbes and Browning. You may be acquainted with my father, the Earl of Morpeth."

"I know him a little," Allan said, having no memory at all of Lord Morpeth, but assuming that he must have bumped into a fellow earl at some point.

"May I present my esteemed colleagues? This is Captain Michael Edgerton, formerly of the East India Company Army. And this is James Neate, who will act as my junior and secretary in this matter, should your lordship be so gracious as to engage us."

Edgerton was a very small man, flamboyantly dressed in the garish blue and yellow striped waistcoat of the Four-Horse Club. Neate was the exact opposite, tall and thin, wearing the sober black of a lawyer, the only sensibly dressed one of the three.

"Gentlemen, you are very welcome," Allan said. "However, I fear there has been some misunderstanding. I did not expect three of you, not for such a delicate matter as this, and certainly not an army man. There will be no need for swords or pistols in this business, I sincerely trust."

"The Captain is retired now," Willerton-Forbes said. "However, his particular skills may be useful to us. For instance, if there is any question of an intruder finding his way into a building, Edgerton can advise on likely points of ingress. As to Mr Neate, it is very helpful when interviewing to have some third party taking notes, so that the interviewer — myself, in this case — may look the interviewee in the eye and thus assess the likelihood that he may be concealing information. Or lying outright. Since this is potentially a hanging matter, there will be strong pressure to lie. And Captain Edgerton has a role in this regard also, for we have found in previous cases that a man with a sword striding about the room has a powerful effect on the lower orders. They become quite garrulous, in fact."

"You have done this sort of thing before, then?" Allan said.

"We have a little experience, my lord, yes. Captain Edgerton and I met when I was working on a tricky ownership question for the Duke of Dunmorton, and we got on well enough to work together on several subsequent occasions. Mostly inheritance questions, but one or two thefts. A possible murder is a new experience, but I flatter myself that we are well placed to assist you. It is, naturally, your lordship's decision."

"You propose to interview people, then?"

"That would be my preferred starting point, yes. Everyone who was in the house at the time in question, initially."

"Initially!"

"It might be necessary to talk to one or two outsiders who have relevant information, such as the physician attending the late Lady Brackenwood."

"This is not going to be very discreet," Allan said. "I had envisaged one man, a lawyer, easily explained, who would ask casual questions of the footmen, that sort of thing. But formal interviews... You will not interview my mother, will you?"

"If she was in the house at the relevant time, yes, my lord."

Allan thought about that, then grinned. "I wish you good fortune with that, Mr Willerton-Forbes. And you will interview me?"

"You must be first on the list, my lord."

"How so? Oh, because I am the most likely person to have murdered my wife, of course."

Willerton-Forbes smiled. "Not at all, or at least, not *solely* for that reason. You must be first to demonstrate that there is no favouritism, and to ensure that no one refuses to cooperate. If the

Earl of Brackenwood agrees to be interviewed, then the housemaids cannot object. Or the dowager."

Allan nodded, taking the point. "You seem to have a well-considered plan of campaign. It will be very disruptive, however."

"My lord, we will proceed according to your instructions. Only you can decide how thorough an investigation you want. If it turns out that your wife truly was murdered, are you prepared for the consequences of that?"

"Of course, but you see, I do not for one moment imagine that there was anything untoward in her death. Who would murder her? I am the only person who stood to benefit from her death, and I know that I did not harm her, so I have no fear that you will uncover any unpleasantness."

"Then may we undertake to investigate, in whatever manner we see fit?"

"You may investigate," Allan said. "We will discuss your approach as we drive north. We will leave London on Monday next, gentlemen."

~~~~~

The travelling party was a rather larger one than had made its way south. Allan shared his coach with Willerton-Forbes, Edgerton and George, while Neate travelled in a post-chaise with the two valets and most of the luggage. This made for an impressive arrival at inns, and since Willerton-Forbes strutted about in his London finery with the dashing Captain Edgerton at his side, one of the two would be sure to be mistaken for the earl, while Allan was happy to trail inconspicuously in their wake.

"All this deference is most soothing to the spirit," Willerton-Forbes said, as a waiter reversed out of their private parlour bent almost double. "I like it very much. It makes one begin to think of murder oneself. If only I had not five older brothers, and if only I liked them less well! Fraternal affection is a great hindrance to advancement."

"It is the very devil being a younger son," Allan said, smiling.

"It is worse being a nobody of a cousin," George said, for once not catching the light mood of the others. "One is neither one thing nor the other. I cannot pursue a career until I am safely supplanted by a son or two, yet I cannot comfortably live the life of a gentleman."

"Oh, are you the heir?" Edgerton said. "I did not realise. Well, you must do as I did, and marry a woman of fortune, Skelton. The Honourable Miss Lucinda Willerton-Forbes and her dowry of fifteen thousand pounds are even now in my tender care."

Willerton-Forbes laughed. "Do not pretend that you only married Luce for her money, Michael, for I know the truth of the matter."

"Of course I did not, but it is not done to admit to a fondness for one's wife. How gauche that would be!"

With such light-hearted companions, the journey could not fail to be pleasant. During the day, they discussed the strategy for the investigation, and in the evenings they played whist for half-crown points, while Edgerton entertained them with an inexhaustible supply of diverting stories. Neate, who was acting as valet for Willerton-Forbes, ate in the tap room with the other valets, a role he would also play at Charlsby.

"One never knows when the servants might talk indiscreetly," Willerton-Forbes said. "A pair of ears below stairs is very useful, and no one would ever take James for a lawyer. He makes a most convincing valet. His father was one for many years, so he knows the ropes."

The days passed in this agreeable manner, and when there was no other entertainment offered, Allan could watch the green fields and woods of England pass by, all in their summer splendour, and be glad he had left the smoky skies and bustle of London behind, and was going home, and would soon see Annabelle again.

Charlsby slumbered under the summer sun. The servants rushed out to greet their arrival, the guests were taken to their rooms to unpack and rest, and Allan was left standing in the hall, his dogs bouncing enthusiastically about him.

"Is her ladyship in the morning room, Plessey?"

"No, my lord. Her ladyship has gone to Chester for the day."

"And... do we have any other guests in the house?"

"Only Mrs Pargeter, my lord, who has gone out in the barouche with Mr Cross."

"With Mr Cross? At least that means there cannot be any urgent business matters requiring immediate attention. I shall go out for a walk, Plessey. The woods are so fine at this time of year, and London has no pleasures so appealing as my own estate on a summer's day."

"Very well, my lord. I expect it will be an hour or more before the gentlemen are downstairs again."

An hour. Long enough to fill his lungs with clean air and soothe his mind with the quiet rustle of greenery above him, the crunch of last year's leaves under his boots and the gentle murmur of the birds. He strode out of the house again, the dogs at his heels, and across the lawn and deer park. Only when he reached the fringes of the woods did he pause, and look back across the grounds to the house. His house and his home. He had never lived anywhere else, and could not imagine doing so. Apart from school and his brief stint in the army, he had never been away from Charlsby for more than a fortnight at a time. It made him feel at ease in a way that nowhere else did, and certainly not London, where he fitted in as well as a sparrow amongst peacocks.

There was a massive and very old oak tree just here, with a seat around its trunk, and here he sat as the dogs chased butterflies attracted by the wildflowers in the meadow. He could just see the schoolroom windows, and wondered whether *she* were in there at that moment, talking French to the girls, or guiding their fingers on the keys of the pianoforte, or watching them walk slowly round the room with wooden rings balanced on their heads to perfect their deportment. His mind brought her sweet face vividly into view, with its softly rounded cheeks, her lips as luscious as strawberries and her hair curling about the nape of her white neck. Annabelle. Delightful Annabelle. How he had missed her! Tonight he would see her again, and perhaps, since all the other guests had gone, he could have the pleasure of inviting her to sit by his side. But no, for Marisa would expect that privilege.

A heavy sigh escaped him. He was getting into deep water with Annabelle. No... Miss Winterton... he must keep reminding himself that she was Miss Winterton. He had made a fool of himself, had proposed marriage in recompense and she had turned him down. She was still in love with that Keeling fellow, however unworthy of her regard he might be. She was not likely to soothe her broken heart with a dull fellow like Allan, that much was certain, however much he might long for her.

Besides, she was a governess and he was an earl and, as Robin Dalton had pointed out, he could do much better than a governess, and better even than Miss Winterton of Woodside. He ought to forget about her, for he should be thinking of the daughter of an earl, at least, and one with twenty or thirty thousand pounds to her name. That was the proper thing to do, if he were minded to remarry. Perhaps he should appear at the assemblies in Chester again, or go back to London in the autumn and try his luck. Or Bath, perhaps. That was a good place to find a suitable wife, and less dreadful than London. Or there was always his friend Carrbridge, whose matchmaking wife might be able to fix him up.

Or he could do nothing, and leave George to inherit. Yes, perhaps that was best, because if he could not have Annabelle, he had no wish to lock himself into another cold, loveless marriage. He must forget about her—

There she was! Down in the meadow, her bonnet shading her face as she picked wild flowers. His heart lurched painfully. She was coming towards him, quite unaware of his presence yet. Bending down to pet the dogs, she was smiling so enchantingly that all his resolutions went out of his head instantly.

It was no good — how could he contemplate giving her up, when he was head over heels in love with her?

# 14: Of Mistletoe

He stood, and the movement drew her gaze. She smiled and waved to him, and his heart lurched even more. Oh dear Lord, she was so open and artless and friendly, with not one whit of consciousness in her face as she hurried up the slope towards him. What was his own face displaying? Everything, he supposed, but perhaps she noticed nothing for her smile never faltered.

"I should have guessed it was you," she said. "The dogs are never so happy when the groom takes them out."

"Miss Winterton." He bowed, and belatedly she remembered to curtsy to him. "I need not ask if you are well, for I can see that the summer air suits you. But you are alone — where are my daughters today?"

"The dowager countess has taken them to Chester to obtain materials for gowns for them. Their half mourning gowns are too heavy for this warmer weather."

"And you did not wish to go with them? You have excellent taste in sartorial matters, and could have advised Mother. She rarely ventures into the higher levels of society these days, so her notions of fashion are rather dated."

Annabelle smiled but shook her head. "Oh, that would never do! The governess putting forward her opinions against those of a countess? No, indeed, I should not attempt it." She sat down on the bench, and patted the seat for him to sit too, in the most companionable way. "But tell me of your travels. Was London quite horrid? It is the most miserable place in the world in hot weather, in my opinion."

They talked of London, and the three men he had brought back with him to undertake the investigation, and then he told her of George and his infatuation with the Lady Grace Bucknell, and she was so sympathetic and understanding that he was overwhelmed by love for her.

"Miss Winterton," he said, too enthralled to be careful in his speech to her, "I wonder if you know your danger in sitting here with me."

She tipped her head on one side, smiling. "I am not afraid of you."

"We are sat beneath the boughs of one of the oldest oak trees on the estate."

"It is a fine tree indeed," she said. "No one could say otherwise."

"Then we are agreed. But this oak tree has one very special peculiarity, very rare in these parts." He pointed upwards. "It is one of very few whereon grows the mistletoe." He pointed upwards. "And I am still desirous of that kiss I was so unfortunate as to be deprived of on an earlier occasion."

She shifted herself a foot or so further from him, but she was laughing, not at all discomfited. "Is it not enough, my lord, that I must endure the dalliance of the persistent Mr Cross without becoming the target of your flirtation also?"

"Why do you suppose I must be flirting with you?" he said, suddenly finding it hard to breathe.

"Because the alternatives are worse," she said at once, the smile wiped from her face. "If I imagined you had any serious intent in mind, then I must conclude you to be either insane or insulting. Since I cannot believe you to be either, then you must only be teasing me. It is unkind in you, my lord, to make me the object of your amusement. You will forgive me if I take my leave of you, for my flowers will wilt if not placed in water soon."

~~~~~

Annabelle walked quickly down the slope, trying to maintain her decorum whilst putting as much distance as possible between the earl and herself. Infuriating man! When he looked at her in that way, she could almost believe— But no, it was impossible. He could not seriously consider marrying her. If she were not his daughters' governess, perhaps it would be tenable, although highly imprudent. But as things stood, it was inconceivable. He must marry within his rank, Lady Something-or-other, with a dowry of twenty or thirty thousand, and the benefit of connections. An alliance with one of the other great families of England, that was his duty, not the penniless Miss Winterton of Woodside.

Yet if marriage was out of the question, there remained only two options: a light flirtation, nothing more than an amusement, or else... She could hardly bring herself to consider it. His mistress. Surely he could not have so low an opinion of her as that? Or was he one of those men who assumed that any employee was his for the taking? She had not thought it of him, and even now it was impossible to believe. Every instinct rebelled at the thought. She had thought him such a pleasant man, and she could not be so mistaken in her judgement, surely.

There was no resolving it, so she determined to put him out of her mind altogether.

~~~~~

*'My dearest sister, I have no wish to keep returning to the subject of Jeremy, for I well know that nothing can bring him back to us, and perhaps it seems maudlin to allow such a sad subject to prey on one's mind so, but I was speaking to Mrs C yesterday after church. It was Mama's birth date and so we were putting flowers on the grave, and Mrs C was at Roger's grave nearby. 'How sad it is that you have no grave but the sea for dear Jeremy,' she said. 'Nor any funeral, although children's funerals must be so distressing, with such a tiny coffin. Not that Jeremy's coffin would have been so small, for he was almost as tall as an adult.' So I agreed with her and said, 'Yes, he was very well-grown for his age, was he not?' and she said, and I have said nothing at all to her of Captain Hunt's words to you, so this was quite unprompted, she said, 'I never saw such a well-grown boy of twelve in my life, and had he lived he would have been a giant.' Upon reflection, I am convinced that Captain Hunt must be mistaken, and it was not Jeremy he saw that day at all. Do you not agree? Your loving sister Rosamund.'*

~~~~~

*'Dearest Annabelle, I have had the most alarming thought concerning Jeremy and the information of his last hours so kindly offered to you by Captain Hunt. Is it possible — is it just conceivable — that the person Captain Hunt encountered was some other party entirely, masquerading as Jeremy? For he was quite certain that the person he saw was indeed called Jeremy Winterton, and yet the description is so greatly at variance with all that we know of the real Jeremy. Is there not a possibility that someone took Jeremy's place, and that he is even now alive in the world? I am so excited at the*

*idea that I can barely write my letters intelligibly. Your affectionate sister, Fanny.'*

~~~~~

Annabelle considered wearing one of her newest gowns that evening, a little more fashionable than those she usually chose. But perhaps it would look too particular, as if she were putting on her finery in honour of the earl's return, and that would never do. Besides, she was still somewhat out of charity with him. She wished he would not talk so, about kisses! It was unkind, and very distracting, for she could not help wondering what his kisses would be like. So she donned a gown she had worn many times before, and pinned up her hair in a simple knot. At the last minute, she decided that was too severe and added a little lace ribbon studded with seed pearls.

That evening was a lively one. Captain Edgerton was a rattle, but an amusing one. When he was introduced to Annabelle, he assessed her with the practised air and appreciative eyes of a rake, but he neither said nor did anything to make her feel uncomfortable. Mr Willerton-Forbes said little, but she had the feeling that he was appraising the company with an acute eye. But George, poor George was so subdued and unlike his usual ebullient self. Her heart went out to him. She understood only too well the misery of a hopeless love.

There was no dancing now that all the young ladies had left, so Annabelle retreated to her corner with her stitchery, while Captain Edgerton drew almost all the rest of the company into a noisy game of Commerce, where he chaffed the gentlemen and flirted outrageously with the ladies. The two aunts twittered in mock horror, Mrs Pargeter blushed like a girl, and even Lady Brackenwood unbent enough to laugh at his jokes. Lord

Brackenwood and George had disappeared after dinner, perhaps to take their brandy in the quieter atmosphere of the library.

The evening was warm, despite the terrace windows standing open, and after a while Annabelle crept outside to find cooler air. The moon was almost full, its silver traces catching every ripple of the lake. The lawn sloped down to the water, where a marble seat was invitingly placed, and there her feet led her. To her right lay the deer park, and to her left the lower lake was shrouded in shrubbery, hiding the Chinese bridge and the Grecian Temple on the far side. But before her was the tranquillity of the upper lake, its perfect symmetry broken only by two or three willows stretching whispering fingers towards the water.

She took a deep breath, allowing the cool night air to fill her lungs. There was hardly a sound, except for the occasional plop of something in the water, the sighing of the willows and now and then a burst of laughter from the saloon.

"Another refugee from the jollity?"

She jumped up, startled. Lord Brackenwood had emerged from the hidden shelter of the nearest willow and was walking towards her.

"I beg your pardon, I did not see you. Do I disturb your solitude? Let me go back inside..."

"Do not let me detain you if you prefer to avoid me, but I should be very glad of your company," he said.

He was so straightforward! She had always liked that about him. And the obvious conclusion to draw from it was that he had not been flirting with her at all. She was aware of a tingle of optimism. But there was no time to consider the implications, for he was beside her in moments.

"Will you stay with me for a while?" he said. "George has taken his misery and a brandy bottle to bed, and Captain Edgerton is too lively for my mood tonight. Your conversation would lift my spirits immeasurably." When she hesitated, he added, "You are quite safe from me, Miss Winterton. There is no mistletoe hereabouts."

She had to laugh at that, and sat down at one end of the bench. He punctiliously positioned himself at the other, sitting, elbows on knees, staring out at the water in silence for several minutes. More laughter trickled out from the saloon. Then, with a sigh, he sat upright and folded his arms.

"How restful your company is, Miss Winterton. You are not a chatterer, as so many women are. You feel no need to fill the emptiness with noise."

"It is fortunate for you, then, that it was not my sister Lucy who became your daughters' governess. The only time she stops talking is when she is asleep."

"Is she the one who writes the ten page letters?"

"Indeed she is. Now, with Margaret, one is lucky to get more than a line or two. And Fanny—" For a moment, the tears were very close to the surface, but, taking a deep breath, she blinked them away.

"You miss them," he said in a low voice. "Of course you do. To be so close, and then to be separated... to be someone of consequence, and then to become a governess... Your situation is hard, but so is mine, in many ways. At least you still have the possibility to marry and leave off being a governess. I can never stop being an earl."

"Is it so troublesome, being an earl?"

"Ah, the title, the deference, the riches, every whim catered for... It seems easy on the surface, but it is a great responsibility also. Not so great as in past centuries, when choosing the wrong side could mean the loss of one's head and everything else besides, but there is still the burden of maintaining the inheritance in good order for the next generation. One must always do one's duty. Sometimes I am so very tired of doing my duty, Miss Winterton. Just for once, I should like to have something for myself, something that is not part of my duty but which nevertheless would make me very happy."

She caught her breath, but he was not looking at her, merely staring out at the water. His tone was so level that she concluded that he was talking about the general, not the particular.

"Few of us are lucky enough to have exactly what we want," she said softly. "If I had had my wish, I would have been Mrs Charles Keeling now. My sister Fanny would perhaps be Mrs Roland Hawes. And my brother Jeremy... Jeremy would still be alive."

"Tell me about your brother," he said, shifting sideways so that he could look directly into her face.

"Jeremy was the best of us, I think. It was as if the most admirable feature of each of us had been given to him, and none of our flaws. He was as handsome as Rosamund, as enthusiastic about lessons as I was, as easy in company as Lucy, as serious and intent as Margaret, and as sweetly good-natured as Fanny. He loved machinery — clocks, locks, the waterwheel at the mill — such things fascinated him. But mechanical devices were not suitable subjects for Papa's son to take an interest in, and Papa decided he needed to be toughened up. He was sent off to sea to make a man of him, and he was dead within days. Poor Papa never recovered."

"But he was the only son, was he not? Why send him into so dangerous a profession? Or any profession at all. The heir is generally kept at home to learn his duties."

"He was the very image of Mama," she said sadly. "It was a daily grief to Papa. Even so... it was a surprise to all of us when he sent him away. Poor Jeremy! He was terrified of the sea, but Papa would have him go, so go he went. He was only supposed to be a Midshipman for a few years, then he would come home to help Papa manage the estate."

"Yet he did his duty in obeying his father, and there is satisfaction in that," he said.

But there was such bleakness in his voice that she shivered. He noticed her discomfort at once.

"Are you cold? May I fetch a wrap for you? Or let me take you inside."

"I should like to go in, but...the saloon sounds very lively."

"Ah, now there I can help. My last attempt to avoid the saloon saw me entering the house by way of the library window, and an unfortunate encounter with the rum supply. I subsequently decided that such a mode of entry was not conducive to my well-being, or yours either, and I remembered that the service stairs have a door by which entry may be gained, if one has the appropriate key." With a grin that made him look ten years younger, he reached into a waistcoat pocket and produced a large, ornate key. "May I escort you home, Miss Winterton?"

"Why, thank you, Lord Brackenwood."

He offered her his arm, and they walked along the lake until they gained the path, then turned towards the house. Half hidden by ivy and overgrown shrubs, the door yielded silently to his key. Inside a lamp burned low, clearly placed ready for the earl's return.

He lit a candle from it and led the way up the spiral staircase, the sound of their feet echoing against the stone walls.

After a half turn, he said, "This is the door to the library."

"A much safer point of entry than the window."

"Yes, indeed. The breeches I wore that night are beyond repair, Portman informs me. He is most displeased with me."

She chuckled, as he moved on up and around until he came to another door and stopped.

"My room. I shall come no further, Miss Winterton. There will be lamps lit inside for me, so take the candle to light your steps the rest of the way to your chamber."

She took the candle from him, and his fingers brushed hers for the briefest moment. Intentionally? Impossible to say, but suddenly she was aware of his closeness, of the silence that had fallen, of the intimacy of standing beside him, quite alone, on the stair outside his bedroom. His eyes were intent, but he kept his distance and, despite the thumping of her heart, she knew that she was safe with him. It was not fear that speeded her pulse and made her breath hard to draw suddenly.

This would never do! With an effort, she said, "Thank you for your escort, Lord Brackenwood."

"For my part, I thank you for your company," he said, with a slight smile. "You have lightened my mood materially."

"You must not be downhearted," she said quietly. "There is much in your life to be thankful for."

"Indeed there is. But there are still moments of deep sorrow, such as now, for instance."

Nervously, she said, "Now?"

"Indeed. For there is not a bit of mistletoe about the place. Good night, Miss Winterton, and sleep well."

And with a smile, his eyes filled with amusement, he opened his door and vanished inside.

~~~~~

*'My dearest sister, Lucy has written me such a long letter, which Lady Harriet had to pay three shillings and sixpence for, upbraiding me for being foolish. She calls me a widgeon and bird-witted and many other things, and I cannot say she is wrong. I am very sorry indeed if I have given rise to hopes which cannot be fulfilled. It is obvious to me now that Jeremy cannot possibly be alive for why would he stay away and send not a word of himself if he is? Rosamund is more gentle, but she too thinks it was silly of me. Your letter was much kinder, in thinking it to be a natural mistake, but I will take your advice and not let my hopes overwhelm my reason in future. Is Margaret all right? I have not heard from her for an age. Your remorseful sister, Fanny.'*

~~~~~

Annabelle's days were rather disrupted once Mr Willerton-Forbes began his investigation. The room adjacent to the nursery was given over to him for the purpose of conducting interviews, so every time Annabelle went out onto the landing outside the schoolroom, there would be a tearful maid waiting to be questioned, or a footman carrying trays back and forth for the gentlemen. Fortunately, they slept in the guest bedrooms on the floor below. Now that most of the house guests had departed, only the chaplain, Mr Penicuik, had a bedroom on the same floor as Annabelle and since his room connected directly to the chapel, she never saw him.

The investigators began their questions with Lord Brackenwood, and then, protesting volubly, Lady Brackenwood, before working their way in rank order through the household, family first and then servants. But on the third day, Annabelle herself was called in. Setting her pupils a passage of Shakespeare to memorise under the supervision of a nursery maid, she knocked tentatively on the door and went in.

The bed and most of the furnishings had been pushed aside, and a long table of unvarnished wood set in the middle of the room. Mr Willerton-Forbes sat behind it, with Mr Neate at one end taking notes. Captain Edgerton sat, arms folded, on the window seat. All the gentlemen rose as she entered.

"Do come in, Miss Winterton, and take a seat," Mr Willerton-Forbes said, indicating a chair by the table opposite his own.

"I am not sure how I can help you," Annabelle said, sitting down and smoothing her skirts. "I was not here when Lady Brackenwood died, and did not even know the family then."

"Precisely," the lawyer said, resuming his seat with a smile. "You are an outsider, as we are, but with the advantage of several months' residency. You have become acquainted with the family — indeed, the whole household — and may give us much valuable information. Are you willing to answer a few questions?"

"Of course, if I can."

The first questions were easy — which servants she had contact with, whether any of them had talked about Lady Brackenwood or raised any suspicions about her death. Then on to the family, and Annabelle remembered something Mr Jeremiah Skelton had said.

"The old gentleman gets very confused, and when I first arrived he thought I was Lady Brackenwood. Then, when it was pointed out that her ladyship was dead, he said, *'Who killed her?'*. But he gets so muddled. I daresay it means nothing."

"And the dowager countess? Does she take an interest in your lessons?"

"Not at all."

"Is she kind to you?"

Annabelle had to smile at that. "Neither kind nor unkind. She ignores me as much as possible, which is entirely proper. I have only talked to her at length once, when her sole concern was to warn me away from thoughts of marrying her son."

"And do you have such thoughts?"

That wiped the smile from her face instantly. "Is that relevant?" Mr Willerton-Forbes made no movement, but she felt as if he were watching her with heightened interest, like a cat, alert and ready to pounce. So she added smoothly, "No, I have no thoughts of marrying her son."

"But he might have thoughts of marrying you, Miss Winterton." Again, she was aware of a tension in the room.

"He got very drunk one night and tried to kiss me. The next day, being an honourable man, he felt obliged to offer for me. I declined." She decided not to make any mention of mistletoe, for how could such a thing be put into words? She hardly knew herself what it meant, if anything.

But after a long silence, the lawyer went on to talk about the doctor and the apothecary and her ladyship's medication. Annabelle knew little of any of them. She had occasionally seen Dr Wilcox coming and going on his visits to the dowager countess, and she had once or twice visited the apothecary for her own needs, but she knew nothing of her ladyship's illness or medicines.

"So you never went into her bedroom? It was not cleared after her death, and one or two of the servants admitted to taking some of her ladyship's tonics and so forth. Did you ever do likewise?"

"I have never been into the bedroom downstairs, no, only the bedroom she used on this floor, since it adjoins the schoolroom, and the supplies of paper and so forth are kept in the closet there."

The lawyer's face, usually so bland, changed to one of surprise. "She had a *second* bedroom? Will you show us, if you please?"

She led the way onto the landing and into the schoolroom, startling the three girls into silence, and then into the large bedroom beyond. The three men at once fell to examining every drawer and cupboard and shelf.

"No medicaments here," Captain Edgerton said.

"There were a great many," Annabelle said. "I put them away for safety, now that the room is generally left unlocked. I did not wish my pupils to find them. They are in a locked box through here."

She took them into the small room and unlocked the box, revealing a score or more bottles, jars and lozenge tins.

"Miss Winterton, you are a wonder!" Mr Willerton-Forbes said, with a beaming smile. "This is exactly what we had hoped to find."

"Then... you believe she took something... that Lady Brackenwood's death was not natural?"

"Natural? No, there was nothing natural about it. Her ladyship was poisoned."

# 15: Of Poison (July)

Mr Willerton-Forbes and his colleagues carefully lifted all the items out of the box, and arranged them in three groups on the floor, two groups containing a mixture of bottles and pill boxes, and one bottle on its own. The lawyer picked up the lone bottle and passed it to Annabelle.

"Miss Winterton, was this bottle amongst the rest? It is not your own, for instance?"

"It was in the drawer with all the others. The label is different, though. This group you have set aside here is from the apothecary, for I recognise Mr Burton's hand. These ones must be from Dr Wilcox and the physician in Chester. But the label on this one is in her ladyship's own hand."

Again they looked astonished. "How do you know that?" Captain Edgerton said sharply. "We found nothing in her ladyship's hand in her room downstairs."

"She kept prodigious notes on everything her daughters were to learn. Do you wish to see her notebooks? I have them in the schoolroom desk."

"Will you show Captain Edgerton where they may be found? Bring a sample here, Michael."

When Annabelle went through to the schoolroom, the three girls were whispering together, paying no attention to their books.

"Would you like to go for a walk?" She turned to the maid. "Matilda, please accompany them. You may walk three times around both lakes, with no dawdling or running, if you please. If you wish to rest, you may sit in the Grecian Temple for five minutes. Remember you are the daughters of an earl."

They followed Matilda demurely to the nursery to find their bonnets and gloves, while Annabelle showed Captain Edgerton the drawer where she had stowed Lady Brackenwood's notebooks. He flipped through one of them, deftly catching a pink dried flower that fell from the pages.

"Hmm. A romantic at heart, then," he said, waving the flower about. "Yet the schoolwork is very dull stuff. Your plan to have them memorising *Romeo And Juliet* is more fun. Shall you act it out when the young ladies have it by heart? If you need a Mercutio, I would be happy to oblige, or if you were Juliet, I could play a most convincing Romeo."

He smiled at her in such an optimistic manner that she could not help laughing. "You are an outrageous flirt, Captain, considering you are a married man."

"Ah, marriage has not rendered me blind, Miss Winterton. I may still admire a beautiful woman, and enjoy her company, but the chains of love are strong, and stretch from London even so far as the wilds of Cheshire. You are quite safe from me. Let us take this back to Willerton-Forbes."

She chuckled at the idea of herself as beautiful. The most she ever aspired to was to hear herself described as a handsome woman, and that when she was in her ballroom finery. Yes, he was a dreadful flirt, but he made her blush a little, and in her present situation, it warmed her heart to be admired, even by such a man as Captain Edgerton.

The lawyer examined the notebook carefully. It confirmed that the handwriting on the label was Lady Brackenwood's, but why she would possess this one sleeping draught with the instructions labelled in her own hand, when all her other medicines were prescribed by physicians or the apothecary, was more than anyone could guess.

~~~~~

The saloon was subdued that night. Willerton-Forbes had told everyone that he was investigating the possibility of poison, either accidental or otherwise, but murder could not be ruled out.

"Nobody would want to murder Eloise," the dowager countess said robustly. "She hadn't an enemy in the world. It must have been an accident. Perhaps she ate some bad shellfish. One can't be too careful when preparing such dishes."

"I shall be talking again to the cook, of course," Willerton-Forbes said. "However, I already know the dishes that were served the night Lady Brackenwood died, and who partook of each one, and I cannot find anything, food or drink, that was served only to her ladyship. I think we must look elsewhere for the cause."

"I daresay she muddled her pills or took too much of one or other of them. She had so many different sorts. Dr Wilcox was always bringing something new for her to try, and always two bottles, one for each of her bedrooms. It would be so easy to make a mistake."

"Let us hope that is the case," Allan said. "It would certainly be very bad for me if it turns out to be murder."

"Indeed! Such a dreadful thing for the family to be associated with that sort of thing," the dowager countess said with a shudder.

"Especially if the head of that family is hanged for it," George said with an attempt at levity. "Can you imagine it — a trial in the House of Lords, and a big splash in all the newspapers. Although... rather good news for me, eh, cousin? Perhaps I had Cousin Eloise murdered in order to get you hanged so that I might inherit the earldom. Have you considered that, Willerton-Forbes? Am I under suspicion?"

"Everyone is under suspicion," Willerton-Forbes said soberly, wiping the smile from George's face.

It was fortunate that Plessey announced dinner at that point, for no one quite knew what to say. Allan led his mother into the dining room, the rest following in unaccustomed silence. They sat, the soup was served and the meal commenced without a single word being spoken. When the footmen had withdrawn, it was Marisa who broke the silence.

"You did not really mean it, surely, Mr Willerton-Forbes?" she said. "It cannot be that *everyone* is under suspicion. Why, Miss Winterton was not even here at the time, and nor was I. You cannot suspect *us*, I am certain."

The lawyer gave a wintry smile. "No, indeed, Mrs Pargeter. You were not here and, even if you had been, you had no reason to wish your sister dead. That is a very important piece of the puzzle, as you will appreciate. If this is truly murder, then the perpetrator must have had a powerful urge to remove Lady Brackenwood from this world, compelling enough to risk being hanged for it. Even if we find out that her ladyship was murdered, unless we can discover *why* we cannot move forward."

"Exactly!" the dowager countess said, speaking loudly across the table. "This is what I've been telling you all along. No one wanted Eloise dead. No one had a reason to murder her."

"Except me," Allan said. "Is it not so, Willerton-Forbes? Who had a better reason to wish his wife dead than her husband, who has no son? If you are looking for someone with a reason to murder my late wife, I must be at the top of your list."

"That is true," the lawyer said easily, laying down his soup spoon. "But yours is not the only name on the list, my lord. The dowager countess also has a reason to wish that you might have a son. Mr Skelton has helpfully provided us with a reason why he might have wished her ladyship dead. There was also her lady's maid, who had been discovered stealing and was about to be turned off without a reference. And Mr Penicuik had quarrelled with her—"

The chaplain dropped his spoon into his soup with a squeak of alarm.

"Then there are the Ladies Dorothea, Florence and Frederica," the lawyer continued relentlessly. "Lady Brackenwood's regime for their education was harsh, and they may have resented it."

"My daughters!" Allan said, horrified. "You cannot seriously imagine that any of them would murder their own mother just because she kept them at their desks for longer than they liked? They are *children!*"

"We must consider every possibility," Willerton-Forbes said seriously. "It would be fatal to assume anything."

"Ridiculous!" the dowager countess said loudly, in a tone which brooked no argument, rendering the room silent again.

Allan had Marisa on his right hand, so he introduced the subject of Devonshire, her husband's county of birth, where she had lived for the past several years. Captain Edgerton had visited the county and was quite willing to do his part in describing its delights, and by this means, aided by the freely flowing claret, the company was brought back to some semblance of good humour. But there was a tension underlying their polite conversation now. Someone in Charlsby, perhaps even one of those gathered around the dinner table, might very well be a murderer.

~~~~~

Annabelle was unsettled by Mr Willerton-Forbes' frank expression of his thoughts. The stark admission that Lady Brackenwood might have died from poison, and his list of those suspected of murder had chilled her to the bone. None of those listed seemed likely to Annabelle. Allan — no, she could not believe him capable of it, nor the dowager countess. George Skelton — again, no, however much he might appear to benefit from such a crime. As for the three girls, the very idea was ludicrous, and Mr Penicuik was the gentlest, most timid man imaginable. The lady's maid, now, that was possible, although murdering one's mistress to prevent her giving a bad reference seemed a little extreme. Besides, her thieving had been widely known, and she could not be certain of receiving any reference if her mistress were dead.

It was the first time Annabelle had thought seriously about the possibility of murder and her dreams that night were filled with amorphous fears. She woke not long after dawn, and as soon as she heard the kitchen door opened three floors below, she got up and dressed herself and went out for a walk through the woods. The cool morning air and brisk exercise could not remove her fears entirely, but it gave an opening for her rational mind, and she remembered that Mr Willerton-Forbes and his colleagues were bent on finding the murderer, if indeed such a person existed. Furthermore, Allan had invited them to Charlsby, which he would hardly do if he had himself poisoned his wife. No suspicion could be sustained against him.

This thought cheered her more than any other. It was very bad to have the possibility of murder in their midst, but so long as Allan was innocent, there was nothing that need concern her in the matter. Then she wondered at herself for such thoughts. Was it possible that she was developing a fondness for him? He was a very likable man, there was no denying it. He had not Charles's looks or stylish air of fashion, but he was such an amiable man, with a charm all his own, and there was no doubt he had driven Charles from her mind to a degree. She was still unhappy, but not as unhappy as she had been before she had met the earl. Had he not shown a certain partiality for her, she doubted she would have taken much notice of him. But now... she considered once again what it might be like to kiss him.

How foolish she was! Even thinking about the earl in such a light was a good way to lead her to another disappointment. She would not be fooled again! Giving herself a mental shake, she returned to the house determined not to give way to any further romantic thoughts about Allan... Lord Brackenwood. Her employer, she reminded herself.

As she reached the landing to return to her room, she caught sight of a wisp of skirt disappearing into the schoolroom, the door closing soundlessly behind the intruder. It was not the hour for the maids to clean, and her pupils were incapable of doing anything silently, so who could it be?

Sudden anger gripped her. It could only be one of the maids, bent on some mischief. Quickly she crossed the landing and followed the mysterious visitor into the schoolroom. The room was empty but the door to the small room stood open, and sounds could be heard from within. Annabelle paused on the threshold in astonishment.

"Mrs Pargeter? Are you looking for something?"

Wearing only a nightgown and wrap, she was engaged in rifling through the chest of drawers, but at Annabelle's words, she jumped, and turned round. "Oh, Miss Winterton! How you did creep up on me! I had no notion you would be up and about so early or I should have asked for your help."

"I am perfectly happy to help now, if you wish it," Annabelle said, calmer now that she knew her visitor was a guest. "Do you want something of the late Lady Brackenwood's? The drawers are full of her things — gloves and stockings and so on. There are gowns in the wardrobe."

"Yes, I see that. The truth is, Miss Winterton, that I could not sleep a wink last night for thinking of all Mr Willerton-Forbes said, of poison, and that it could not have been in the food or drink, and so it must have been one of her medicines. There was nothing out of the ordinary in her usual bedroom, where I sleep, but then I discovered that she sometimes slept up here and I could not rest until I had looked for myself. Just imagine if the very poison that had killed my poor sister were still lurking here, undetected."

Annabelle was not sure that she should be discussing what had been found in the room, for Mrs Pargeter did not strike her as the most discreet person in the world. She might mention it in the strictest confidence to her maid and within an hour every servant in the house would know of it. She contented herself, therefore, with saying only, "You may be easy in your mind, ma'am, for there are no medicines in this room."

"Ah." Mrs Pargeter gazed at Annabelle, as if assessing her trustworthiness. "Well, that is a relief. I have been worrying myself unnecessarily, it seems."

"We are all prey to these sudden fears," Annabelle said. "I doubt anyone slept well last night, after all that Mr Willerton-Forbes said. The sooner this matter is resolved the better."

"Oh, yes, indeed," Mrs Pargeter said. "Well, I had better go back to my room. Perhaps my breakfast tray will have arrived by now."

So saying, she glided out of the room.

When Annabelle heard Mr Willerton-Forbes, Captain Edgerton and Mr Neate come up the stairs to their office, she met them on the landing, and told them what had occurred.

"I did not feel it was wise to disclose every detail," she said.

"You were quite right, Miss Winterton," Mr Willerton-Forbes said. "The less said the better."

"Although... it makes me uneasy to withhold information from Mrs Pargeter, for she is not under suspicion, is she?"

Mr Willerton-Forbes smiled. "I am naturally suspicious of everyone, but in this case I cannot see how Mrs Pargeter might have poisoned her sister when she was at the other end of the country, nor why she might wish to do so."

Annabelle nodded. "Exactly. I am sure that Lady Brackenwood's death was an accident, but if anyone murdered her, it must have been someone who was here. Her maid, for instance."

"Indeed. The maid has been traced, and invited to come here to tell what she knows," Mr Willerton-Forbes said.

"If she does not come, we will have our murderer," Captain Edgerton said grimly.

~~~~~

*'Dear Annabelle Aunt Letty has died Margaret'*

~~~~~

### *JULY*

Annabelle was wrestling with some number work with Dorothea, while Florence and Frederica flew through their own sums. They had such a great facility with mathematics, but struggled with reading and writing, whereas Dorothea was very much the opposite. Since Annabelle had similar affinities, she was far more inclined to sympathise with poor Dorothea's sufferings and dismiss the younger girls' struggles. It was hard to remember that not everyone felt that books were the answer to every problem ever conceived of, and most of those yet to be imagined. Dorothea, Annabelle had discovered, wrote poetry and prose to a commendable degree, and might one day aspire to be a published author, while her two sisters had yet to grasp the point of writing at all, except as a means to torture innocent girls.

While they were thus engaged, the schoolroom door opened with a subdued snick, as if the person entering were trying to avoid notice. Annabelle assumed, therefore, that it was one of the maids, and ignored the newcomer. It was Dorothea who looked up and squealed in delight.

"Papa! You have come to see us! *Please* will you help me, for I cannot manage this work at all."

"Another time, perhaps, Dody. I am come to take the three of you out for a walk. Go and get your bonnets and gloves on."

"Oooh, yes!" Florence cried. "Three times round the lakes—"

"No running or dawdling!" Frederica said, laughing. With a whisk of muslin skirts, the three bounded off to the nursery.

Annabelle had the greatest foreboding. The girls saw only an unexpected treat, but she could read Allan's face rather well now. His expression was filled with... sadness, perhaps. Sympathy. It was bad news, she knew it.

He laid the London newspaper on the table in front of her. "Page two. Take the rest of the day off, Miss Winterton." Then he left as quietly as he had arrived. A few minutes later, she heard the girls go chattering out to the landing and down the stairs, Allan's low rumble mingling with their high voices.

Terrified, she fumbled with the pages. A death — it must be a death. One of her sisters, surely. It could not be about Aunt Letty, for the notice for that had already appeared. Rosamund, perhaps. Or Robin — oh God, no!

She spread the page open and scanned the columns as fast as she could. Then she caught her breath.

*'The engagement is announced between Mr Charles Keeling, eldest son of Mr Thomas Keeling of Littlemarsh, Brinshire to Miss Cynthia Lorrimer, eldest daughter of Mr David Lorrimer of Chester.'*

Not a death, then, or at least, not that kind of death. Only the death of all her hopes and dreams.

# 16: Of Kisses

Annabelle could not say how long she sat, staring at the notice in the paper. For three years she had been in expectation of this news, yet it was still a shock to discover that Charles was betrothed. And to Miss Lorrimer, who was the shyest young lady in England, and had the most protective parents. How had it been managed? With Charles's boundless charm, she supposed, and persistence and determination, and an inexperienced young lady who could not help responding to his wooing. That at least she understood, and perhaps there came a point where even the most hard-hearted father might crumble, in seeing his daughter swept up in the throes of love. Charles was not, after all, a fortune hunter, merely a man who must marry prudently, and perhaps Miss Lorrimer, her family only recently established among the gentry, was glad to have so eligible a husband. She would—

"Miss Winterton?"

She jumped, not having heard him come in. "Back already? That was a short walk."

The earl smiled in his gentle way. "We were gone for two hours at least. Five circuits round the lakes, no running or dawdling, and then up to the woods to see the wild strawberries. May I get you anything? Some brandy?"

"Thank you, but no. I am perfectly well. This is not unexpected after all."

"No, but..." He hesitated, one hand on the back of a chair. "May I sit?" She assented, and he carefully lifted the chair so that the legs did not scrape against the wooden floor, and sat down. "Miss Winterton, if it is of any comfort to you, I believe he will come to regret you. Miss Lorrimer may be a charming young lady, but she is far from your equal in quickness or temperament."

She managed a small smile. "Yet she is far beyond me in wealth, and the marriage is not as mismatched as many, in terms of rank and family. And in temper, for she is amiable and he has no bad habits that I ever discovered. They will deal together admirably."

"Perhaps. I thought her father very much opposed to the match, if only for the disparity in wealth, but perhaps he feels that Mr Keeling's expectations justify the risk."

"Twelve hundred a year?" she said, puzzled.

"There is a cousin, a sickly child of five, who holds the family fortune presently. If he should die, then Mr Keeling will stand to inherit a great deal more. Another two thousand a year, eventually, according to the industrious researches of Mr Cross. With Miss Lorrimer's dowry, that will give Mr Keeling an income approaching four thousand a year, a very comfortable sum."

"He mentioned something of the matter, although I had forgotten it until now," she said thoughtfully.

"You may be sure that Mr Keeling has not, however," the earl said. "He is a man who is very mindful of monetary matters. Forgive me... I do not mean to disparage a man you hold in high esteem. In his position, such mindfulness is no more than good sense."

She nodded, but said nothing. What was there to say? His interest in money had shocked her, but she understood it.

The earl cleared his throat. "It pleases me to find you so composed. I hope you will be able to put him out of your mind, in time."

"If this had happened two or three years ago, I would have been distraught," she said quietly. "Now... it is a shock, of course. Nothing quite prepares one... but at least I have the comfort of knowing that he did not, in the end, regard me with dishonourable eyes. It remains only to regret my foolishness in falling in love with him in the first place."

"But that is perfectly understandable," the earl said, leaning forward to rest his elbows on the table between them. "He is handsome, well-dressed, with excellent manners and an open, trustworthy demeanour — how could any young lady help falling in love with such a man?"

She laughed at that. "But I know fifty such men, at least. One meets them all the time. You yourself fall under the same description, Lord Brackenwood. One does not fall in love with a man solely on account of his good manners."

He cleared his throat again. "You mean, I suppose, that it is his underlying goodness that makes the difference?"

"Ultimately, perhaps. One grows to know a man and thus learns whether he be worthy of one's love. But falling in love is not about looks or manners, it is far more unconscious than that. I liked Charles well enough, and his attentions flattered me, but it was not until Willowbye that I fell in love. Willowbye, my lord, is one of those old houses that looks to be thrown together by some mischievous spirit. Wings here, wings there, tossed out whenever the owner had a little money to spare, and at the heart of it, the medieval great hall, with bare walls and arched wooden roof, just as it must have looked four hundred years ago. There was a ball there, three years ago next month. I danced with Charles, and then with several others, and finally with Charles again, and somehow, on our way to the supper room, we found ourselves in a little ante-room, quite abandoned and dark. There in the shadows he kissed me and poured his ardour into my ears. No man had ever kissed me before, or held me that way, as if he would never let me go, warming me right to my toes. I felt as if I were drowning in his love. For perhaps half an hour we were quite alone, and at the end of it I was so deep in love that I could not tell the difference between up and down. And the reason was *passion* — what we felt in that room was passion, and his was just as great as mine. That is why I have never quite been able to forget him. Or to forgive him for abandoning me in the way he did, not instantly, but by means of a slow withdrawal, a gradual fading away. It was months before I understood what he was about, months of agony. If he had only told me, openly and honestly, that he could not marry me... It would still have hurt, but at least I would have known. There would not have been the endless waiting and hoping... That is what women do, *all* we can do. We wait and hope."

He nodded, saying nothing. Once or twice as she talked, his hand moved across the table towards her, as if he wanted to touch her but dared not. She was struck by the impropriety of talking so to her employer.

"Good gracious, I am treating you very much as a friend, Lord Brackenwood. Forgive me, I should not talk so."

"I shall always be your friend," he said, with such simplicity that her breath caught in her throat. "I am honoured by your confidence, Miss Winterton. You may tell me anything you wish, and to show you that I mean what I say, I shall share a confidence with you, if you will hear it."

"Of course."

"Mine is also about a kiss. When I first came into my honours, my mother wished me to marry at once. George was at the time an unpromising twelve-year-old whom I had barely met above twice, so it seemed sensible. Mother hauled me off to Wales to meet her distant kin, including two sisters, Eloise and Marisa. Like you with Mr Keeling, I was not in love, but there was a strong attraction, on both sides. Even with my lack of experience, I was aware of the way she looked at me, the little signs. And then one evening she drew me into an empty room and... and kissed me. Very thoroughly. Very expertly, I now realise. And I was lost."

"But how charming!" Annabelle said. "And so you fell in love with your wife."

"Oh no," he said, and there was a bleakness on his face that shook her to the core. "I fell in love with Marisa. The next day, I offered for Eloise, because my mother wished it and her father wished it and there was a dowry of thirty thousand pounds that came with her which I would not get with her younger sister."

"Oh," she said, sitting back in her chair abruptly. "But you could afford to marry for love, surely?"

"Perhaps, but I did not know that at the time. The estate was still tied up with the lawyers. My mother told me we needed money, she told me it was all arranged with Eloise's father and that I could not renege on those arrangements. You think me foolish, I daresay, and indeed, sometimes I think so myself, but at the time... I was two and twenty, and I had lost my career, my adored older brother and my father in very short order. I was adrift and unhappy and had always done as my mother commanded, and so I married Eloise. And I can tell you, Miss Winterton, that it takes a very long time to stop regretting the love thrown away. Mr Keeling will be unhappy for years."

This time she was the one who reached across the table, and he did not flinch when she took his hand. So warm, the fingers so soft... "I am so very sorry. Have you been dreadfully miserable?"

He smiled, then. "No, not exactly. Just... empty. Aware that there ought to be something more to life. For a long time, I was sure I could make her happy, that she would turn to me... but she wanted nothing I could offer her."

His words wrung her heart. She had seen the sadness in his eyes when she had first arrived at Charlsby, but had ascribed it to grief. Now she saw it again, the raw pain of a marriage without love, of endless enduring.

"As for Marisa..." He stopped, and she held her breath, unwilling to force confidences, but curious what he would say of her, the woman he had loved many years ago and had only recently rediscovered. He gave a wry smile. "One discovers eventually that the dream of perfect felicity is no less ephemeral than any other dream, or perhaps one's ideal of the other sex changes with time. I am not sure that I would have been any happier with Marisa than with Eloise. But I shall never know, now. I made my choice, and it cannot be unmade."

She understood him. Mrs Pargeter was his sister, and could never be his wife.

"Prudence has a great deal to answer for," she said, idly stroking his hand as it lay passively in hers. "Charles prudently turned away from me, and you prudently married the older sister.

Both decisions were sensible, at the time. There is no blame to attach anywhere."

"Not in your case, perhaps," he said, shifting restlessly, so that his hand slipped away from hers. "In mine, my mother was the instigator. She chose Eloise for me, although I have no idea why."

"Have you not?" Annabelle said, smiling at him. "Having met Mrs Pargeter, I can imagine that she would have ruled the roost here, and the dowager countess would have been obliged to give way. Was the late countess a more biddable creature?"

He laughed then. "The timidest soul alive! Yes, she never dared to stand up to Mother. Do you think that was it? That Mother wanted no rival in the house?" Then, abruptly, the bleakness was back. "Aye, that would be like her. She loves to... how did you put it? Rule the roost. She certainly rules me."

"Only where you allow yourself to be ruled, I think," Annabelle said.

Something crossed his face then, a look that she could not interpret, and he sat upright in his chair again.

"Miss Winterton..."

He got up and paced restlessly across the floor to the window, his footsteps echoing on the wooden floor. The house was quiet in these afternoon hours, everyone resting before the dressing gong, or engaged in peaceful occupations. There was no sound from the nursery, so perhaps the girls had gone out with the nursery maids. Mr Willerton-Forbes had left the house early, and Captain Edgerton was away on some secretive business of his own. Mr Penicuik would be in the chapel. There was no one else on this floor, and probably no one on the floor below. Annabelle was alone with the earl in the schoolroom, the door closed, and yet she felt utterly safe with him.

"Miss Winterton..."

He flopped down onto the chair again and ran a hand through his hair, which disordered it not at all. He was not one of those men who spent an hour arranging his locks into a carefully contrived state of seeming naturalness. His hair owed nothing at all to artifice. If he did more than run a comb through it each morning, she would be surprised.

"Miss Winterton..." Now his fingers drummed on the table. She waited. With a heaving breath, he began, "I beg your pardon. Impulsiveness is not my besetting sin, but I must speak. You have said that you value openness and honesty, and so do I, so I *will* speak, and thus you will understand and will not be surprised when—" He stopped again. "This is awkward."

She said nothing, hardly knowing what to say to such words. It was almost as if... but surely he could not be on the point of offering for her again? Had she not scotched that idea sufficiently? But she coloured up, all the same.

With another deep breath, he said, "Very well, then, openness it is," almost as if he had been conducting some internal argument with himself. "Straight at the fence, and no jibbing," he added in an undertone. Then he continued in a stronger voice, "Miss Winterton, I wish you to understand that when this ghastly business of Eloise's death has been resolved, and if I am not hanged for it, I intend to make you an offer of marriage in due form."

"My lord, I—"

"No, no, say nothing!" He raised a hand, alarm written all over his face. "Pray say nothing at all. I only wish to make you aware of my state of mind, so that... you will not be surprised, and will not be in any doubt of my intentions. The peculiar nature of your position here makes it improper for me to show you those little attentions which would... or, at least, *might* lead you to— But I cannot, as you will appreciate. I cannot say or do anything which might harm your reputation, or... or raise speculation in other quarters. It would be unendurable for you. But I wish you to understand, do you see?" He was almost pleading with her, but she was too shocked to speak. "There! I have said it and now you know, and we will not speak of this again until... afterwards. When this business is settled. But we are still friends, I hope, and even if I appear to treat you in public as merely the governess, you will know that you are much more than that, to me. And now I will leave you. I shall see you at dinner?"

She heard the question in his tone, and nodded.

"Good. Until then, Miss Winterton." And without another word, he was gone.

Annabelle could barely breathe. It was the strangest conversation she had ever had. She had been the recipient of more than one offer of marriage, and one gentleman she recalled had made it very plain a few days before that he intended to speak. He had followed the proper form, of approaching her father and obtaining his permission to pay his addresses, which he then did, very prettily. Her reply was perhaps less pretty, for it is hard to make a refusal sound sweet. Then there was the impassioned gentleman who had proposed in the rose garden and then in the summer house and again in the morning room and finally in the drawing room. He had not been to see Papa, and he had given no warning, either, simply blurting out his admiration and wishes. Her refusals there became rather short. And the sweet parson from the neighbouring village, a man she might well have accepted for himself, but not when she would be sharing the marital home with his five children, his mother, his two maiden aunts and a stipend insufficient for their needs.

But never before had she encountered a gentleman who announced that he was going to offer for her, but not yet. And she had not the least idea what she felt about it, or even what the earl felt. Was he in love with her? His attempts to kiss her suggested some kind of attraction, but nothing more. And he had not talked of love or any of the proper things that a proposal should contain. Because, whatever it was, it was not a proposal. Oh, it was vexatious! Idiotic man, to tease her so! And yet she smiled, even as she thought it. Such a lovely man, and she could do worse. Far, far worse.

~~~~~

Allan was shaking as he left the schoolroom, but when he had regained his library and poured himself a large measure of brandy and drunk some of it, he began to laugh. That would put Mother's eye out! There could be no drawn out argument to sap his spirit, no futile attempts to persuade him. She would rule the roost no more. She would sulk, naturally, for she always did when her will was thwarted, but he could cope with that. Now he could tell her openly that he planned to offer for Miss Winterton and he could not be denied, for it was a matter of honour. He had announced his intention and he could not honourably withdraw. He sipped his brandy and chuckled.

Annabelle, meanwhile, would have time to consider her response and he hoped — oh, how much he hoped! — that her thoughts might be turned away from the unworthy Mr Charles Keeling and towards someone who would value her as she should be valued, who would cherish her for ever. She deserved something better than the unworthy Keeling.

The business was unorthodox, of course. How improper to say that he planned to offer for her, but not to do it! But she was the most sensible woman he had ever met, and would understand his motives. He could not leave her to wait and wonder, but nor could he court her in the conventional manner, not when he was her employer... No, he must be honest with himself. It was his own nature which drove him to such an expedient. He could not flirt, or pay a lady those delicate attentions which she would understand to originate with love. He did not have it in him to write poetry or offer posies of flowers or even to talk in the easy, teasing way he had heard some men employ. Inevitably he would end up talking about the weather, or whether the duck was as well cooked as the fish. He was a dull dog, and would never be anything else, but perhaps now that Annabelle's hopes of Keeling were quite gone, she would settle for a dull life as a countess. He could make her happy, he was sure of it, if only she would give him the chance. Would she like jewellery and silk gowns? Or travel? Perhaps it would amuse her to see the beauties of England, or the Continent? He would give her anything her heart desired, if only...

By the second glass of brandy, his pleasant reverie of married life with Annabelle had expanded to include several children, all with her delightful features and calm demeanour. Her sisters were there, too, for naturally she would want to rescue them from the ignominy of paid employment. They would walk each afternoon round the lakes, no running or dawdling, and end up, perhaps, in the Grecian temple where, somehow, the merry band of children and sisters had vanished, and he was alone with his sweetheart and might kiss those soft, warm lips until—

A knock on the door disrupted this pleasant scene. He sighed. "Enter."

It was Mr Willerton-Forbes. "Do you have a few minutes to talk, my lord?"

He repressed another sigh, but he was far too polite to send him away, however much he might prefer to be alone with his daydreams. He was shown to a seat, Madeira was poured and cakes sent for, since Willerton-Forbes was one of those thin men who was perpetually hungry. But eventually he came to the point.

"I have spent the past three days in Chester with two of the apothecaries there," Mr Willerton-Forbes said. "I asked them to look at all the medicines found in the late Lady Brackenwood's rooms to determine whether each one contained the designated substance, and to the correct degree. They found only one which differed from the label — this one." He produced the bottle labelled in Eloise's own hand. "This bottle, my lord, contains a substance which, in minute quantities, may soothe a heart which beats irregularly. In larger quantities, it will cause the heart to stop beating altogether. This bottle contains the larger quantity. If a person were to take the dose prescribed, it would invariably be fatal."

Allan stared at him. "Then this is what killed her?"

"Almost certainly. The question is why. My lord, I regret to say that I must pry into matters which should not be the concern of anyone but the two people concerned. I must ask about the exact state of relations between you and your wife."

# 17: Of Marriage

"Wait," the earl said, bewildered. "I should not drink brandy in the afternoons, for none of this is clear to me. You went to Chester to see two apothecaries there? To examine my wife's medicines? Surely Mr Burton and Dr Wilcox could have given you all this information? They made up these mixtures, after all. Or are they under suspicion too?"

"Everyone is under suspicion," the lawyer said solemnly. "Even if it were merely a simple mistake in making up a lozenge, say, the two gentlemen might feel pressed by loyalty into saying nothing. What is done cannot be undone, after all, and what is the point in disrupting lives after the event? There was no intent to kill, and therefore no need to destroy a man's livelihood. That is how they might argue."

"And I would have some sympathy with such a view," Allan said.

"But imagine, if you will, that Mr Burton had a secret, and your wife discovered it. If all were to be revealed, he would be ruined, quite ruined. In such circumstances, a man might be tempted to make a small mistake in preparing her ladyship's medication."

"That is preposterous," Allan said, laughing. "Burton has lived in the village all his life, and his father before him. He can have no secrets."

"Everyone has secrets, my lord," Willerton-Forbes said heavily. "Will you tell us something of how things stood between you and your wife?"

He hesitated. It was so personal, and yet, having brought Willerton-Forbes to Charlsby, it would be foolish to cavil at his methods. Besides, he was innocent of any wrong-doing, and therefore had nothing to fear from honesty. "What do you wish to know?"

"Was she happy?"

Allan frowned, considering that. "She never complained," he said eventually. "Not to me, at any rate. Not publicly. Perhaps she talked to her maid, as many ladies do. Eloise simply... drooped. Some days she seemed lively enough, as if she were privy to some inner joke, and other days she sank into apathy."

"And was she... welcoming when you went to her at night?"

"This is necessary?" Allan said sharply. "It is a very intimate matter to be discussing."

"My intent is only to determine her ladyship's state of mind," Willerton-Forbes said. "The mixture which killed her is, after all, in a bottle labelled in her own hand. It is possible, therefore, that her death was also by her own hand. If, perhaps, she found the continued attempts to produce an heir irksome—"

"Hardly that!" Allan spat, before he could stop himself. With an effort, he moderated his tone. "The efforts could hardly be irksome, Mr Willerton-Forbes, since there were none. After the twins were born, Eloise soon found herself increasing again, but she was unwell almost from the start. The birth itself was dreadful for her, quite dreadful. The child — a boy — was born dead, and Eloise was never quite well afterwards. Dr Wilcox told me that another child might well see her into her grave, and that I should not claim my marital rights if I wished to spare her."

"And you accepted that?"

"Naturally."

"Then you have... a mistress? Some... alternative arrangement?" Willerton-Forbes suggested tentatively.

Allan smiled ruefully. "Not all men are immoral, sir."

"I beg your pardon, my lord. No offence was intended. But you will wish to marry again, now that God has taken your wife from you."

It was not framed as a question, but nevertheless the lawyer waited for an answer. Allan hesitated. They were back at the crux of the matter — his lack of a son, which they imagined would give him a reason to murder his wife.

"There is little point in prevarication, my lord," Willerton-Forbes went on relentlessly. "I can ask the servants. And... forgive me, but anyone can see the direction your wishes take."

Allan was not offended. He had invited Willerton-Forbes to Charlsby precisely for his perception, so it would be churlish to quibble at it when applied to himself, but he could only hope his attachment was less obvious to others.

"I intend to make an offer of marriage to Miss Winterton, it is true," he said easily, unable to suppress a smile at the thought. His heart gave a little skip at this public acknowledgement of his private wishes. "But since I did not meet her until long after my wife was dead, that could hardly have been a cause for murder."

"In the particular, no," Willerton-Forbes said. "But in the general — the requirement for a son — it is clear that none would be forthcoming from the late Lady Brackenwood. You cannot be crossed off the list yet, my lord, or the dowager countess. Or Dr Wilcox, come to that. Did you know that he prescribes the same heart medicine for your mother as killed your wife?"

"Oh, the physician is suspected now, is he?" Allan said testily. "What reason he might have for killing his most profitable patient is hard to fathom, however. And poor Mr Penicuik, I suppose he is still on your list? A man of God, who steps aside rather than squash a beetle on the path before him — you cannot seriously suspect him of murdering Eloise, just because she found out something from his past and teased him about it. You had sooner find Eloise's maid, for there was a close-mouthed woman, if you please. She and Eloise spoke Welsh together, and they always had some secret going on. I never liked her, and I would believe her capable of any mischief."

"Captain Edgerton has located Miss Hancock," Willerton-Forbes said. "She is to arrive here the day after tomorrow. I undertook to send a conveyance to Chester for her. I trust that is in order, my lord?"

"Of course. I beg your pardon," Allan said. "I should not vent my anger on you, but it is so... *humiliating* to have everything dragged up like this, with everyone suspected, and everyone's motives for every action questioned. My wife and I married from duty, not love, and we were not even good friends, if the truth be told, but we rubbed along well enough. I was not an unkind or negligent husband, and she was not a faithless or wasteful wife. It never troubled me to be excluded from her bedroom, or to have no son. That is not something that can be proven to you, but nevertheless it is true. I was not unhappy with my situation, merely a little bored, I suppose, and probably she was much the same. My mother has long since accepted that no grandson of hers will inherit the title. As for the others on your list, one has to grasp at straws to make a case for any of them feeling so strongly as to kill someone. It makes no sense to me. No one in this house would have killed Eloise."

"That, my lord, remains to be seen," Willerton-Forbes said unsmilingly.

~~~~~

*'Holly Lodge, 15th July 18— My dear Annabelle, Here we are back in Brinshire at last, a little later than expected, but the garden is so green and refreshing after London that it quite lifts the spirits. Travelling is such a chore with the children, but it would be so dreadful to leave them behind when we are away for months. Your last letter made me think that you are growing very fond of the pupils in your charge. They sound a lively trio! We had thought we might be able to travel north to see you over the summer before I am confined, but Robin's father is no better and although he makes no complaint when we are in town, we do not like to leave him again just yet. Robin has a number of books that he feels you will enjoy, which we had hoped to bestow on you with our own hands, but we will not make you wait. I shall pack them up and send them to you by the mail. I have— Mrs Greeves has just brought in all the mail awaiting us. Four letters from you, dear Annabelle! Of course you expected us to be home long since. I shall read them at once, and write more when I have learnt all your news. ~ Annabelle! Such shocking developments! I am quite alarmed for you, living in a house where there might be a murderer hiding. Surely there must be some mistake? Please write at once to assure me that you are well and that it is all some dreadful misunderstanding. Send word at any time if you wish Robin to come and take you away from*

*there. We shall squeeze you in with us somehow. Yours in dread, Rosamund. P S Have you had any word from Margaret? I have heard nothing at all since Aunt Letty died. It is most concerning. Do let me know if you have any news of her.'*

~~~~~

Annabelle was rather stunned after her talk with the earl. He wanted to marry her! It was not mere drunken ramblings or idle flirtation, but a serious offer. Or it would be, in time. How strange it was to know that the offer would be made, and not to have to wonder about it! She had time to get her thoughts in order, and decide how to answer, for this time her response was not immediately clear. With her three previous offers, the only question was how to frame her refusal in the kindest way possible. And there was the offer never made, from Charles, and there again she had known exactly what she wanted. But this time...

How she wished her sisters were there! She missed their whispered bedtime conversations, the candle burning down to nothing. They would go over everything that had happened that day, and needless to say the subject of most interest concerned their gentleman acquaintances. The sisters would discuss every aspect of their admirers, and speculate endlessly on whether this one or that one would come up to scratch, and how much they wished it. How many hours had they wasted drawing delightful pictures of the future Mrs Charles Keeling? How happy she would be, they told her. How many pretty children she would have, and fine carriages, and splendid gowns. Annabelle had blushed and smiled and let them conjecture all they liked, for those dreams were hers, too. It was all nonsense, of course, for Charles had never offered, and had besides not enough money for half the dazzling images the sisters conjured up.

This time, though... She shivered. To be a countess, entitled to wear the coronet and ermine! How grand she would be. There was a fine estate and no shortage of money. She would never have to earn her bread again, never have the humiliation of seeing pity in people's eyes. She would be *somebody*, and that was almost temptation enough.

Then there was the earl. He was not a splendid figure of a man, someone to turn heads as he walked in the room, but he was good and kind and generous, he had no bad habits and would make her an excellent husband. She was not in love with him and her heart refused to turn somersaults when he walked into the room, but she was always pleased to see him. He was a friend, and perhaps that was as good a foundation for marriage as any.

There was one other aspect that gave her a thrill of pleasure. She would be rich enough to offer some help to her sisters. One, perhaps, might come to live at Charlsby as her companion and friend. The others could be helped in innumerable little ways — a length of fabric sent or a jewelled comb, a pound of tea or little gifts of money slipped under the seal of a letter.

And as she followed this line of thought, she realised the truth — that she would marry the earl because she must. There would never be another offer so good as this one, she would be comfortably situated for life and she would be in a position to help her sisters. No, she would not refuse the offer when it came. Even so, she decided to say nothing to her sisters yet. There was no point in getting their hopes up until the offer was made.

*If* it was made... perhaps he would think better of it? But no, he was too honourable a man to renege on a promise given. He had told her that he would offer for her, and so he would do it, once the small matter of murder was cleared up. Assuming he was not hanged for it. But that was impossible... surely? She tried to set such thoughts resolutely out of her mind, but whenever she thought of the earl, there was a niggle of worry in the far corner of her mind. Such a gentle, unassuming man, but perhaps he was a murderer? And with that possibility unable to be extinguished, how could she marry him? It was a nightmare of a situation to find herself in.

~~~~~

The first evening after her talk with the earl she felt a little awkward. However, he neither said nor did anything to distinguish her in any way, and so she gradually became more comfortable. Even so, when she looked at him, often his eyes were on her before he turned his gaze away.

The following day, the seamstress was at the house to fit the girls for their new gowns, so Annabelle stole away into the gardens with a book to find a quiet spot to read. It was the hottest hour of the day, and the cool woods being some distance away across the park, she chose to settle herself in the Grecian Temple, where the view of the lake was refreshing to the eye and the dense shrubbery all about provided both privacy and soothing shades of green to balance the bright eye of the sun.

The temple was pleasantly shaded. She cast aside her bonnet and gloves, and sat, feet up, on the marble bench that lined the interior. Near the entrance, a trio of pillars provided a support for her back and screened her from anyone who should happen to pass by. She opened her book and settled down to read. She had no fear of being disturbed for she was not visible from the house, and the gardeners had gone inside for their dinner. For a while, the only intrusion was from the occasional bee buzzing past on its own important business, and the heat was such that before long she found her eyes closing.

She woke to the sound of voices very close.

"Of course he won't marry the trollop! Her ladyship's seen to that."

The voice was that of Denby, the dowager countess's lady's maid. It was the day for her sister to visit from the neighbouring estate where she, too, was a lady's maid. Normally Annabelle would have made her presence known, but she was still only half awake, not entirely sure if Denby's words were real or part of some strange dream.

A deep-throated chuckle. "Quite right! As if his lordship could be allowed to breed with *that* little baggage."

Annabelle froze. Could they be talking about her?

"Well... not that her ladyship's from the top drawer, exactly, but don't tell anyone I said that."

Another chuckle. They were very close now, almost level with the temple and not moderating their voices at all. "But what can anyone do to prevent it? These men, they do get these strange fancies... Wait, is there anyone in here?"

Annabelle froze, as the two stopped and peered into the gloom of the temple. The two pillars mostly hid her from their view, but if they looked closely they would see her bonnet on the seat... It was still not too late to declare her presence...

"No, no one's there." They started to move on. "So what can she do? I don't see how she can stop him if he sets his mind to it."

"Oh, but he's so particular, his lordship. He'd never marry anyone... you know... impure. So if he gets ideas, she's going to tell him that that Keeling fellow had her. Dr Wilcox will back her up, he'll say she went to him for help afterwards."

"Wilcox? He'll do that, will he?"

They were almost beyond the temple now, their voices fading. Annabelle strained to catch their words.

"Aye, he'll do whatever she wants. She knows all about what he was up to with—"

They were gone, too distant for her to catch even the echo of their words, leaving Annabelle a curious mixture of emotions. She was furious that the dowager countess would stoop to blackening her reputation to keep her away from Allan, but also terrified that she would succeed. He would believe it, of course he would. Charles had been in the house, the entire company knew their history and must guess at her feelings for him. Why, he had even intimated to George that he wanted her as his mistress. No story the countess invented could be more plausible. So that was the end of her pleasant little dream of a happy future. Allan would never offer for her now.

# 18: The Lady's Maid

Allan had been tied up for hours with Mr Cross, dealing with paperwork that had accumulated while he was in London and which he had been putting off ever since. Cross was well enough as a secretary, but he never used his initiative. He simply opened the mail and arranged it in presumed order of importance, and then left it for Allan to deal with. Much of it was tenant business, which could easily be passed directly to Mr Pratchett, but no, Allan himself had to read every letter and note, and decide what was to be done about it. It was very tedious.

Now that he was released, the library was far too stuffy to while away the afternoon hours in. Even the dogs had disappeared from their usual place on the hearthrug. The glorious summer weather drew him out of doors. He collected a book and his spectacles, and headed down the lawn to the lake, mirror smooth in the stifling heat. He walked dutifully around the upper lake — no running or dawdling, he thought with a smile — and then into the cooler environs of the lower lake, its giant shrubs towering above his head. Their blooms were all but finished now, but here and there a few stray blossoms lingered with the faintest hint of fragrance, and the air hummed with bees. Some bushes had grown so mighty that their roots protruded into the path, so he stepped onto the stretch of lawn that edged the other side of the path and walked as silently as a cat.

So it was that he came to the Grecian Temple just as a lady in grey shot out of it and barrelled into him, sending his book flying into the air. Another book flew skywards, and, with an exclamation of dismay, the lady in grey jumped after it. She was not quick enough to prevent it from sailing into a bush.

"Oh no!" she cried, trying to rescue it and finding her arms would not stretch high enough.

Allan laughed, admiring the fine view of Annabelle's form as she reached upwards.

"Oh, I do beg your pardon!" she said, turning round. "How rude of me to— Oh! It is you." And, to his great delight, she blushed. "I am so sorry, Lord Brackenwood. Are you injured?"

"Not in the least," he said, still laughing, as he retrieved her book, and then his own. "Only my pride, to find that I am rated in lesser need of preservation than a book."

She bit her lip, but her smile was warm. "I am so sorry. I did not hear you coming, you see."

"That was my fault. In avoiding the rhododendron roots, I was walking on the grass. But you were running... is there something amiss?"

The smile died away. "Oh... but I cannot tell you, for it is something I overheard and it was wrong of me, but it was so shocking that I could not move or speak a word, and then they were gone..."

Her expression was filled with such distress that he could not help himself from taking her hand and lifting it to his lips, making her blush even more. How delightfully she blushed! "If it troubles you, then it is best shared, is it not? Surely we are good enough friends that you can trust me with any secret?"

"Oh, yes, of course! But... it concerns your mother and I should not—"

He laughed again. "Then I must definitely hear it. What now has she been up to? She has taken you in dislike, I fear, but I would not for the world have you troubled by anything she says or does. You need not regard her. Come, let us go into the temple and you may tell me all about it."

And so, by degrees, he persuaded her back into the temple she had left so precipitately only moments before, and settled her on the marble seat, and then collected her bonnet and gloves, which she had been holding as she fled and had been scattered about. Only then did she recover some of her composure and tell him of her favoured reading spot, hidden by the pillars, and the shocking words she had overheard from Denby's lips.

"And none of it is true!" she cried fretfully. "I have never... I would never... you must believe me! The very idea is abominable. As if I would ever do such a thing!"

"Naturally you would not," he said calmly. "No one who knows you could believe such a thing for an instant."

"But if Lady Brackenwood says so... and Dr Wilcox supports her..."

"Annabelle, when we have guests in the house, at night there is always a footman stationed on the landing on the bedroom floor. It is more convenient for anyone who needs anything in the night than ringing the bell and waiting half an hour for the scullery maid in the basement to hear the bell and rouse someone. It also serves to discourage any nocturnal wanderings. I can prove that Mr

Keeling never left his room at night, and that no one entered it. Your reputation is quite safe."

"Oh." Her eyes were wide. "I had no idea."

He smiled at her, seeing her hunched shoulders relax a little, and a tremulous smile play about her mouth. She was so adorable when she was worried, with the little frown between her eyebrows and her lips slightly apart. Ah, her lips! And they were barely an arm's length away from him. If only he dared to cross that divide… but more than thirty years of gentlemanly restraint held him in check. He still held her hand, however, lying warm in his own, and he was determined not to relinquish it.

"It does not surprise me that Mother would play such tricks," he said, his smile vanishing abruptly. "But this is infamous! You are a guest in this house, and I will not have any slur cast upon you. And Wilcox, too. Why would he support such lies?"

"The dowager knows something to his detriment," Annabelle said. "He has been up to something with… something. Or someone, perhaps. So Denby said. I did not hear what it might be, for she moved away then."

"Hmm. Interesting. I have not heard anything scurrilous about Dr Wilcox. There are whispers about a woman, but that is always so with a single man. Still, if there is any secret to be uncovered, Mother will find it out. She and Eloise were two of a kind in that regard. They both had their maids digging around for every little rumour. That is how Eloise found… well, whatever it was she discovered about poor Mr Penicuik, something so mortifying that he wished to leave Charlsby. I had the greatest difficulty dissuading him. If there were any secret in Wilcox's life, one or other of them would have ferreted it out. Still, whatever Wilcox may have done, he cannot harm *you*, so it does not matter much."

But her face was serious, and for the first time she would not look him in the eye.

"Annabelle? What now are you thinking?"

She hesitated, withdrawing her hand from his grasp. "I have been thinking of what Mr Willerton-Forbes has said — that everyone is under suspicion. If Mr Wilcox has done something dreadful that would ruin him if it were found out, what might he do to keep such information secret? Might he kill someone?"

"You think he killed Eloise because she found out something about him and threatened to expose him?"

"I do not *think* it, no, but it is a possibility. Or else your mama forced him to do it, as she is forcing him to say bad things about me. He has access to the same type of medicine that killed her, after all."

"The fox-glove is a common plant, anyone might have made up that mixture, and it is widely prescribed. Why, Wilcox prescribes it for Mother." He stopped, considering the implications of that. "So she might have interfered with Eloise's medicine herself." He sighed. "Really, the more one considers, the more one begins to look at everyone with suspicious eyes. Anyone might have given Eloise that medicine. Except that it is her handwriting on the label. That I do not understand."

"That is easy to explain," Annabelle said. "I dare say that someone gave Lady Brackenwood a receipt for a sleeping draught and she made up the mixture herself, or perhaps her maid did it for her. Then she wrote the label herself. Later, when someone wished to poison her, the sleeping draught was thrown away and replaced with a potent fox-glove mixture."

"Or she made the poison herself so that she might take her own life," Allan said.

"But then, why mislabel the bottle?" Annabelle said. "Indeed, why label the bottle at all?"

Allan laughed suddenly. "You are so logical, Annabelle. Yes, suicide does not seem plausible. But all this does not help to narrow the field of possibilities. It seems to me that there are only three people who could *not* have murdered Eloise — you, me and Marisa."

"And to everyone else, it is only me and Mrs Pargeter," Annabelle said quietly, her eyes fixed on his with sudden intensity.

He was about to laugh at the absurdity of her words, but then the implication of them hit him in full force, like a dousing in icy water. "Even to you?" he said, his voice harsh suddenly. "I did not murder my wife, Annabelle, trust me." He found he was shaking. If she had the slightest doubt of him—!

"It is not a matter of trust," she said, dropping her gaze. "I believe implicitly in your innocence, naturally. Everything I have seen of you, everything I understand of your nature confirms it. But perhaps my judgement is faulty, for which of us is perfect? Or perhaps you are such a persuasive hoaxer that you have convinced everyone of your honour while secretly hiding a black heart. Such things have happened before. I do not know — I *cannot* know — what is truly in your heart. No one can. Only God sees and understands all. We mere humans must go by appearances only. So although I cannot — I *do not* believe that you murdered your wife, there is still the tiniest sliver of doubt in my mind, and so it will always be, until the true murderer is unmasked. Forgive me, but it cannot be otherwise."

He was silent for a long time, as rage tore through him. How could she doubt him? And how could they possibly marry with such mistrust hanging between them? It was impossible... She was lost to him now... And then his anger melted into grief. She would never be his, never sweeten his life and walk by his side through the years to come. His delightful daydream fizzled into nothing.

"Allan..." she said timidly, and to his surprise she reached out and willingly took his hand. "There is only one way to get past this obstacle, and that is to find out who truly killed your wife. I will do everything in my power to help, because only thus can we move forward and begin to consider the future."

"But what can anyone do?" he said. "It is up to Willerton-Forbes now. If he decides that I am a murderer—"

"Then we must help him to decide otherwise," she said crisply. "And we must share whatever we find out ourselves, and bring our own powers of logic to bear on the problem, as we have done here. I believe in your innocence, Allan, but I want to prove it, too."

He nodded, and gave her a tremulous smile, but he had never felt so helpless in his life.

~~~~~

The next day, Annabelle was in the schoolroom with the girls, working on some Latin with Dorothea, while Florence and Felicity practised scales on the pianoforte. For several days the heat had infected them with summer torpor and little had been achieved, but today the skies were grey and damp, and they all had more energy for their labours.

A sharp rat-tat-tat on the door was followed by the smiling face of Captain Edgerton, who had returned from one of his mysterious journeys the day before. "Miss Winterton. Lady Dorothea. Lady Florence. Lady Frederica." He executed ostentatious bows to each in turn. "My deepest apologies for the disruption, but might I have a word with you outside, Miss Winterton?"

She followed him out onto the landing.

His voice dropped, abruptly becoming serious. "We have Miss Hancock here, the late Lady Brackenwood's lady's maid, but she will not agree to be interviewed by three gentlemen without a lady present. I wonder if—?"

"Of course, but... would it not be better to call upon someone Miss Hancock knows? She must have friends amongst the staff."

"You are the only person we can be sure has no connection to the death of Lady Brackenwood."

For an instant she was taken aback. The only person? Surely not. But there was no time to consider what his words might mean. "Very well, then. How long will this take?"

"I cannot say. Several hours, perhaps."

"Give me a few minutes to arrange for the nurse to keep an eye on the girls, and then I shall be at your disposal, Captain."

And for once the serious face remained, and he had no flippant answer to make.

Miss Hancock was a solidly built woman approaching fifty, with the first hints of grey in her hair. She nodded curtly to Annabelle as they were introduced, her eyes raking her up and down.

"The governess, eh?" she said with a sniff. "I wouldn't have guessed by your appearance."

"Miss Winterton is a gentleman's daughter," Captain Edgerton said. "Lord Brackenwood is very fortunate to have engaged her services."

Miss Hancock sniffed again, then settled herself in the chair indicated by Mr Willerton-Forbes. Captain Edgerton placed a chair for Annabelle nearby, arranged, she noted with interest, so that she could observe Miss Hancock's face. Then he himself lolled in the window seat, apart yet watching with keen interest. Mr Neate, the lawyer's valet and secretary, sat at one end of the table, his pen poised over the paper to record Miss Hancock's words.

"Miss Hancock," Mr Willerton-Forbes began, "pray tell us first about your employment. You had been with Lady Brackenwood for a number of years, I understand."

"Since she was born," Miss Hancock said, lifting her chin proudly. "I was a nursery maid, just fourteen years old, when Miss Eloise was born, and never left her. Nursery maid and chamber maid for twelve years, then her personal maid after that."

"Would you say you were friends?"

"Friends? Not my place to be friends with my mistress," she said with another sniff. She had a strong Welsh accent, and Annabelle wondered if the late Lady Brackenwood had had a hint of it too, despite her gentler birth.

"But you were loyal to her," the lawyer said. Miss Hancock inclined her head regally. "Yet she was about to turn you off for stealing from her."

"Ha! Not her!" Miss Hancock said, a grim smile on her face. "She knew me better than that. I'd never steal from her. That were just Mrs Hale misunderstanding."

"Oh? Yet she found you with Lady Brackenwood's purse open and the coins in your hand."

Miss Hancock sighed heavily and rolled her eyes, as if irritated by some particularly unintelligent child. "*Of course* I had her purse in my hand. I took care of all her money. If she wanted to buy something, I took the coins for it and brought the change back later. She never left Charlsby, poor lady, her health being so uncertain. So I used to do all her shopping for her."

"So why did Mrs Hale think you were stealing?" the lawyer said blandly.

"How should I know? You should ask her. She's always had it in for me, although I don't know why. *I've* never done anything to her."

"So you were not in any fear of being turned off?"

Miss Hancock gave a bark of mirthless laughter. "Never! Miss Eloise couldn't manage without me, she said so often enough. *'You're indispensable, Lena,'* she'd say to me. *'Quite indispensable.'* No, she'd never have turned me off."

"So you were very much in her confidence, I suppose?" Mr Willerton-Forbes said.

"Of course!"

"You must have been a great comfort to her ladyship during her years of illness," he said.

Miss Hancock smiled knowingly. "Ah, her illness! She wasn't so ill as all that, not when she didn't want to be. If it was something his lordship wanted, or the dowager, no, Miss Eloise was too ill for that. But if it was something *she* wanted to do, she'd be well enough. Not that she was putting it on, or anything of the sort. It was just that certain things weighed on her, and she could barely leave her room then."

"We have been told that she was too much of an invalid to pay calls or to entertain, is that correct?"

"That's true enough. Sometimes callers came here, but she gave up on returning their calls. She'd be in bed for a week afterwards. She never liked the gentry round about. They looked down on her, they did. Talked about her behind her back. Said she wasn't fit to be a countess. Spiteful, they were. And the London folk were worse. No, she kept herself to herself, that was the way she liked it. Nice and peaceful, and no one wearing her out. But she'd go for long walks through the woods. There were days when she was well enough for that. Out for hours, she'd be, and come back with roses in her cheeks, looking as lovely as a girl. But this house got her down, what with the dowager telling her she'd failed her husband, and him not caring tuppence about her, and the servants whispering about her. That's what made her ill. She'd be lying on her daybed for hours, the curtains drawn against the sun. Poor lady! She had a terrible life."

"Were you familiar with her medicines?"

"Oh, no. She saw to all that herself. Well, her and Dr Wilcox. She never stuck to what he prescribed, though. She'd take something for a day or two, then decide it wasn't working or she felt better, so she'd leave off that one. Then, a week or two later, there'd be something else she'd try. She used to send away for things, too. Tonics and such like advertised in the London Post or the Chester Chronicle. There were always things arriving in the mail."

"Do you recognise this bottle?" Mr Willerton-Forbes said, dipping into a drawer and producing the bottle labelled in Lady Brackenwood's own hand.

Miss Hancock sniffed disparagingly. "I never took no notice of such things. If she left them out, I'd tidy them away so the maids didn't run off with them. They're a light-fingered lot, they'd lift anything not nailed down, they would."

"So you have no idea what she was taking just before she died?"

Miss Hancock shook her head firmly.

Mr Willerton-Forbes sighed, and obviously decided to change tack, for he said, "How did Lady Brackenwood get along with her husband?"

"Oh, him! She had no time for *him*. Not much of a man, she said. Of course, he married her for her money, everyone knew that. Set himself up nicely, he did, but he never cared what happened to her. I'm sure he was glad when she died. Mind you, I'll say this for him, he did his duty by her as a husband, right to the end."

"Did he?" Mr Willerton-Forbes said in neutral tones.

"Aye, that he did. Got her with child again, didn't he?"

"Really? No one else has mentioned such a possibility," the lawyer said, with an edge of surprise in his voice.

"Well, she never said nothing about it, but a mistress can't hide that sort of thing from her own lady's maid. I knew, all right. Miss Eloise was with child when she died."

# 19: A Walk In The Woods

Mr Willerton-Forbes and Captain Edgerton both raised their eyebrows, exchanging surprised glances. Mr Neate's pen hovered in mid-air, a drip of ink poised to fall and blot the page.

Annabelle wondered at their surprise. Despite the description of her as an invalid, Lady Brackenwood did not sound terribly ill, and she could not have been much above thirty. It was hardly surprising, then, that she had been blessed with another child. Did it make a difference to the question of murder? Not if no one knew about it, perhaps. But if Allan had known… yes, that would take him off the lawyer's list, surely? He could hardly be suspected of killing his unborn child. But George…

No, that was foolish. Even if George were minded to dispose of a threat to his inheritance, the murder of Eloise would merely free Allan to marry again. It was illogical. But then murder was illogical. Who would care so passionately that they would kill? And what could arouse such feelings? Was anything worth the risk of being hanged?

"Miss Hancock, that is all we wish to discuss with you for the moment, but we shall have more questions, I am sure. Are you prepared to stay here for a few days?"

"Aye, my new mistress is very happy for me to assist you gentlemen. I can stay until Monday next, if required."

"Thank you. You may go now. And Miss Winterton, also. Thank you both for so graciously giving us your time."

Annabelle found herself unexpectedly free. Finding that the girls had gone out for a walk with the nurse, she took the opportunity to do the same and clear her mind after the sourness of the maid's words. Such an unpleasant woman! She liked no one, and had little respect even for her own mistress. Perhaps she truly was stealing from Lady Brackenwood, and undoubtedly she listened at keyholes and picked up all sorts of hearsay and lies. Allan had said something of the sort — that Lady Brackenwood sent her maid to dig up rumours. And now, presumably, she would relate everything about the investigation to her new mistress and the story would be everywhere.

She walked briskly across the lawns and across the bridge between the two lakes. Somewhere around the lower lake the girls' high voices could be heard, but they were hidden by the shrubbery. Smiling, she walked on, across the park, the wet grass soaking her boots, and up to the woods. The trees still dripped after the rain and the air was humid but pleasantly cool.

The exercise was refreshing but it did not succeed in its objective. Her head was still full of the interview she had witnessed, and the impression it gave her of the late Lady Brackenwood as a sad, disappointed woman, finding very little to enjoy in her life. Her husband, her mother-in-law, the neighbours — all had displeased her. Mr Willerton-Forbes had not enquired into Lady Brackenwood's feelings for her daughters, but then he had read her schoolroom notebooks too, and could see for himself how little patience she had with them. No, she was not a maternal woman.

Yet she had conceived another child, and perhaps it would have been the son that everyone expected of her. Allan had said that he was quite content with George as his heir, and Annabelle believed him, but still, he would have been pleased to have a son of his own, surely? And she wondered again if he had known about the child. The maid thought she was the only one to know, but perhaps Eloise had told her husband? It would be perfectly natural to do so. And if he had known, then no one could suspect him of murdering his wife. But if he had not known, then he must stay on the list...

With these thoughts, a terrible idea struck her. She did not believe for one moment that Allan had murdered his wife, but supposing he had? Her stomach churned at the thought, but she had to consider it dispassionately. If he *had* murdered his wife, then he could not possibly have known that his wife was with child. No man could kill his own child. If he now discovered that there had been a child, what would he do? An innocent man would be overwhelmed by grief for the loss of his unborn child, but a guilty man would at once see that all he had to do to demonstrate his innocence was to claim that he had, in fact, known of it.

And, understanding this, she knew that she had to tell Allan of this new discovery and see how he responded. If he were grief-stricken, she would know once and for all that he was innocent of the dreadful accusation levelled at him, and she would be free of this ache inside her whenever she saw him. It was the horridest feeling in the world, wanting to trust a man absolutely, yet having no notion whether he was a good man or a murderer. She wanted so badly to put her faith in him, to surrender her freedom to him... to surrender her *heart*. More than anything in the world, she wanted him to be a man of honour, worthy of her confidence. Worthy of her hand and her love.

It was so difficult.

She had been so engrossed in her own thoughts that she had walked further than she had ever ventured before. She had reached the end of the woods that fringed the estate, and had come to the fields that separated it from the village of Charlsby Wooton. A little distance to her right, the lane to the village wound through the fields. To her left, she could see the smoky haze of Kenford away in the distance. Just in front of her was a small cottage, seemingly abandoned, for its garden was overgrown and there were no signs of habitation — no smoke from the chimneys, no chickens scratching in the dirt, no washing laid out to dry. Yet the path from gate to front door was free of weeds, and there were recent hoof prints in the muddy track that connected the cottage to the lane.

And the garden was ablaze with familiar pink flowers. She could reach over the wall and pluck them at will to confirm that, as she had suspected, this was the flower dried and preserved so many times in Lady Brackenwood's notebooks. So she had come here, then. Miss Hancock had said that her mistress liked to take long walks, and this place, clearly, was one that she visited, picking a flower or two as she passed by as a reminder of a pleasant outing, perhaps.

Annabelle picked a large bunch of the flowers to take back to the house. They would brighten up the schoolroom, and the girls could practise their skills with the brush and paint them. She toyed with the idea of walking back by the lane, but decided it would be too muddy after the rain and turned instead to retrace her steps through the woods.

She had not gone far when a rustling in the undergrowth was followed by the familiar shape of a panting dog. He came straight up to her and flopped at her feet.

"Hello, Dusty!" She crouched down to pat the creature, who was immediately joined by his fellows, bouncing around her excitedly. "Blackie, Lively, good day to you. Are you out with Henderson today or—"

She had her answer immediately, and it was not Henderson the under-groom who was smiling down at her with that look on his face that made her rather flustered.

"Good afternoon, Miss Winterton. I see you have been past Drummond's Cottage."

"Good afternoon, Lord Brackenwood." She jumped up and dipped a curtsy. "Drummond's Cottage? Oh, the flowers! I have never been there before and they were so pretty... Mr Drummond will not mind, I hope. There were so many..."

He laughed and shook his head. "He will not mind. He has been dead these... oh, twenty years or more. The original Mr Drummond was gamekeeper to the estate, but the last of that name was assistant to Mr Wilcox's predecessor and bequeathed him the cottage when he died."

"So Mr Wilcox owns it now?" He nodded and she pondered that. "But no one lives in it?"

To her surprise, he went rather pink, but shook his head. "There was a woman living there for a while but she left a few years ago. Are you walking back to the house? I am just about to turn back myself, so perhaps we may walk together?"

She acceded to it, and he offered his arm. It was agreeable strolling along together in that comfortable way. He was just the right height for her, she decided, not so tall that she had to twist her neck to look at him, yet tall enough to be a comfortable support. The dogs bounded on ahead, snuffling in the undergrowth, and digging through the half-rotted heaps of last year's leaves. This was how it would be, she supposed, when she was his wife — pleasant walks in the woods, then home in time to dress for dinner and an evening when she would no longer have to sit in the corner with her stitchery, but could play cards if she wished or simply sit with a book. She heaved a sigh of pleasure.

"Now what was that for?" he said, smiling down at her so warmly that she blushed and lowered her eyes. "I beg your pardon, Miss Winterton, I did not mean to pry. Your thoughts are your own. How are your sisters? Suffering from cramped fingers, I suspect, from all the letter writing they do."

That made her laugh. "They are all well enough, although their lives are not smooth at the moment. They all have... difficulties to contend with. Well, not Rosamund, I think, apart from the usual minor complaints to do with her condition."

"Rosamund is Mrs Robin Dalton, is that right? Her husband is heir to Lord Westerlea, a baron, I think? But he was a younger son, too, as I was, whose brother reached adulthood before he died. It is strange how these things come about. Illness can strike any of us, at any age."

"Or accident," Annabelle said. "Mr Richard Dalton was thrown from his horse and broke his neck while hunting, just a few days before he was to marry Rosamund."

He stopped and half turned. "But how tragic! And so she married the younger son, instead. That was sensible."

"Rosamund was always the practical one of the family," she said, smiling fondly. "When Richard died, she had never met Robin and the two were very different, yet they were married within a month. I thought her very cold-hearted at the time, although it has worked out very well for them both and they live in perfect harmony together."

"That is a great joy when it happens," he said. "She sounds like a sensible lady, so I imagine she had very good reasons for her decision."

"For the marriage, yes, but I cannot see why she could not have waited a little. It seemed so disrespectful to Richard's memory. Oh look, the sun is coming out at last."

They had come to the point where the oak tree stood with the seat around its trunk. He gestured towards it. "Miss Winterton, will you sit with me for a while? I promise not to mention mistletoe."

She laughed and agreed to it, and he spread his coat on the bench to preserve them from its dampness. She was both pleased and disappointed that his coat was large enough to permit him to sit well away from her. The mistletoe above her head made her wonder, not for the first time, what it would be like to kiss Allan — to be kissed by him. Would he sweep her away to some magical place where nothing else existed but the two of them? Would he warm her insides and make even her toes wriggle in delight? Or would it be a prosaic, mundane experience? And if so, could she put herself into the hands of so passionless a man? She could not say. She wanted to, for marriage to Allan would be a pleasant and comfortable life, with nothing to trouble her, but could she live without love? Without passion?

"You are very thoughtful today, Miss Winterton," he said. "But perhaps I can alleviate one concern, at least, since we have agreed to share whatever we discover on the matter of my wife's death. I talked to Mr Willerton-Forbes first thing this morning, and he is coming to the view that my wife's death was an accident. The mixture which killed her was so strong that there were few people with the knowledge to create it deliberately. It would involve picking just the right part of the plant at the proper time in the growing cycle, and then treating it in a certain way… only a trained apothecary, well versed in the latest thinking, would be capable of it, and he can find no evidence of such knowledge in either Dr Wilcox or Mr Burton, nor have they the slightest reason to wish Eloise dead. So Mr Willerton-Forbes is minded to suppose the whole incident to be an accident. Perhaps it is as you said, that Eloise obtained a receipt from someone and made the mixture herself, inadvertently selecting the wrong plant for her needs. After all, the label is written in her own hand."

"That is indeed a great relief," Annabelle said. "I wonder, however, if Miss Hancock's information will make a difference to his opinion."

"I had forgotten about her," Allan said. "I confess, my dislike of her creeping ways allowed me to suspect her of murder, and that was wrong of me. Just because she sneaks about eavesdropping does not make her culpable of anything worse, and her willingness to come here to tell her side of the story is testament to her fundamental honesty. It seems her journey was wasted, for she can have nothing of interest to say now."

"I would not be so sure," Annabelle said. "Mr Willerton-Forbes and Captain Edgerton seemed very surprised by her information."

"Oh, she has been questioned already? And you know of it?"

"I was asked to act as chaperon to Miss Hancock. She was nervous about being alone in a room with three gentlemen."

He laughed. "How very particular! But why you, and not one of the servants? Oh, but you are so conveniently placed, with the schoolroom being next door. What did she have to impart? Something scurrilous, I dare say, for she knew all the gossip."

Here was the opening Annabelle had hoped for to implement her plan. Yet now she had second thoughts. It had seemed a clever way to determine to her own satisfaction that he was innocent, but now, it seemed, such a stratagem was no longer necessary. If Lady Brackenwood's death was deemed an accident, there was no threat of Allan being hanged, and the revelation of his child could only grieve him to no purpose.

"Annabelle?" Allan said gently. "Is it something bad? It must be if you do not want to share it with me."

"I do! I do want to share it, but... it will distress you, I fear. Miss Hancock believed that Lady Brackenwood was with child when she died."

To her great surprise, Allan laughed. "No, she is mistaken on *that* score, I assure you. It is impossible."

Annabelle looked at him in amazement. "She seemed very confident about it. She said that a personal maid always knows about these things."

"No, no, she is quite wrong," Allan said. "There is no—" He stopped and his face changed, reddening. "*No!* She would not—? Surely not." He looked so dismayed, almost angry, that she was shocked and could say nothing. He jumped up and paced about, muttering, "No, it cannot be," from time to time. It was almost as if he had forgotten Annabelle's presence.

Abruptly, he mastered himself, and said, "Forgive me, I am neglecting you shamefully. Shall we walk on?"

Willingly, she jumped up but at once, he turned to her, one hand to his forehead. "No, I cannot pretend this is nothing. You must think me insane, but I assure you that my reaction is a natural one in the circumstances."

She could not prevent herself from saying, "Is it?" in surprised tones.

He looked at her fully then, his eyes softening as he smiled at her. "Ah, Annabelle, you do not know all. This news from Hancock would distress me, you said, and so it has, but not in the way you expected. May I explain? I would have no secrets from *you*."

She nodded her agreement, and they sat down again.

"I must be blunt, and I therefore beg your forgiveness in advance for mentioning subjects that no delicately brought up young lady should discuss, still less with a man. But I cannot explain it in roundabout terms, so therefore I will come straight to the point. If Eloise had got herself with child, it was none of my doing."

"Oh!" Annabelle's hands flew to her hot cheeks. "Oh, but then..."

"Yes. She must have had a lover. It is an irony, is it not? You expected me to be despondent at the loss of my child — a son, perhaps, who knows? Instead, I am despondent for a different reason entirely."

"You did not suspect her condition?" Annabelle said carefully. "Or the existence of a lover?" For if he had... *that* might drive a man to murder.

"Not in the slightest. Nothing in her behaviour gave me the slightest cause for alarm, and she never went anywhere or stayed away from home, not even for a single night. I cannot imagine how she managed it or who it could be."

Annabelle looked at the flowers still clutched in her hand, and recalled the other flowers picked from the garden of that isolated little cottage, and later pressed between the pages of the notebooks for remembrance. She recalled, too, that the dowager knew something bad about Dr Wilcox. With a heavy sigh, she said sadly, "But I can."

# 20: *The Merest Trifle*

Allan was so abstracted as Portman dressed him for dinner that night that the valet said, "Are you quite well, milord? Do you wish to see Dr Wilcox?"

This made Allan laugh so hard that his cravat was quite spoilt, and he had to begin again. Yes, indeed he did wish to see Wilcox, but not for any medical reason. *'Good morning, Wilcox. What fine weather we are having, are we not? Is the road from the village abominably dusty just now? Shall we have a good harvest this year, do you suppose? And by the way, were you bedding my wife?'*

He was still laughing when he went down to the saloon. Marisa was the only person there.

"I am pleased to see you in better spirits, Allan," she said. "You have been too long-faced these past weeks. It does my heart good to see you enjoying life again. Shall you share the joke, or is it some secret amusement?"

She rested one elegantly gloved hand on his arm, and it was a testament to his good humour that this did not irritate him as it normally would.

"It is my experience that a joke loses much of its entertainment when spoken aloud," he said.

"What, even when shared with a very good friend?" she said, simpering coyly at him. "Come now, do tell."

"No, indeed, for it is the merest trifle, not strong enough to withstand scrutiny," he said pleasantly. "How have you occupied yourself today, sister? Have you been out walking? I can recommend the exercise now that the heat has dissipated a little."

As he watched her pretend not to mind the snub, and half-listened to her answers to his polite questions, he wondered for the hundredth time why she lingered on at Charlsby. Three months it had been, now, and there was no sign that she wished to be elsewhere or cared much about the children she had left behind in Devonshire. He had thought he understood her reasons for coming, but since their last shocking conversation on the subject of marriage, she had neither raised the topic again, nor shown any other possible reason for her presence. Yet here she was. It was vexing.

Gradually, the others trickled into the saloon. Annabelle had left off her black gloves again, he saw, after a month's mourning for her aunt. That was not long, but then she had never met the lady, so it was hardly surprising. He trusted his Annabelle to follow the correct form.

His Annabelle… how proprietorial he was getting! And yet she might still turn him down, he knew that. She might look at him, at the dull, boring Earl of Brackenwood, and remember the handsome, fashionable, oh-so-personable Mr Keeling, and his kisses that roused the sleeping maiden, and decide that she would far rather stay single. And then what would he do? How could he go on being distantly correct with her, when he wanted so badly to sweep her into his arms and smother her with kisses of his own. Just because a man was quiet and restrained and not articulate did not mean that he was insensate. He looked at her softly rounded shoulders and way her hair fell so gently and her smooth cheeks, and he ached to hold her, to touch her, to run his hands over her and—

"Dinner is served, my lady," Plessey intoned.

Were all butlers so pompous, he wondered irritably? He had no idea. He remembered one from his boyhood who had been a pleasantly unassuming, paternal figure, but all his replacements since had been stiff and unapproachable. Eloise had gone through three of them in the eleven years she had been mistress of Charlsby, but they were all the same — so full of their own importance, grander, in many ways, than he was himself. Still, as long as the house ran smoothly and meals were served on time.

The difficulty with sitting at the head of the table was that he could see everyone clearly. His eyes would keep wandering to Annabelle's dear face. Lord, but he was in trouble there. He had never wanted a woman the way he wanted her. Even Marisa. His eyes turned to his sister-in-law, chattering animatedly to George, and he could not deny that she was a very handsome woman. Handsome, lively, quick-witted — everything that her sister was not. Yet he could barely remember now his youthful love for her. That had been nothing but a rush of excitement brought on by her kiss, for he had known her only a matter of days. One could not truly love a person so quickly. One might fall in love, in a heart-stopping, stomach-churning moment, but a love that would last for years could only be founded on the respect that grew from time and friendship. In the six months he had known her, his feelings for Annabelle had grown slowly, from early admiration to respect for her teaching skills and modest demeanour until he was utterly enchanted by her, helpless to resist. And again his eyes were drawn to her, listening composedly to Aunt Beth.

Marisa turned her attention to Mr Willerton-Forbes, sitting across the table from her. She had to raise her voice to be heard. "How does your investigation go on, Mr Forbes? Have you added any names to your list of possible murderers?"

"Fortunately not, Mrs Pargeter," Willerton-Forbes said politely. "I have, however, managed to remove a few. I am now satisfied that the Dowager Lady Brackenwood had nothing at all to do with the death of her daughter-in-law, for although Dr Wilcox prescribed medicine of the same type that killed Lady Brackenwood, it was in fact merely sugar water."

"What?" the dowager said. "You mean Wilcox has been charging me five guineas a bottle for sugar water? I shall have words with him about that, you may be sure. But what about my granddaughters... you cannot still suspect them?"

"No, I do not believe the Ladies Dorothea, Florence and Frederica had anything to do with their mother's death. They had not the knowledge or opportunity to make or obtain the fatal mixture."

"You're beginning to show some sense, then," the dowager said sourly. "Have you taken Allan off your ridiculous list yet?"

"I must always be at the top of the list, Mother," Allan said equably. "At least until the true murderer is known, or it is determined that Eloise's death was not murder." And as he spoke, he wondered why Willerton-Forbes did not announce to the whole company that he now suspected an accident rather than murder.

"And I expect my name is still there," George said cheerfully. "I stand to gain if Cousin Allan is hauled off to be hanged."

"Hanged? What nonsense!" the dowager said robustly, but Allan laughed.

"Have no fear, Mother, I shall not be hanged, since I am innocent of any crime."

"Ah, such confidence," George said. "Men are hanged every year for crimes they did not commit. I can but hope, eh?" And he winked broadly.

Allan was pleased to see George making the effort to appear like his normal self. In company it was hard to tell there was anything weighing on his mind, as he flirted with Marisa and joked raffishly with the men. But when he thought himself unobserved, the convivial expression vanished to be replaced by a look that Allan could only describe as despair. Poor George, in the throes of unrequited love!

He knew that feeling well enough. For years he had wondered what might have been, if he had only had the courage to defy his mother and marry Marisa. And yet two days after meeting her again, he had developed such a disgust of her as could never be overcome. How glad he was now that he had not been trapped with a wife who had so few moral scruples, and so little understanding of his position. It still astonished him that she could imagine he would defy the church's ruling and marry his late wife's sister. Such marriages happened amongst those of lower rank, but in the nobility it would be madness.

"And what about me?" Aunt Beth said timidly. "And my sister? And Uncle Jeremiah? You have not mentioned us. Surely you do not—"

"Oh, no! Not at all, Lady Elizabeth," Willerton-Forbes said. "You and Lady Anne and Mr Jeremiah Skelton have never been under the least suspicion." Mr Penicuik cleared his throat, his eyes wide. "And I am satisfied that Mr Penicuik was not involved, either.

He has been... very helpful. I have talked to Miss Hancock today, and have taken her name off the list, too."

"Your list is getting rather small," Marisa said.

"Indeed it is, and perhaps it may vanish altogether soon, for I am not certain that this is a question of murder at all. The sleeping draught which killed Lady Brackenwood resided in a bottle labelled in her own hand."

"Exactly!" Marisa said, in triumph. "Written in her own hand, and what could that mean except that she made the contents herself? There is no other explanation."

"But there is," Annabelle said, then hastily lifted her napkin to her mouth, as if to unsay the words. "I beg your pardon, pray forget I spoke."

"You are quite right, Miss Winterton," Willerton-Forbes said gently. "It is possible a harmless sleeping draught concocted by Lady Brackenwood herself was poured away, to be replaced with the potent mixture which killed her."

"But anyone might have done so," Marisa said. "Anyone in this house might have done such a thing."

"Indeed," Willerton-Forbes said. "It is a puzzle, is it not, Mrs Pargeter?"

~~~~~

After dinner, Mr Willerton-Forbes asked to speak to Allan privately, so they withdrew to the library.

"Brandy?" Allan asked him.

"Thank you, but no."

"Not a social visit, then," Allan said, stoppering the decanter regretfully. He had a feeling that he would need brandy before the night was over.

Willerton-Forbes gave a wintry smile, waiting politely until Allan had seated himself in one of the large wing-chairs beside the hearth before taking its pair for himself. "Did you know your wife was with child?" he said abruptly.

"No, I did not." He could not quite keep the anger out of his voice.

"You are not surprised by this news, from which I surmise that Miss Winterton informed you of it?"

"Was it confidential? She did not want to tell me of it, for she thought it would distress me to learn that a child of mine had died with my wife. My response was not what she expected."

"You maintain, then, that you were not intimate with your wife? That this child could not be yours?"

"I do."

"Then Lady Brackenwood had taken a lover?"

"It must be so," Allan said. "How shaming that my wife felt such a need."

"Lord Brackenwood, do you realise that this gives you a powerful motive for murdering your wife? She carried another man's child, a child who, if male, would inherit the earldom."

Allan stared at him. "Do you think I would have cared about that, even if I had known? Half the great families in the land have a child or two who looks nothing like his father. No one makes a fuss about it. But even if I were such a man as to care, I had not the least idea of it. However she managed the business, it was discreetly done. Miss Winterton has a theory about that, by the way. Something to do with dried flowers, which grow at Drummond's Cottage, which is owned by Wilcox. From that she makes the leap to supposing that Eloise visited him at the cottage. I do not see it, myself, but then I am finding it difficult to imagine Eloise with any man. She was such a timid creature, Willerton-Forbes. And yet, it must be so, and the strange part of it is, that I am glad that she found some happiness in her life. God knows, she was not happy with me."

"I will talk to Dr Wilcox again, of course, but I know that Lady Brackenwood's last confinement was distressing."

"Distressing? She nearly died. Or so Wilcox said." He grunted in exasperation. "You see what you have done, Willerton-Forbes? You have got me looking askance at everything for hidden meanings and secret intent. I much preferred it when I thought the best of everyone."

Willerton-Forbes gave a wintry smile. "Indeed. But I have talked to the Chester physician who attended Lady Brackenwood on occasion, and his reports coincide with Wilcox's. So is it possible that, finding herself once again facing the same dire prospect, she might have chosen to end her life in her own time, to lessen her suffering?"

Allan pondered the point. "It is possible, I suppose," he said slowly. "Yet she was very devout, and would have abhorred the very idea. But then I would have thought her the last person in the world to take a lover, so perhaps I knew her less well than I supposed. Poor Eloise! I could have tried to make her happy, if she had only confided in me. I am not a cruel man, I hope, and I was fond of her. Certainly I never wished any harm to befall her. Poor Eloise."

~~~~~

Annabelle was twice more called upon to act as chaperon to Miss Hancock, while Mr Willerton-Forbes and Captain Edgerton tried to convince her that the late Lady Brackenwood had had a lover. She would not have it. Her mistress had been a woman of Christian principles to the core, she asserted, and would never even have considered such a thing, nor would she have taken her own life. It was unthinkable, and nothing would shake her. In the end, the lawyer gave it up.

It was clear, however, that he believed Allan's story that the child could not be his. How humiliating for a man to be forced to admit that his wife had a lover! Although he seemed unwilling to accept that it was Dr Wilcox. Annabelle herself was convinced of it, if only because of the little pink flowers.

But what a coil it was! If Lady Brackenwood had conceived a child by a man other than her husband, then there were immediately three men with a reason to want her dead: her husband, who might be jealous and not wish to accept a cuckoo in his nest, his heir, who might see his own chance of a title slipping away, and the lover himself, who might wish to destroy the evidence of his wicked deed.

Allan. George Skelton. Dr Wilcox. Three men who might have wished Lady Brackenwood dead.

Until that point, Annabelle had never thought murder very likely, but now, with a chill of fear, she realised that an illegitimate child might be just the impetus that would do it. And she had to face the horrible prospect that the man she was seriously considering marrying might very well be a murderer. She wrote long, despairing letters to her sisters, and then burnt them. How she longed to talk to them, for there was no one in the house she could call a friend. Only Allan.

It was just as well she had her duties in the schoolroom to keep her busy now, for otherwise she would have run mad. The three girls were not, of course, perfectly well-behaved at all times, and Dorothea, in particular, was still inclined to odd shifts in mood, but on the whole they worked hard, and she could truthfully say that they would, in time, be accomplished young ladies and a credit to their papa.

She was supervising their drawing one morning when there was a knock on the schoolroom door and Allan crept in. Annabelle could see at once that there was something badly amiss, for his face was ashen, as if he had sustained a great shock.

"Whatever is the matter?" she cried.

"May I—?" he croaked, then cleared his throat and tried again. "May I have a word with you outside, Miss Winterton?"

She followed him out in silence, her stomach roiling in fear. It must be bad news! A death, at least... one of her sisters! Nothing else— Unless Allan was to be accused of murder after all! Terror speared through her — no, he could not be hanged! Please God, no!

And then he spoke the last words in the world she had ever expected to hear.

"Mr Keeling is here to see you. He wishes to speak with you privately. He is awaiting you in the library."

*"Charles?"*

"Yes. In the library. I will sit with the girls. Go, now."

She went, in a dream, hardly knowing what she was doing. Charles here? Wishing to speak with her privately? What could it mean? Her heart pounded and she knew perfectly well what she hoped to hear — that his betrothal to Miss Lorrimer was at an end and he had remembered Annabelle, his first love, and realised that he could not live without her.

But was it likely? Was it possible that there could be a happy ending for her, that all her heartache could be erased in a moment? And at the back of her mind was the treacherous thought — was this even what she wanted now? Charles would be the choice of her heart, but now there was another choice, a more prudent choice. She could marry Allan instead, and rescue all her sisters from poverty, and have a man who had never wavered in his devotion, even for a moment.

She descended the stairs and crossed the hall, still in a dream of disbelief. She opened the door of the library and went in, and there he was, as handsome as memory had ever made him, and smiling at her so warmly, with such joy in his face.

"Annabelle!" he cried, rushing forward to take her hands. "The most wonderful news! No... it is sad news, of course, but wonderful for me. For *us.* You remember, I am sure, the circumstances of my family... that my uncle held the family estate. But he died two years ago, and his eldest son not long after, leaving only a sickly child. And now that poor child, too, has gone to meet his maker and so my father inherits all, and I after him. Is it not the greatest good fortune?"

"For your father, and for you, of course. I am happy for the improvement in your circumstances." Her heart pounded so loud in her ears she could barely think, but she was puzzled, for he made no mention of Miss Lorrimer.

"So you see, the way is finally clear, my dear Annabelle." He raised one hand to his lips and then the other. "I always knew it would be so. Fate has been kind to us." He lifted one of her hands to his cheek, and held it there, eyes closed. She could barely breathe for happiness. But still there was no word of Miss Lorrimer.

"Ah, Annabelle," he murmured. "Make me the happiest of men. Say you will be my wife. Sweet Annabelle, love of my life."

He leaned towards her, and in a moment he would claim her lips and then she knew she would be lost.

"Wait!" she said. "What happened to your betrothal?"

"Never mind that," he whispered, his lips brushing against her ear in a way that turned her to jelly. "Say you will be mine, darling Annabelle."

Abruptly, she pulled out of his grasp. "No. Tell me about Miss Lorrimer. Are you or are you not betrothed to her?"

He sighed. "Annabelle, please..."

"It is a simple question, Mr Keeling," she said coldly, although she shook from head to toe. "Has your betrothal been ended?"

"No, but as soon as you say you will marry me, I—"

She slapped him so hard that his head snapped to one side. He jumped back, one hand lifted to his cheek.

"What was that for, you little termagant?" he said in sudden anger, his brows lowering.

"You are no gentleman, sir. You are betrothed to Miss Lorrimer. Go away and marry her, and do everything in your power to make her happy."

He sucked in his breath sharply, and his anger drained away into a look of fear. "But Annabelle, I love *you*."

"Then I am very sorry for you." She strode to the door and flung it open. "Out, sir. I hope I never see you again."

"Annabelle, please! For God's sake marry me or I shall run mad! How can I live without you?"

*"Out!* Ah, Plessey, pray show Mr Keeling out."

"Certainly, madam. This way, sir."

"Annabelle..." he whispered, and the anguish she saw in him mirrored her own. Her first love, her *only* love, and now he could never be hers, never. How could she marry a man who cared so little for honour? He was lost to her.

"Go," she said.

And he had no choice but to leave, his face flooded with torment.

Annabelle shut the library door, hurled herself into Allan's wing chair, and burst into wild, painful sobs.

# 21: An Announcement (August)

Despite her distress, Annabelle was aware of the precise moment Allan entered the room. Even through her own weeping, the soft snick of the door was clearly audible, and she knew it was him. Her spirits lifted at once. It was strange how he always had that effect on her. Allan was such a reassuring presence in her life, so calm, so matter-of-fact, and that was just what she needed at that moment.

A chink of glass and the glug of liquid, then he was there before her, a brandy glass in his hand. "Here... drink this, my dear."

She could not move, so he pressed the glass into her hand, curling her fingers round it. Then, his own hands firmly around hers, he helped her raise it to her lips. Shakily she took a sip, feeling the liquid burn its way down her throat. Then a second sip. Her hands were trembling too much for safety, so he took the glass from her and set it on the side table amongst his many books. Then he knelt in front of her, proffering a handkerchief. He said nothing more, asked nothing, for which she was profoundly grateful.

After a while she mopped her eyes, blew her nose and said, "Thank you. I beg your pardon for my weakness. It was such a shock, you see."

"No need to apologise. Perfectly natural, but... you refused him?"

"Of course."

"Oh." He sat back on his heels. "I assumed... Your pardon, this is no concern of mine."

"He is still betrothed!" she burst out, and could not keep the anger from her voice. "He is still betrothed to Miss Lorrimer, but he comes here to offer for *me*, if you please, and thinks to break his engagement once he has secured my hand. But if I should refuse him, why, he still has his heiress, does he not? What a contemptible specimen of humanity he is! And to think I was once so foolish as to imagine him worthy of my affection. How ashamed I am of those feelings now! He is no gentleman, and I hope I never see him again as long as I live."

"Oh," he said again, and she saw a dozen different emotions chase each other across his face. Hope... perhaps that was the most dominant. Well, now he had reason for hope. She had finally shaken off her obsession with Charles, and understood his true character. And there before her, now that she could see clearly at last, was the man of true worth, the man who would never betray her or shame her, who was the real gentleman.

She knew then that she loved Allan and would marry him whole-heartedly, gladly and with faith in their future happiness.

~~~~~

### AUGUST

Allan left word with Plessey that he wished to speak to Dr Wilcox whenever he should next be in the house. He rarely spoke to the man, except on those occasions when he felt obliged to invite him to dinner, but now it was necessary.

Wilcox was one of those wiry, nervous men whose very presence made Allan feel exhausted. The physician was never still, shifting from foot to foot if he stood, and crossing and uncrossing his legs if he sat. At the dinner table, when his hands were unoccupied he drummed his thin fingers gently on the table. But he was a sensible man, highly regarded both as physician and neighbour, and Allan had never had any quarrel with him.

He did not intend to quarrel with him over Eloise, either, for confrontation was not his way, but there were things that had to be said and matters that had to be understood between them.

Wilcox came regularly to the house to see Allan's mother, so it was not long before Plessey showed the physician into the library.

"Ah, Wilcox, do come in. A glass of Madeira? Yes? And some cakes perhaps?"

Wilcox accepted the Madeira, refused the cakes and settled himself in the other wing chair as Plessey silently withdrew.

"Now then, my lord, what can I do for you? Is it a touch of this summer flu that is afflicting so many of our neighbours just now?"

"No, no, it is not my health. Nothing ever ails me, thank God. No, I wanted to talk to you about my wife, since you were attending her in the weeks before she died and must have as good a notion as anyone may of her state of mind."

"Of course, my lord, although we talked at some length of this matter at the time, and it is hard to see what more may be said now."

Allan smoothed an imaginary crease in his breeches, not quite willing to look Wilcox in the eye. But he must, he absolutely must. "There has recently been an unexpected development. Miss Hancock has suggested that Eloise was with child when she died, and—" Wilcox stilled abruptly, his face shifting almost imperceptibly to wariness. "—since I had not visited the marital bed for some considerable time, I must suppose that my wife had taken a lover." Allan spoke as calmly as he could, for it was imperative not to alarm Wilcox. "As my wife's physician, it may be that you were aware of her condition, and very kindly refrained from adding to the family's grief by mentioning the fact, for which consideration I must thank you. Or perhaps you were not aware of it at all. However it may be, I should be glad to know if, in the light of this new information, you have any insight into my wife's innermost thoughts at that time. For it would lessen my sorrow to know that she had enjoyed some happiness before she died."

Wilcox licked his lips, but his face was chalk-white. If Allan had wished for confirmation of Annabelle's suspicions, he could not have had stronger proof of it. He had not really believed it possible, yet everything in Wilcox's manner proclaimed it so. He had been Eloise's lover.

But he was not intent on shaming Wilcox into a confession, quite the reverse. It would be enough for him to know more of Eloise in those last weeks before her death. Had she run eagerly through the woods to the little cottage surrounded by pink flowers? Was she in love? Or was it boredom or desperation or loneliness that had driven her in this unexpected direction? And how had she felt when she realised she was to bear a child which her husband would know was not his?

"Was she happy, would you say? Or distressed?"

Wilcox cleared his throat. "Not happy, no. Despondent, I should say. She… was so gracious as to… to confide in me, so I knew of… of the child."

"Then I can only reiterate my thanks for your kindness in withholding that information from me. From all of us. My mother would have been greatly distressed to know of it."

"But you are not?" Wilcox said, quivering with nervous energy.

Allan chose his words with care. "Surprised, certainly. Shocked, even. But distressed? Every child is a blessing from God and I would have welcomed this one into the family, just as I did my daughters."

Wilcox looked startled. "Then you would not have—?"

"Repudiated the child? Shamed my wife and brought scandal upon the family? No, certainly not. And if my wife had been happy in her choice, then that would have been a matter for celebration, to me. It has always been a great grief to me that I could not bring Eloise the joy she deserved. But you say that she was despondent?"

"Latterly, yes. When she knew for certain that there was to be a child. My lord, Lady Brackenwood had the greatest fear of *pain*, and after her last confinement, she swore she would not subject herself to such agony again. She... forgive me, my lord, but she asked me to tell you that she came close to death so that you would not— Forgive me!"

That was a surprise. Was it pain she disliked, or Allan himself? Perhaps that was her way of expressing her distaste for her husband's attentions? Yet she had taken a lover... He shifted restlessly, not sure what to make of it. "You did as she asked, so you cannot be faulted for that," he said slowly. "Yet if she had such a fear of pain, I wonder that she exposed herself to the possibility by taking a lover." Wilcox's knee jiggled restlessly, but he said nothing, so Allan went on soothingly, "But I suppose it was not intended. An accident of over-enthusiasm, perhaps. Poor Eloise! Do you think, then, that she took her own life?"

Wilcox swallowed convulsively. "I... I believe it possible, my lord. I... Oh, my poor lady!" And to Allan's embarrassment, Wilcox covered his face with his hands and wept softly.

"There, there, man," Allan said, not quite knowing what to do. "It was not your fault." Which was, perhaps, a spectacularly stupid thing to say, for who else could be blamed except her lover and the father of her child?

"I beg your pardon, my lord." Wilcox scrubbed his face with his hands. "You see... I loved Lady Brackenwood deeply, and treasured every moment in her presence. Her death... it was the greatest affliction to me. I considered taking my own life, but... after praying for guidance, it seemed to me that my penance for entertaining such inappropriate sentiments must be to live on, with the pain of her loss my constant companion. I do not mean to suggest that my sufferings are in any way comparable to your lordship's, but to this poor lonely physician, they were great enough."

"Have you told any of this to Mr Willerton-Forbes?"

"Oh yes! He also wished to know... if I had been aware of her ladyship's condition and her feelings on the matter. I have told him everything I have told you, trusting that you would wish me to be entirely open with the gentleman."

"Indeed, that is for the best, for otherwise you might have been suspected of being her lover, and murdering her to conceal the evidence for it," Allan said, with brutal frankness. "As it is, your obvious affection for Eloise must remove you from any suspicion of that nature."

But he thought bleakly that Mr Willerton-Forbes' list was growing short indeed. Only his own name and George's still remained.

~~~~~

That evening, however, brought all his fears to an end. As soon as everyone gathered in the saloon before dinner, Willerton-Forbes asked permission to address the company.

"My lord, ladies and gentlemen, I have good news. Today sees the conclusion of my investigation. After thorough questioning of everyone in this house and connected with it, and after long consideration, I have concluded that there is no evidence that Lady Brackenwood was murdered. It is my belief that her health preyed upon her mind to harmful effect, and brought her to such a state of low spirits as to be called lunacy, whereupon she took her own life. There is, therefore, no blame attached to any person here present."

Allan was so thankful that he ordered champagne to be brought up from the cellar, and dinner passed in a very convivial manner.

"There, is that not a relief?" Marisa said, as they drank their soup. "Now you can begin to entertain again, for you have invited no one to dinner for weeks, apart from Mr Wilcox and that stuffy parson from the village."

"That is true," Allan said, with a sigh. "We owe hospitality to so many people. I hardly know where to begin."

"Why not throw a party?" she said, smiling. "That way you might fulfil all your obligations at once."

"A party!" Allan said, appalled.

"Would it not be fun? I dearly love a good party, and you are such a dull old dog these days, Allan, that it would do you the world of good. I should be happy to arrange it for you, if you find it too much trouble. If you make a list, I can send out the invitations for you, and talk to Mrs Dawkins, and if your mama is not up to the exertion, I should not mind playing hostess in her stead, you know. What could be more fitting, since Eloise is no longer here to stand by your side, than that her sister should take her place? No, do not thank me, for I should be happy to do it."

"I *do* thank you for the offer, Marisa, but your assistance is entirely unnecessary, I assure you. If I wish to hold any kind of entertainment, my secretary and my mother are perfectly capable of arranging matters between them. And let us be clear — only two people will ever stand at my side to receive guests. One is my mother and the other is the next Lady Brackenwood."

Allan had spoken louder than he intended, and the table fell silent. From his seat a few places down, Mr Willerton-Forbes watched them intently. Annabelle was studiously drinking her soup.

Marisa tittered. "The *next* Lady Brackenwood? How intriguing! Are you making an announcement, Allan?"

"Hardly that. It is customary to ask the lady first before announcing a betrothal."

"But I can barely contain my impatience to know the identity of the lady in question. Is she someone we know? Is she, in fact, seated at this table even now?"

"She had better not be," the dowager said in a low growl.

Allan only smiled at Marisa. "My dear sister, you forget that Miss Winterton is the only lady here present who is unrelated to me. Plessey, remove the soup, if you please. I am ready to begin carving the mutton."

Marisa flushed an angry red and subsided into sulky silence, but Allan was very conscious of Willerton-Forbes' perceptive eyes flicking back and forth between them.

~~~~~

Allan knew that his mother would summon him to her room that night for a lecture, for he could not come so close to declaring his intentions without suffering her wrath. He was not minded to be summoned like a child, however, so when the dowager declared herself tired and ready for bed, he followed her out of the saloon.

"Mother? Five minutes of your time in the library, if you please."

"I am going to bed, Allan."

"Library. Five minutes. If you please."

With a huff of annoyance, she took the arm he proffered. He settled her in the wing chair opposite his own, her back rigid with disapproval, her mouth pursed.

"Now, Mother, since the subject has arisen, I wish you to know my intentions for my future happiness."

"You're going to marry the governess," she said in tones of utter disgust.

"I plan to offer marriage to Miss Winterton, yes. I cannot presume to know her answer—"

"Of course she'll take you! Why wouldn't she? It's what she's been scheming for ever since she entered this house, the conniving little hussy."

"I will not have her spoken of in that manner, Mother," he said calmly. "It is not what you want for me, I am aware of that, but my admiration and esteem for her have grown to such proportions that my life will not be complete without her. I can only hope she will have me."

Not long ago, he would have been shaking in fear at speaking so to his mother. She had terrified him when he was a boy, and not a great deal less as a man. But now he was not afraid. He had already told Annabelle of his intentions, and he was therefore irrevocably committed. Honour compelled him to offer for her, and now that Willerton-Forbes had concluded his investigation, it could be soon. Soon! Perhaps tomorrow, perhaps the day after, but before too long he would know his fate, and perhaps, if he were lucky, he could look forward to the day when he might call her wife. Even his mother could not deter him from his course.

The dowager snorted in derision. "She's got you wrapped around her thumb, that's clear enough. Men are such fools, to see the meek as milk exterior and not see the devious mind at work, drawing them in. You'll regret it, you know."

"I think not," he said. "We are very well suited, much better suited than Eloise and I were, and considerably better suited than some of *your* suggestions."

"But at least they would have brought some money to the marriage. What does this chit bring with her? Nothing but a family history of wastefulness and dissolution. Her father was a gambler and a whore-monger who threw away everything he had, and she has his blood in her. She may seem demure enough now, but she'll lead you a merry dance once she's got your name to protect her. You do know that she's no innocent, I take it? That Keeling fellow —"

"Oh, is this the story you cooked up with Wilcox?" Allan said, amused. "Sorry, but that is a faradiddle, Mother, and you know it."

Her mouth dropped open momentarily, then snapped shut. "You're determined to disgrace the family name, then. Stubborn, that's what you are, just like your father. Pfft. If only Duncan had lived, then—"

"Yes, if only!" Allan said with sudden passion. "Do you imagine I ever wanted this? I can never take his place, never! He was everything a man ought to be — lively, handsome, a good dancer, gallant towards the ladies, and that magnificent voice when he sang... He was everything I am not. He enjoyed life and made everyone happy, not like me, drifting through the days, doing my duty. Well, no more, Mother. I did my duty with Eloise, and made us both miserable. Now God has seen fit to bestow on me the grace of a second chance, and I intend to grasp that opportunity wholeheartedly, with regard for my own happiness as much as for the future of the family. Miss Winterton will make me an excellent wife, should she choose to do me that honour. I can only hope I may be worthy of her, in time, and bring her the happiness she deserves."

The dowager pressed her lips into a thin line, but, to his great relief, she argued no more and rose wordlessly to quit the room.

Two minutes after she had left, while Allan was still contemplating whether to have a small brandy to celebrate his triumph, a knock at the door announced Mr Willerton-Forbes.

"Might I have a little word, my lord?"

Allan's heart sank at the serious look on the lawyer's face. "Must you? I am in a particularly good mood tonight, and I have a feeling that your little word will reduce me to gloom." He sighed, then went on, "I beg your pardon. Do come in." He ushered him in and poured brandy for them both, a large measure for Willerton-

Forbes and a smaller one for himself. Then, gloomily, he poured more into his own glass. "Now then, what is on your mind?"

"Mrs Pargeter is on my mind," the lawyer said starkly. "Something occurred to me at dinner... something I had not previously considered, since it seems impossible, but... My lord, let me speak plainly."

"Oh, please do."

"Is it conceivable that Mrs Pargeter might mistakenly believe you could marry her?"

"Difficult as it may be to imagine, she did indeed have some thought of that when she first arrived here," Allan said. "Naturally, I disabused her of the notion very quickly. Any marriage between us would be forbidden by the church, even had our feelings drawn us in that direction."

"Quite so, and perhaps I am not speaking out of turn if I say that the direction of *your* feelings is plain to see. But as to Mrs Pargeter's feelings... Again, I must be blunt, my lord. Is Mrs Pargeter in love with you?"

Allan shook his head. "I cannot think so. When we first met, years ago... there was some attraction between us then. But I married Eloise, Marisa married Jacob Pargeter and I did not see her again until a few months ago, although she and Eloise wrote to each other constantly, as sisters do."

"Really? We have found no letters from Mrs Pargeter to her sister. And she never came to visit, nor did Lady Brackenwood wish to visit her sister? Hmm. I wonder what impelled Mrs Pargeter to visit you after so long apart?"

"Mr Pargeter died in April last year, and once her year of mourning was over, she wished to travel," he said easily. "There is nothing odd in that. A lively young woman married to a much older man — naturally she wanted to spread her wings a little."

Willerton-Forbes nodded thoughtfully. "Spread her wings... I see. So she flies straight to you, thinking you might marry her, you explain that you cannot and yet... she is still here? Why do you suppose that is, my lord?"

"I have no idea," he said. "Not from any encouragement from me, you may be sure, nor from my mother. And she is a rich woman now, she need not play the poor relation at my table. Perhaps she just likes it here."

"Perhaps. She is very friendly with Mr George Skelton."

"She will have no luck there," Allan said. "He is smitten with the Lady Grace Bucknell, a duke's daughter, and most unlikely to be interested in a widow older than he is."

"Stranger things have happened. Widows have... a certain fascination for young men."

"George has been on the town long enough not to be taken in," Allan said with a smile.

Willerton-Forbes nodded. "Hmm. Mrs Pargeter often goes into Chester for the day, so there may be a gentleman friend," the lawyer said. "For a moment there, I wondered if I had overlooked another name for my list. If Mrs Pargeter had nurtured a secret passion for you all these years, and had not realised you would never countenance such a match, perhaps she murdered her sister to marry you yourself. But I do not see how it could be done if she was in Devonshire the whole time. If she had sent poison to Lady Brackenwood by way of the mail, then the label could hardly be in her own hand, and Mrs Pargeter was not here to decant poison into an existing bottle."

"What a devious mind you have, to consider such possibilities."

"I have a lawyer's mind, my lord. We see the worst of humanity in the courtrooms of England, and it makes us unduly suspicious of human nature. But in this case I believe I may keep to my previous opinion. Lady Brackenwood died by her own hand."

# 22: Questions

Annabelle felt oddly calm. The investigation had concluded, no one was to be hauled off and hanged for murder after all, and especially not Allan. Not that she had ever imagined him guilty, but once one started asking questions and rooting around in the past, one never knew what might be unearthed. It was a relief that it was all over at last, and in a few days, after Mr Willerton-Forbes had compiled his final report, he and Captain Edgerton and Mr Neate would take themselves back to London, and everything would be tranquil again.

And now... now she waited. One day soon, she would receive a summons to the library, and Allan would make his offer in form. Or perhaps he would ask her to meet him in the Grecian Temple, as he had done once before. Or the schoolroom door would open and there he would be, and her whole life would change. The moment she accepted him, she would no longer be the governess, tucked away in her secluded corner or shut away with her pupils. She would be Miss Winterton of Woodside again, and the future Countess of Brackenwood.

It was as well that she had developed a firm routine for her lessons, for without that anchor to keep her in place she might have drifted into lassitude, doing nothing as she waited. But the girls bounced into the schoolroom each morning for their lesson in French conversation — they had progressed beyond the baby house and now looked through books with pictures for their inspiration. After that, there were reading, writing and ciphering lessons, and then music, singing and deportment, followed by their walk around the lakes or into the woods, or a riding lesson. Then the hour in the library with Allan before they went back to the nursery for supper and baths and bed. There was little time for reflection or nervousness, and if she lay awake at night wondering just how she would manage as mistress of this great house, and how she would get along with the dowager, she supposed such worries were normal.

But the hours flew by, and the days, and still he did not speak. In fact, they hardly exchanged a word which did not relate either to the children or to the food on the table. On one particular day, the only time he spoke to her was to ask her to pass the buttered mushrooms at dinner.

The summer heat had become oppressive, and after dinner the ladies drifted onto the terrace, where cushion-strewn sofas and chairs promised a cooler spot to await the gentlemen. They sat, fanning themselves, making desultory conversation, as moths blundered into the lamps. A thin band of colour lightened the horizon, but distant rumbles heralded a storm.

Annabelle was too hot to sew, and felt awkwardly out of place under the disapproving glare of the dowager, so she wandered down the lawn to the marble bench beside the lake. There was no breeze, but it was mercifully quiet and she could fan herself and think her own thoughts in peace.

"May I join you?"

Her heart leapt at the sight of him. He was correctly dressed, as always, but there was something careless about his evening coat, knee breeches and stockings, made more for comfort than fashion, as if he were doing his best, but would really rather be wearing buckskins and top boots. Dear Allan! So much more at home in the country than in town.

He sat down beside her, a proper distance away, but then he lapsed into silence. She dared not look at him, for fear of what she might see there, so she hung her head, staring at her fan. Was he regretting his impulsive declaration? Perhaps now that he was free of the threat of trial for murder, he wished to look higher for a wife than the penniless second daughter of nobody in particular.

"Annabelle, will you marry me?"

So abrupt, so plain-spoken. That was his way, of course, for flowery words never came easily to him. But still, to say nothing of admiration... affection... or love. There should be something said of love.

"Please, Annabelle. Please."

She lifted her head, still not looking at him. "May I ask you a question?"

"Of course." He was slightly breathless.

"Is this driven by a sense of obligation? Because of the rum?"

"No. No. Nothing like that. I offered *then* as much from obligation as anything else, but you refused and so I feel that honour is satisfied on that score. This time I offer from my own wishes, Annabelle."

She turned to look at him, and what she saw in his face made her tingle with joy. So much anxious hope written there, as he leaned slightly towards her, his hands twisting restlessly. At once she understood. His reticence was all due to nerves. He was not a man who made speeches easily, and his hesitation was no more than an indication of his shyness.

Before she could speak, he rushed on, "Forgive me, you deserve a more articulate proposal than that, but somehow I cannot make my foolish tongue shape the words. I have been struggling for days to find the proper phrases, but I can wait no longer. I must tell you what is in my heart, however unadorned the speech. All I know is that I want you with me always. Please, please tell me that you will be my wife."

She took a deep breath, but there was no hesitation in her answer. "Yes, I will. Thank you for the very great honour you do me, my lord. I should be delighted to marry you."

"Dear Annabelle!" he cried, his face alight with happiness. "But do you really mean that? Oh, forgive me, that is impertinent. I mean only that I should not like *you* to feel under an obligation, either. To... to marry me from gratitude or... or because your recent experience with a young man has left you despairing of making a match of the heart. Because I must tell you that your beauty and good nature must always attract admirers and, in truth, you could do much better than a dull specimen like myself."

It would be so easy to make a flippant answer, or to flatter him, to tell him that he was as lively, as handsome as any man of her acquaintance. But it would be wrong to begin her life with Allan with anything less than perfect honesty.

"I cannot refuse you, naturally," she said, with a little laugh. "Despite your flattering words, I shall never have such a good offer again. But that does not mean that I have the slightest reservation about my answer. I accept you willingly, whole-heartedly, joyfully."

"Oh," he breathed. "Then, come, my dearest. Let us go back to the house and impart the good news to all our friends."

"And to your mother," she said, raising her eyes to his with a demure smile. And he laughed, as she had hoped he would. They would not fall out over the Dowager Countess, in any event.

He stood and offered her his arm, and they walked slowly back up the lawn to the house to receive the congratulations, with greater or lesser sincerity, of everyone present. Annabelle was kissed by the aunts and Allan had his hand vigorously shaken, champagne was poured and the couple's health was drunk, and only the dowager glowered and said nothing.

Before long, the first heavy splashes of rain fell, and the servants rushed about retrieving cushions and moving chairs to shelter. The terrace was partly covered and so the whole group lingered on outside, drinking champagne steadily as rain poured from overflows and gurgled through drain pipes, and lightning flickered over the lakes. Only when thunder crashed almost overhead did everyone begin to drift indoors again.

Annabelle smiled and blushed, head lowered, yet was fully aware that her happiness was tempered by disappointment. There had been no kiss to seal the bargain, no mention of love and no passion. Could she live the rest of her life without that glorious, shiver-inducing passion that she had felt once before? Could she survive with only politeness and kindness? Was it enough? It might have to be.

~~~~~

Annabelle had expected her life to change instantly, but nothing of the sort occurred. The girls were told — her step-daughters, as they would be before long — and they reacted with pleased surprise. "Oh good, now you will never go away!" Dorothea said, which made Annabelle cry. The servants displayed a new respect. She set aside her plain governess gowns and brought out her finery for the evening, taking her place beside Allan and finally joining him at the card table. But otherwise, her life went on as before. Once the news got about, she supposed she would be expected to receive callers and make calls of her own, and perhaps there would be invitations, but her first day as the future mistress of Charlsby was spent in the schoolroom, as always.

She wrote long letters to all her sisters, telling them her news. It was awkward, for she had said very little about Allan before, apart from the occasional mentions that arose from his position as her employer and a central figure into the investigation into his wife's death. Her own feelings had been too nebulous, and the prospect of a resolution seemed too unlikely to be worthy of relating. Even when he had declared his intentions, she had not wanted to raise her sisters' hopes of a reprieve from their penury. But now, it could all be told, and they must know of her happiness...

Here she quailed. Was she happy? Yes, naturally she was happy, for how could she not be? She would have a kind and gentle husband, a position in society, a lovely house, a family... In fact, she would have a family the instant she left the church. And here a lowering thought assailed her. How often had Allan complimented her on her management of his daughters, and praised her teaching skills? Perhaps, after all, that was her greatest attraction — that she would make a competent step-mother. Yet he had told her more than once that he wanted to kiss her, and not always when fuelled by rum. He liked her a little, then. He felt some attraction towards her.

But not love. And if he did not love her, then she could never show him how much she loved him. If he chose to be polite and restrained, that was how she must be, too. Yet how much she longed to kiss him, to touch him, to feel his warm arms around her.

~~~~~

On the second morning after her betrothal, Annabelle woke later than usual, yet there was no chocolate awaiting her, nor any sign of her hot water for washing. She washed in last night's cold water, and was half dressed before a maid Annabelle had not seen before came in at a run, carrying the ewer of water.

"So sorry, Miss," she said. "We're all at sixes and sevens this morning."

"Where is Milly today? She is usually so prompt with the water."

"Sick, Miss. Sorry, gotta rush. Breakfast tray at the usual time, I hope."

"Will you just lace my stays before you go? It is the only part I cannot easily do myself."

"Oh... course, Miss." She laced them so loosely that Annabelle might as well not have been wearing stays at all. Then, with a quick bob of a curtsy, she rushed away.

Annabelle went out for a morning walk. She told herself it was to take advantage of the cooler air, but a corner of her mind hoped to meet Allan. However, she returned to the house without seeing a soul, and ate her breakfast in solitude in her room. How she hated those breakfast trays! She had grown up eating breakfast in company with Mama and Papa and all her sisters. Whatever else they did during the day, that hour in the breakfast parlour was an affirmation of her family's affection. She and her sisters would giggle and whisper together about their new bonnets or the chance of a sighting of the handsome new neighbour, Mama would laugh and tell them they should think about their music practice, not young men, and Papa would chaff them for making so much noise. And Jeremy... no, she could hardly remember Jeremy. He always had his nose in a book. Poor Jeremy, who had never wanted to go to sea, yet there he was, his bones lying amongst the fishes.

Now she was getting maudlin. That would never do! She must not repine, for was she not on the brink of matrimony to a kind man... If only he would kiss her! If only he would take her in his arms and tell her he loved her, that he wanted her for herself and not just as a mother to his daughters. If only...

She took a deep breath. Once she was safely married, then she could begin to draw out her husband a little, and look for the affectionate man that she hoped lay hidden inside the formal exterior. And she would start by proposing that they eat breakfast together, and the girls too. They would be a proper family. That would please him, surely?

Before she began lessons for the day, Annabelle sent to enquire after Milly, and received encouraging news. She had collapsed unnoticed in one of the store-rooms while fetching fresh candles the night before, and had been quite ill at first, but Dr Wilcox had seen her and cupped her, and she was a little better.

Late in the morning, Mrs Hale came to the schoolroom. "His lordship's apologies for interrupting the lesson, but would you be so good as to attend him in the study, Madam."

"Oh. Of course. Thank you, Mrs Hale. Dody, you may continue your writing. Florry, Freddy, when you have completed your translation, you may begin memorising the next sonnet in the sequence. I shall hear you recite when I return."

They rose to curtsy as she left the room. They, too, were more deferential now that she was betrothed to their father.

The study adjoined the library. Once, the two rooms had been laid out in the usual arrangement for all the corner rooms of Charlsby, with one larger portion for the library and one very much smaller as a study, set alongside the spiral service stair. Sometime in the past, however, these two had been rearranged, and half the library given over to increase the size of the study. Here Allan and Mr Cross had matching desks, and here the business of the estate was carried on.

Allan rose to greet Annabelle as she was shown in with such a smile on his face that she could not mistake his affection. He took her hand and raised it to his lips, and that small touch, that warmth on the back of her hand, relieved all her anxieties. When she was alone, all her doubts flooded in to haunt her, yet when she was with him, when he looked at her with such obvious admiration, she was perfectly happy.

"My dear! Come in, come in. Mr Cross and I are finalising the notice to be sent to the newspapers, and we wished you to see it first, to be sure that we have everything correct. We have put ' *..second daughter of the late Mr Winterton of Woodside in the county of Brinshire.'* Is that as you would wish? Should we mention your mother's family also? What was your father's Christian name?"

"Edmund," she said absently. "I do not know about mentioning my mother. She was a Tilford, a long-established family in Shropshire, but she is not connected with the nobility. I beg your pardon, I have never done this before. I do not know what is proper."

"Generally speaking, Miss Winterton," Mr Cross said, "one might mention the mother's family if it is grander or wealthier than the father's, but in this case...?"

"Oh, no, I do not think so. Mama's family is perfectly respectable, but the estate is very modest."

"Then I believe it should not be mentioned. Is there anyone you would wish his lordship to notify of the marriage?"

"No, I believe not. I have told my sisters, and there are no other close relations."

Allan stroked her hand gently. "Miss Winterton, you will wish to have time to obtain your wedding clothes, so how would you feel about a wedding in three months' time? In November. That will be more than a year since Eloise died, and, for myself, I should like everything to be settled before Christmas, but I will abide by your wishes in the matter. If you wish to wait until the spring—"

"Oh, by no means. Let it be November."

"Excellent. I plan to invite your brother-in-law to visit, to discuss the settlements and so forth, but you have no mother to advise you. Perhaps you wish to have one of your sisters here with you, to help you and bear you company, for my mother is perhaps not the best person to take care of you."

"You are all kindness, my lord, but my sister Rosamund is unlikely to wish to travel so close to her confinement, and Lucy, Margaret and Fanny cannot leave their posts just now."

"Hmm, and my own sisters cannot be spared either. So what is to be done?"

She smiled at the thought that she must now have a companion. "If she is willing, Mrs Pargeter would be well suited to advise me on new clothes, for her taste is excellent."

"Ah, that is true. But still, she is a stranger to you. Surely you wish to have a congenial companion?"

"I have no need of company beyond yours," she said simply, looking into his eyes.

"Ah, Annabelle," he said, squeezing her hand, and she felt rather breathlessly that if Mr Cross had not been there perhaps Allan might at last have stepped beyond mere politeness. Perhaps he might even have kissed her.

~~~~~

Allan was dizzy with happiness. She had said yes! He had been terrified that it was too soon after her quarrel with the despicable Mr Keeling, terrified that she might refuse him and then... then everything would have been awkward, and she might have felt obliged to go away. But she did not refuse, and all was well.

Now there was just the interminable three months until the wedding to be got through. Three months. Thirteen weeks. Ninety days or thereabouts. He could barely contain his impatience, but he must. For ninety days, he must tiptoe around her, do nothing to remind her of her worthless suitor, do nothing to alarm her or send her running. She was only marrying him because she must, after all. *I cannot refuse you.* Eloise could not refuse him, either. That was the damnable part of being an earl, of being wealthy and respectable and worthy, there were few women wealthy enough or powerful enough to spurn him. Well, he would take Annabelle however he could get her, and he would do everything in his power to make her happy, but please Lord, let her not cry off. And please Lord, let Miss Lorrimer not cry off, either. Let her marry Mr Keeling and take him out of Annabelle's life for ever.

But it was so difficult to keep his distance. Allan hardly dared trust himself alone with her, yet he had to see her as often as possible. The evenings were wonderful, for he could take her into dinner on his arm, sit beside her, talk to her, look at her, admire the whiteness of her smooth arms, the brightness of her eye, the rosy lips... Ah, those lips! How they tormented him! So luscious and enticing, but he dared not kiss her, so he tried never to be alone with her.

Still, there were ways of seeing her, even during the day, so that he could feast on her delicious curves and welcoming smiles. Long after Annabelle had returned to the schoolroom, he emerged from his seclusion with Mr Cross to find a letter for her sitting on the hall table. Smiling, he picked it up, and took the stairs two at a time.

Florence was reciting when he entered the schoolroom, so he waited politely until she had finished and praised her performance.

"Shall you hear it all, Papa? I can easily begin again."

"You may recite it all for me this afternoon, if you like, when you come to the library. I only came to bring Miss Winterton her letter."

"Ooh, who is it from?" Dody said excitedly.

"It is from one of my sisters," she said, looking at the writing.

"Which one? Is it the married one who goes to London?"

"I cannot tell until I open it, although there is a blot on the direction, so that might be Lucy."

"You cannot tell?" Allan said in surprise. "They sound such different people that I would have imagined they wrote in very different hands."

"No, indeed. We all write in exactly the same manner, just as we were taught by Mama. Sisters always write alike. You have seen your daughters' writing and you cannot tell one from another, can you?"

"No, but... I had supposed that temperament affected such matters."

"A little, perhaps, but if sisters are taught in the same way, and learn well, they will always write in the exact same style. I imagine brothers are the same, if they have the same tutor, or attend the same school."

He acknowledged that it might be so, and, having no further excuse to linger, he left them to their work.

It was hours later, as he was in his library, trying to read and finding his thoughts preoccupied with his future bride, that her words came back into his awareness.

"Sisters... Oh, great heavens, *sisters!*"

And finally he understood.

He leapt up, casting his book aside, and rushed into the hall, where Portman stood patiently. "Mr Willerton-Forbes — is he is his office upstairs?"

"I believe so, my lord. He rang for more paper just an hour ago."

Allan ran up the stairs, and tore into Willerton-Forbes' office without knocking.

The lawyer was at his desk, scratching away with a pen, but he looked up as Allan burst in. "My lord?"

"Sisters! They are—"

From somewhere not too far away, a pistol shot cracked in the still air.

# 23: The Grecian Temple

*'Dear, dear Annabelle, How happy your news makes me! I suspected long since that there was an attachment between you, for you talked so highly of Lord B and his many fine qualities as bespoke a great regard, and you are so charming and clever that he must be a simpleton not to fall in love with you instantly, so this is perfect and I am so, so happy for you! I wish you the greatest joy, my dear sister. Pray write soon with all the details of the wedding date and what clothes you are buying and whether you will make any changes to the house and if you will have to keep the Dowager Countess or may pack her off to the Dower House at once. Is there a Dower House? These noble families always have a Dower House, do they not? Shall you have a wedding tour? And if so will you come to Yorkshire? I should so very much like to see you again, for although I have made all these new friends, there is no one like family and one's own sisters, is there? Do write again very soon. Your delighted sister, Fanny.'*

~~~~~

The girls were to have their riding lesson that afternoon, so, after she had sent to enquire after Milly and learnt she was sleeping peacefully, Annabelle was able to retire to her room to read her letter at leisure. She wrote a long reply, before folding the letter away neatly and putting it in her box with all of her sisters' other letters. Sometimes she would take out a batch to reread, and try to divine whether each sister were as content with her lot as she claimed, or merely putting a brave face on her situation. Perhaps before too long she would be able to rescue them from their impoverished situations and bring them to Charlsby... But no, for then they would be poor relations and just as impoverished as before, and besides, Allan would not want all three of her unmarried sisters descending on him, especially Lucy, whose chattering would drive him mad. She sighed. It was difficult to know what to do for the best.

She had just picked up a book to read when a knock on the door heralded the entrance of Mr Penicuik. He coughed discreetly, his face crimson with embarrassment.

"Beg pardon, Miss Winterton..."

"Good day, Mr Penicuik. May I be of service to you?"

"No, no, nothing like that, Miss Winterton," he said, his Adam's apple bobbing in his throat. "I have brought you a message."

"Oh, I see. What is the message, pray?"

"Lord Brackenwood would like you to meet him in the Grecian Temple."

"At what hour?"

"Oh. I do not know. I suppose... now."

She laughed in delight, thrilled at the prospect of an assignation. At last, she would be private with Allan and surely now he would kiss her and hold her and—

Mr Penicuik cleared his throat.

"Oh... thank you, Mr Penicuik."

Throwing down her book, she grabbed a bonnet and rushed down the stairs and out through the saloon. With quick steps, she crossed the lawn and made her way along the upper lake, across the bridge and a little way round the lower lake.

The Grecian Temple was empty. She tried not to be disappointed, knowing that Allan would be there soon. It was pleasantly cool inside, so she sat on the marble seat and waited as patiently as she could. It would be worth the wait, for the temple was very secluded, the towering shrubs around the lake screening it from the house. She would have Allan all to herself, and they could talk, and hold hands, and kiss and—

A figure came into view, strolling slowly along the path edging the lake, her elegant skirts swaying, a parasol shielding her from the sun. Mrs Pargeter. Of all the unlucky coincidences, that she should pass this way just now! If she spotted Allan approaching, she would be sure to engage him in conversation, and then perhaps she would sit with them in the temple and Annabelle's precious time alone with her betrothed would be lost.

But perhaps she would be lucky, for Mrs Pargeter was gazing out over the lake, quite oblivious of Annabelle sitting, as quiet as a mouse, in the gloom of the temple. She wished she had tucked herself behind the pillar, where she would have been hidden from view, but perhaps she might not be noticed if she held her breath...

Mrs Pargeter stopped, and the parasol tipped slightly as if she were leaning forward, gazing into the water. After a moment, she straightened and turned to move on. Unfortunately, she closed the parasol at that moment, and as she did so she caught sight of Annabelle sitting inside the temple.

"Why, is it Miss Winterton? What are you doing all alone? Isn't Allan with you?"

"I expect him to arrive at any moment, Mrs Pargeter," Annabelle said, with as good a grace as she could muster.

"Then I will not linger, for who would wish to come between two such love birds?" She gave a little trill of laughter, which sounded oddly false to Annabelle's ears. "But before I go, do come and look at this odd thing that is in the water just here. Why, it looks like gold, as if it might be jewellery."

"Jewellery? In the lake?"

"So it seems to me. Do come and look, and give me your opinion, Miss Winterton."

Annabelle rose, and went to stand at the edge of the lake, in the spot indicated by Mrs Pargeter, the place she had stopped a moment earlier.

"There! Do you see? Glinting in the water — is it gold, do you suppose?"

"I see nothing glinting, only a few mossy pebbles."

"A little further out... no, you will have to lean further than that..."

Annabelle leaned. "No, I—"

Something hit her hard in the small of the back, and she fell with a cry into the lake. As her face plunged into the water, a great weight on her back pushed her down, down... something was forcing her head beneath the surface. She could not breathe. She tried to cry out, but her mouth filled with water. Gasping, struggling to take in air, she wriggled and heaved to dislodge the heavy weight on top of her...

There was nothing but water, and stones against her face, and no air.

No air...

She could not breathe, could not move, and not all her efforts could dislodge the weight that held her down.

No air... No air...

Only water and peacefulness and surrender...

Abruptly, the weight was gone, and something lifted her and tossed her aside. She drew in a great gasp of air, coughing up lake water, spluttering, taking great heaving breaths. She was on her hands and knees, head down, a pool of regurgitated water beneath her.

Somewhere nearby, for unfathomable reasons, there was shouting, then a scream, then, horrifyingly, a gunshot. More shouts, and running feet.

She spat out more water, breathing, breathing... Thank God for air to breathe.

More running feet, and someone beside her, a hand on her back. Was it Allan? Her heart surged with joy — he had come!

"Annabelle! Are you all right?"

Not Allan. It was George Skelton, mystifyingly. How had he come there? Why was there so much shouting? She was too busy breathing to care.

"Annabelle? Miss Winterton? Nod if you are all right!"

George again. She managed a nod.

"Thank God! You look terrible! Have no fear, Edgerton will catch her." Her? What her? "Someone has gone for Wilcox. And blankets. You must be frozen."

She coughed, and more water spewed out.

"There now, get it all out of you," he said cheerfully.

"Allan," she croaked. It was meant to be a question, but somehow it came out wrong.

"He has been sent for," George said, his voice softening. "He will be here directly."

In the distance, another scream. What was happening? She could not move, crouched on hands and knees, her lungs gradually coughing up half the lake.

Then another voice, so familiar, so dear, and gentle hands lifting her, wrapping something soft around her. "Annabelle? Oh, dear God, is she…? Oh my darling, do not die, please God, do not die! I could not bear it! Please, my love, stay with me, stay with me, never leave me. There now, my dear one, you are safe now."

"Safe…" she whispered, knowing it to be true.

When she opened her eyes, there he was. He picked her up and carried her into the gloom of the temple, and she rested her head against the reassuring solidity of his shoulder. Settling himself on the marble seat, he laid her across his knees, his arm tucked around her back. His coat was round her shoulders, and tenderly he tucked it a little closer about her.

"Allan," she murmured, reaching out one hand and grasping his shirt.

"I am here, my darling, and all is well. Nothing can hurt you now."

He rocked her gently, and with a great cough, she spewed water all down his waistcoat.

"Better out than in," George said cheerfully.

Annabelle felt Allan shake a little, but when she opened her eyes again and gazed at him, she realised that he was laughing. "Darling girl," he whispered, and kissed her gently on the forehead.

"Allan..." she sighed, snuggling closer to him. She was perfectly safe now.

~~~~~

For the rest of that day, and through the night, and all the next day and night too, Annabelle was never alone. Allan carried her back to her room, Mrs Hale and two of the maids undressed her and put her to bed, and one or other of them stayed with her constantly. Dr Wilcox gave her something to help her sleep, and sleep she did, off and on for thirty six hours.

When she woke, one of the aunts was dozing beside her bed.

"Lady Elizabeth?" She pulled herself up to a sitting position, yawning.

Aunt Beth grunted, and startled to wakefulness. "There now, you look a great deal better, dear. Are you hungry? Let me ring for broth."

The broth arrived, and then there was a bath, and a clean gown, and after that, an hour in her sitting room, an aunt on either side of her, with Allan and George and Mr Willerton-Forbes explaining just what had happened.

"I always wondered about Mrs Pargeter," Mr Willerton-Forbes said. "Why did she come here after all this time, and then linger on? It was odd. But she was in Devon when her sister died, and there seemed no method by which she might have had a hand in the matter, nor any reason for it. So she was never on my list, not officially, but I wondered very much about her. But then, the other night at dinner, she hinted that she would like to take her sister's place, which raised my suspicions. Was she perhaps in love with

Lord Brackenwood, I wondered? Again, though, how could she have murdered her sister?"

"She was not even here," Annabelle said. "Surely you cannot think—?"

"I did not, not at first," the lawyer admitted. "But Captain Edgerton's enquiries of friends in Devon had revealed that Mr Jacob Pargeter had suffered from dropsy, and had been prescribed exactly the kind of medicine which killed Lady Brackenwood. What is more, he had been given a new bottle the very day he died."

"You do not mean that she murdered her husband?" Allan said sharply.

"Probably not, but perhaps the new mixture was unusually strong — a mistake by the apothecary, perhaps, or it may be that the gentleman took more than he should have done. Mrs Pargeter realised that she was now free, and also had the means to hand of disposing of the only obstacle keeping her from her heart's desire. Undoubtedly she relabelled the bottle as a sleeping draught, and that was what confused us, for the hand was identical to Lady Brackenwood's. She sent the bottle to her sister by mail, her sister died, and as soon as her year of mourning was over, Mrs Pargeter set off to secure her prize."

"She took a terrible risk," Allan said. "Anyone might have known that she sent that particular bottle."

"Even if they had, what of it?" Mr Willerton-Forbes said. "Lady Brackenwood had been ill for some time. Her death was sudden, perhaps, but not such as to arouse suspicion. And the handwriting was, we thought, Lady Brackenwood's own. Mrs Pargeter realised our mistake, and probably destroyed all her own letters to her sister so we would not realise the truth. The real risk Mrs Pargeter took was in staying on after the letter was found, putting the idea of murder into your head. You were bound to investigate, but—"

Annabelle gasped. "Not *found!*" she cried. "Mrs Pargeter *wrote* that letter! She must have done. If Lady Brackenwood had written it, she would have put some direction on it, to her sister, perhaps, or *'To whom it may concern, to be read after my death'*. That sort of thing. Otherwise, the housemaid might simply burn it, finding a half finished letter lying about after her death. No wonder we could not make out the purpose of it, at the time. It made no sense. But if Mrs Pargeter wrote it, then it makes perfect sense."

"I have to agree," Mr Willerton-Forbes said. "To be truthful, I had forgotten the letter, imagining it irrelevant to the matter in hand. But it is clear now, and the reason for it."

"I hope you will explain it to me," Allan said plaintively, "for I do not see why, if Marisa killed Eloise, she would draw attention to it in that way."

"I would wager she brought the letter to you very soon after you rejected her advances."

"The very next day, but—"

"There you are then!" Mr Willerton-Forbes said. "Mrs Pargeter successfully released you from your marriage, and gently suggested to you that she might replace her sister in your affections. When you spurned her, and in a manner allowing for no possibility of a change of heart, she no doubt looked at George and saw how she might still win her way to a title."

"You mean, I suppose, that she intended me to hang for Eloise's death, leaving George to inherit? Good God!"

George snorted in derision. "She must be insane if she ever imagined I would marry her. I ignored her hints often enough. I took to keeping my bedroom door locked, just in case of nocturnal wanderings."

"I knew you were a match for her," Allan said, with the first sign of a smile.

Mr Willerton-Forbes smiled too. "And when that did not work, she decided to try to get you hanged for Miss Winterton's death, instead. She would have concocted some story — that Miss Winterton had trapped you into a betrothal, but you realised you loved Mrs Pargeter all the time and tried to do away with your betrothed."

"As if I would ever hurt a hair of her head!" Allan said indignantly.

"Of course you would not! But she was desperate by then, I think. She tried to poison you first, Miss Winterton, by meddling with the wine in your sitting room. Milly was lucky there, for seemingly she liked a drink after seeing you to bed, but she only took a very little, so she will make a full recovery. But then Mrs Pargeter gave up on stealth and tried an open assault, and perhaps she might have succeeded if Edgerton and I had not already realised the possibility, and set a watch on her. Either Edgerton or Neate followed her everywhere, and we alerted Mr Skelton, too, and a select few of the footmen and grooms that Neate suggested were trustworthy. In the event of any problem, a pistol was to be fired to summon help, and everyone would converge on the spot. Edgerton was therefore on hand to pull Miss Winterton from the water, and Mr Skelton to attend to her until you could be fetched, my lord."

"You might have told *me*," Allan grumbled. "All this going on under my nose, and Miss Winterton's life in danger, and you never thought to tell either of us?"

Mr Willerton-Forbes smiled. "My lord, you and Miss Winterton are too honest and open to be involved in any deceit. Your countenances would have given the game away instantly. Miss Winterton was quite safe, and I was awaiting only a letter from Devon, final confirmation of events there, before informing you fully. Another day would have seen her locked away and no one at the least risk of harm from her ever again."

"Where is she now?" Annabelle said, hesitantly.

Allan hesitated. "Dr Wilcox has taken her to an asylum. We thought it for the best."

# 24: Congenial Company

That evening, Annabelle was well enough to take dinner with the family, the aunts solicitous on either side of her, and Allan watching her anxiously. The following morning, when she went to the schoolroom as usual, she found the three girls already hard at work, with the nurse stitching away on the window seat.

"Look, we have followed your regular lesson plan," Dody said eagerly. "I have written the chapters to be studied and the verses to be learnt on the board, you see? We can take care of ourselves until you are quite better."

"I see that I am not needed," Annabelle said, laughing.

"Oh no! We *do* need you," Florry said seriously. "Dody will run out of ideas in a few days, but Papa said you are to rest for a while and we are not to be troublesome."

"We are not being troublesome, are we?" Freddy said anxiously.

"Not in the least," Annabelle said. "Very well, you may manage by yourselves for the rest of this week, and then on Monday I shall return to my usual tasks."

"There, you see?" Dody said. "I told you she would not mind. Now you may go and rest, Miss Winterton."

Annabelle felt she had rested enough. What she needed most was some brisk exercise and congenial company. She collected her bonnet and went to the library, and then, finding it empty, to the study next door. Mr Cross and Allan had their heads bent together over the desk, with such twin expressions of pain that Annabelle almost laughed. The dogs bounded across the room to meet her, and Allan jumped up and followed them just as eagerly.

"Annabelle! Miss Winterton... going out? Not alone, surely? You will not go out alone?"

"I will not, if Mr Cross can spare you to me for an hour."

Allan's face lit up with such delight that it quite took her breath away. She could not be mistaken in the affection he felt for her, surely? It was genuine, it must be. He could not dissemble, she knew. He was too open for such falsity.

He collected his hat and gloves, and with the dogs bouncing excitedly around their feet, they set off across the lawn.

"Around the lake?" he asked.

"I should like to go up to the woods," she answered.

"So far? You will not overtire yourself by walking such a distance? It is almost all uphill."

"It is a very gentle slope, and there is a seat to rest upon at the top."

He fell silent for a while, but she kept up a patter of meaningless conversation until they had gained the edge of the woods, and the seat around the oak tree. Here Annabelle sat, and gazed out across the deer park and the lakes and the lawns and gardens beyond, at the house. Charlsby. Her home, now. In a few weeks, she would be mistress here and might order the household as she chose, for Allan was such a gentle, unassuming man that he would not gainsay her wishes. Not that she planned to change much. She might use the Italian room to receive callers, perhaps, since the dowager had the morning room. And a little more entertaining might be pleasant, if Allan had no objection.

Allan had lapsed once more into silence, tossing his gloves into his upturned hat and seating himself at arm's length from her, but she was not to be deterred.

"May I ask you something?"

"Of course," he said, but he would not look her in the eye. He must be aware that her choice of direction for this walk was no accident, and that they now sat directly below the mistletoe.

"You have several times expressed a wish to kiss me, Allan, but naturally I could not permit it before. Yet now, when we are betrothed and it would be perfectly allowable, you make no approach. I do not know what to make of that."

His head lifted abruptly, but he had the hunted look of a deer about him. "It is not from any lack of desire, if that is what you fear. But..." He stopped with a sigh, and again silence overcame him.

She moved a little nearer to him and took his hand. He looked at her warily but made no move to escape. "Allan... my dear Allan, do we not know each other well enough to be open? There should be no secrets between us, do you not agree?" He nodded miserably. "Then will you not tell me what the matter is? Why you flirted with me before, but now—"

"I was not flirting!" he said. "I have no idea how to flirt. All I was trying to do, in my bumbling, inarticulate way, was to see if you held me in any regard, however slight. It was the only way I knew how to approach you. But now..."

"Now you do not need to flirt?" she hazarded.

"Flirting… I wish I knew how." Absently, he stroked the back of her hand. "I never know what to *say*, Annabelle. Words do not come easily to me, or those little gestures that tell a lady how much a man admires her. I watch George sometimes, or even Captain Edgerton, and envy them that easy way with ladies."

"There are no words needed for a kiss," she said softly. "Here we are, sitting under the mistletoe and all you need do is lean forward—"

"But I can never be *him!*" he burst out. "I can never kiss you the way he did, and pour ardour into your ears, and warm you to your toes, and make you love me so much you hardly know which way is up. I cannot forget the words you spoke of him. I wish I could, God knows, but I cannot. I dare not kiss you, Annabelle, because I will inevitably fall short and then perhaps you will leave me and how could I possibly bear it? Do not ask it of me, I beg you!"

It was so irrational she could hardly take it in. And yet, she understood it, in a way. "Allan, Charles will always be a part of my past, just as Eloise is a part of yours. Think how much you have shared with her, both happiness and sorrow, in love and friendship and companionship. I shared one kiss with Charles, just one, and it changed my life for ever and blinded me to anyone but him. I have wondered a great deal lately if he did me a very bad turn by kissing me in that way, like a lover. I would have been far happier, I believe, if it had never happened. But it did happen, and we can none of us change the past, nor can we go back to what we were. I loved him once, but I love him no more, believe me. My future is with you. I have pledged myself to you, body and heart and soul. I am *yours*. Let us seal the pact once and for all. Please, please kiss me."

He was listening so intently that he had insensibly leaned nearer to her, so that his face was a bare few inches from her own. She could feel his breath on her face, still sweet and heavy with his morning chocolate. His eyes were fixed on hers, and she saw longing there, she was sure of it. Yet still he hesitated.

She could wait no longer. There was nothing else for it, for if there were to be any kissing done, she was going to have to start things off herself.

Slowly, oh so slowly, she moved nearer to him. His lips were parted, and, just at the moment when she feared he might move apart, he closed his eyes, waiting. With the softest touch imaginable, like two waterlilies drifting into each other, her lips brushed his. He gave a little whimper, although whether of pleasure or distress she could not tell. She pressed against him a little more, and he yielded to her touch, but still his restraint held him back.

She moved a little apart, gazing into his eyes. His breath was ragged, but he made no move to place himself closer or further away. He simply sat, holding tight to her hand, and waited. Cautiously she lifted her free hand to cup his cheek. Now, if at all, was the moment when he would draw back. But he did not. With a little groan, he closed his eyes and turned his head to kiss the palm of her hand. "Annabelle, Annabelle..." he murmured. He stopped, opened his eyes again and looked at her, breathing heavily, his head resting in her hand.

And then, to her great joy, his free hand crept around her back, warm and solid and comforting. At last! She smiled at his dear face, and, very slowly, his own answering smile spread across it. Pulling her nearer, he closed his eyes and rubbed his nose against hers, and then kissed it, oh so softly. Then her forehead, her cheeks and, tantalisingly, all round her mouth. And finally, when she felt she would explode if he did not kiss her properly, this minute, *at once*, he pressed his lips onto hers. Without hesitation, she melted into him with all the ardour that had built up inside her over many weeks and months, all the fervency of her nature that had waited patiently for the chance to express itself.

And he kissed her back just as passionately, and the world was nothing but warmth and need and love and passion.

Some unknown time later, when she gradually became aware of herself and Allan as two separate beings again, instead of a single vine twined together, and could feel the breeze gentle on her cheek and hear cattle lowing distantly, she smiled happily up into his face and he gazed down at her with unmistakable delight. She was half lying on his knees, although she had no memory of getting there, but it was quite delicious to be held so, with his arm sturdy around her back, and one hand resting warmly on her leg, his lips still close to hers.

"Sweet, darling Annabelle," he whispered between kisses. "My beloved, my only love, my sweetheart, my dear. I love you, I adore you, I worship you. My sweetest, loveliest Annabelle…"

He continued for some time in this vein, kissing her and murmuring of love, and she was not in the least minded to interrupt him. It was so pleasant, in fact, that she sighed for the sheer joy of it.

At once he shifted. "Are you chilled, my love? Or uncomfortable?"

"No, how could I be, with you to hold me and keep me warm?" He chuckled, a low rumble that rocked her gently. "Very effective, that mistletoe, so never again tell me how inarticulate you are."

That brought another laugh. "I have been very foolish, my darling. I was so afraid..."

"There is nothing to be afraid of," she whispered, stroking his cheek softly. "We are together now. We will always be together. We will always love each other."

Abruptly he froze, and she wondered with a spear of terror if she had said the wrong thing, and broken the mood.

"Do you mean it?" he said huskily. "Can you possibly... love *me?* I am so... boring."

"You are *not* boring," she said fiercely. "Reliable, perhaps. Dependable. Constant. Loyal. Trustworthy. Reassuring. Faithful. Honest. Punctilious. Kind. Generous. Steady. *Safe."*

"Hmmm." He was silent for a while, then he said, "Sounds pretty boring to me."

"I feel," she said slowly, "as if I have come home to safe harbour after a long and turbulent sea journey."

"Ah," he said. "And I feel as if I have found a friend. A friend of the heart."

And she was satisfied with that.

~~~~~

Annabelle spent a morning walking round the house with Mrs Hale and the dowager, to determine if she wanted any changes made. Allan trailed along behind them, but his only contribution to the discussion was to say periodically, "You must do whatever you wish, Miss Winterton. Anything you want, you may have." Each time, the dowager would roll her eyes and make tutting noises.

There were few changes that she wanted to make. The dining room could be freshened with new wallpaper, she decided, and perhaps the music room, too, but little else needed attention.

"I do not wish to redecorate the Italian room, but I might rearrange the furniture a little," she said.

"The Italian room?" the dowager said, looking down her nose at Annabelle. "What is wrong with it, pray?"

"Why, nothing at all. It is a very stylish room. However, it is not very comfortable at present for receiving callers. It needs some more soft chairs and so forth."

"Receiving callers? What nonsense! The Italian room is only used when we have large formal functions."

"Indeed, but I intend to use it to receive my own callers."

The dowager stared at her. "But why? You will receive in the morning room, naturally, as Eloise did, and as I do still."

"The morning room is your room, Lady Brackenwood. I shall have my own room."

"Allan, tell her that the Countess of Brackenwood always receives in the morning room."

Annabelle did not wait for Allan to respond to this appeal. "On the contrary, previous countesses received in the Italian room, and I intend to revive that tradition," she said crisply. "You will be welcome to join me there, or you may continue to use the morning room. I shall not object to that, you may be sure, for this is still your home. But if you do not like my dispositions, the Dower House is empty."

And that silenced her very effectively. Allan tried, not entirely satisfactorily, to hide his laugh, and when the dowager moved out of earshot, he whispered, "You see? I told you I would marry the woman who could stand up to Mother."

The only room Annabelle wished to transform utterly was the bedroom which would be hers. She had never seen inside it before that day, but she wanted nothing left to remind Allan of his dead wife, or of her sister, who had so recently slept there.

"Are you sure you do not prefer a different room altogether?" he asked her quietly, as Mrs Hale and the dowager exclaimed over the gowns still hanging in the wardrobe. "I do not wish you to be made uncomfortable."

"With new furniture, wallpaper and hangings, it will be perfect," she said. "Besides, what other room has so convenient a connecting door?"

He smiled, a smile of pure joy and anticipation that she could read perfectly well. "Then let it be so," he whispered, as his arm reached around her waist and pulled her close.

~~~~~

A few days later, Allan had just finished his session with Mr Cross, and was settling down with relief in the library, when Plessey came in. Plessey had been employed at Charlsby for several years, and Allan would have thought him quite imperturbable. Now, however, he was unusually discomposed.

"My lord..." he began. "My lord..."

"Whatever is it, Plessey?"

With shaking hands, the butler proffered a silver salver bearing a small card. Allan took the card, read it and laughed. The reason for Plessey's unsettled state was now clear.

"Show him in, Plessey."

A minute later, the butler returned and intoned with the utmost reverence, "His grace the most noble the Duke of Camberley."

The duke was not, as so often happened, a man grown to corpulence on the excesses of wealth. He was thin to the point of emaciation, and dressed in plain, sober black. He wanted only the Geneva bands at his throat to make him a clergyman, or lawyer, perhaps. Unlike most of his rank, he eschewed the carriage with footmen and postilions and outriders, and travelled about on horseback with no more than a couple of grooms to protect his dignity.

After the business of greetings and refreshments had been accomplished, and Plessey, bowing deeply, had withdrawn, the duke laughed. "Good Lord, Brackenwood, ain't your butler ever seen a duke before?"

"Probably not. We live very quiet here. Plessey has been living in hope of the Marquess of Carrbridge for some years, but a duke is beyond his wildest expectations. He will die a happy butler now. But do sit down and tell me what brings you all this way to the wilds of Cheshire."

"That nephew of yours... or cousin, whatever he is. George Skelton."

"Ah. The Lady Grace."

"You know all about it, then? I tell you straight, Brackenwood, I don't like it above half, but she is my youngest and the very image of her mother, and such a taking little thing, my Gracie... well, I shall not refuse him out of hand, not if we can come to terms."

Allan raised an eyebrow. "Duke, George has no more than eight hundred a year of his own. Furthermore, although he is presently my heir, his expectations have taken a turn for the worse lately, since I shall shortly have another wife myself, and he will likely be cut out of the inheritance. He cannot possibly aspire to Lady Grace's hand."

"Is that why you took him away from town, then?"

"I had nothing to do with it. George saw that the young lady was beginning to show a partiality for him, and withdrew himself immediately from her society. He is no fortune hunter, Camberley."

"That is what I wished to hear. Never go to town myself — too rackety a place by half, these days — but my older daughters brought Gracie out and that is what they told me. The boy was obviously head over ears, and who can blame him for that? Not I! But he behaved just as he ought, they said, never put himself forward or gave them the least concern, and if he had had a title or a decent estate... But then he left town and ever since then, my lovely girl has been all in the dumps. Tries to hide it, of course, for she is a good girl and not one to mope, not in company. But I can see how pulled she is, and I want none of it. Lord, we have had enough of that with Ramsey, drooping about after that girl. Three years she kept him waiting before she said yes, and the best part of a year to get her to the altar, and I am not going through that with Gracie, and so I tell you. I cannot bear to see her in the dismals."

"I am very sorry for it, for she sounds a delightful young lady, but I do not quite see what may be done about it. George has an allowance from me at present, but I can hardly afford to set him up in the sort of style that would allow him to raise his eyes so high."

"No, and one would not wish to be endlessly funding a man. Gracie is used to the very best, and will be expensive to keep in comfort. Does your nephew... cousin, I mean, have any other expectations?"

"None that I know of. He has always wished to take up a career, but so long as I was deficient in sons, I could not countenance the scheme. Would you like to meet him? He will be back from his morning ride by now."

The duke assented, and Plessey was summoned, all agog, and told to fetch Mr Skelton to the library. Allan could almost see the wheels spinning in the butler's brain as he tried to work out why the Duke of Camberley should have arrived unannounced and, furthermore, why Mr George Skelton should be sent for. It would not be long before they worked it out, for George's valet might have some suspicion, but it amused Allan to see Plessey stumped for once.

George crept in, plainly terrified, but he made his bow and said all that was proper. But then he burst out, "The Lady Grace? She is well? There is no... bad news?"

"No, she is *not* well, not at all well, thanks to you, young man," the duke said firmly.

George went ashen, and Allan could see that he had not observed the twinkle in the duke's eye.

"Lady Grace is suffering much as you are, George," Allan said. "The duke wishes her to be happy, and so he comes here to talk to you, and see if matters may be arranged to the satisfaction of all parties."

"Happy... arranged... satisfaction..." George repeated, eyes wide.

"Do sit down, boy, before you fall down," the duke said genially. "True enough, Gracie is moped to death on your account, and I hate to see the child unhappy, so if we can come to some agreement, you can have her, with my blessing. But you will have to take good care of her, mind! I shall not see her made miserable, you may depend upon it."

It was fortunate that George was standing right beside a chair, for his legs seemed to give way at this point and he plumped down like a deflated balloon, his mouth round with astonishment.

"Now then, Skelton," the duke said. "It appears you are unlikely to be an earl after all, so what else can you do, eh? And do not say the church, for I'll not have a prosy clergyman in the family, that much I tell you."

"I... I..." George squeaked, before regaining some control over his voice. "The army, perhaps?"

"No, that will never do," the duke said briskly. "Why, you might have to fight. You might even be injured or killed, and Gracie would not like that."

"Oh. A government post, perhaps?" George hazarded.

"Ah, now that is more the thing. Gracie would like to live in London. I have a few houses she might choose from, and you will come to Marshfields for the summer, naturally. I tell you what, Skelton, how would you like to go into Parliament? I have two or three seats that might suit you. What do you say, eh?"

"Oh... I should like that very much. Thank you, your grace... thank you..." He swallowed. "When may I see her? Please?"

"She is staying with friends not ten miles from here, waiting for me to bring you to her. Get your horse saddled and I shall take you straight there."

George made a strangled sound in his throat, and rushed out of the room.

"Ah, young love," the duke said complacently. "I remember it well. This is the most awkward stage, naturally, but once that is got over,  it only gets better. With every year, it gets better."

# 25: The Streets Of Chester (September)

September brought incessant rain, but Annabelle could not be downhearted, for it also brought the first truly welcome visitors she had received at Charlsby in the persons of her sister Rosamund and her husband Mr Robin Dalton. For the first time, Annabelle stood beside Allan on the steps to greet the arrivals, and the smiles on both sides, mingled with just a few tears, were the greatest delight to her.

Their meeting was, as is so often the case with dear friends, a protracted affair, for they all stood for some time in the entrance hall, Rosamund chattering to Annabelle and the two men just as easy together. The carriage had gone to the stables, the luggage was unloaded and carried away up the stairs long before the party finally began to move up the stairs themselves. Then there were three faces peering through the upper bannisters, and Allan's daughters had to be called down to be introduced.

But eventually, Annabelle detached Rosamund and showed her to the room that was to be hers. "Robin is just next door, but we have no other guests just now so we can give you the best rooms."

"But this is so delightful, Belle!" she cried, casting her bonnet onto the bed and flopping with a sigh of relief into a chair. "Everything is exactly as you described it, yet I could not quite see it in my mind's eye. And Lord Brackenwood all that is amiable and kind. I am so glad to have met your earl at last, for I was a little concerned... But now that I have seen you both, I can see the affection between you and my mind is quite at ease. Letters are all very well, and you have written a great many, it is true, but it is not the same. I needed to see the two of you together, and observe the manner in which you look at each other, and those little gestures that are so speaking. One cannot judge at all from written words. Words are a screen by which the heart may be concealed, but when we stand in the same room and I can look you in the eye, nothing may be hidden from your sister, dear. I see the little blush on your cheek when you speak his name, and the brightness in your eye when you gaze at him. I see the devoted way he looks at you and the delicate way he offers you his arm, and then touches your hand when he thinks himself unobserved. In short, I never saw two people more in love, and it delights me more than I can say after— But we need not speak of that."

"You refer, I suppose, to Mr Keeling," Annabelle said coolly. "You need not give him another moment's thought, for *I* have not, I assure you. He has behaved abominably, and I am quite ashamed that I ever thought so highly of him, or wasted so many tears on such a worthless man."

Rosamund tipped her head on one side. "You truly retain no warmer feelings for him at all?"

"None," Annabelle said, with a decisive shake of the head. "He has forfeited all right to my regard. Miss Lorrimer is welcome to him. They are to be married later this month, I hear, and I do not envy her one bit. I am well rid of him, for mine is by far the better bargain."

Rosamund laughed. "You are quite right, dear. Now, have you many entertainments planned for us, or is this to be a quiet visit? We must make the most of it, for we cannot stay above ten days, and I shall not be able to travel again for some time."

"A dinner and card party is the only social event we have planned, although we may receive invitations once your presence here is known. But most of all I should like your help with my wedding clothes, for I have not got very far as yet and there is no one else here whose judgement may be depended upon."

"Not the dowager? But of course, dear, although we shall have to take Robin shopping with us. His taste is impeccable."

So it was that Annabelle found the purchase of her wedding clothes was to be supervised by a gentleman, and even Allan reluctantly agreed to be advised on the purchase of a new coat to honour his bride.

Annabelle had always thought Mr Robin Dalton something of a dandy, but she had to admit that Rosamund was right. His taste was indeed impeccable. On their first visit to the warehouses and shops, every modiste and milliner and glove maker and purveyor of silks divined at a glance that he was a person of sartorial distinction such as Chester had rarely seen before. The finest materials were produced for his inspection, the prices offered were far lower than Annabelle herself had received just one week earlier and it was, apparently, no trouble at all to make up an elegant ensemble in just three days.

"Oh, there is no need to rush so," she protested, only to be told that it was no trouble at all, and they would be quite delighted to oblige her.

"Well, that was interesting," Annabelle said, as they made their way through the crowded streets to an hotel for some refreshments before beginning the journey home. "There is nothing else for it, Robin, but you will have to move to Cheshire and accompany me on every shopping expedition in future. I have never been so well attended to."

"Did you mention on your previous visits that you were about to marry the Earl of Brackenwood?" Robin said, eyes twinkling.

"I do not believe I did," Annabelle said.

"And you asked for the bills to be sent to you, I suppose?"

"Naturally. I shall pass them to Allan, of course, but—"

"And you wore one of your oldest and least fashionable gowns, I daresay?"

"Certainly, in these dusty streets. I would not have worn anything so pale today if you had not insisted. I understand you, I think. Better service is provided to those of higher rank, so Miss Nobody of Nowhere-in-Particular is left to wait, like that poor widow in the milliner's shop, who was quite neglected while three ladies attended to me. It does not seem entirely equitable, for she was elderly and looked quite tired and out of sorts. It would have been a kindness to attend to her first."

"She had a chair to rest upon, and I believe she enjoyed watching you order five bonnets at once more than she would enjoy her own purchase of a new ribbon or a couple of feathers. If one has a position in society, one must provide a spectacle for those of humbler rank to amuse themselves at one's expense." His eyes twinkled merrily as he spoke. "As for the tradespeople, you forget, sister, how much value they derive from your custom. A gown for Miss Winterton, the governess, is of no interest, but to be able to speak of the future Lady Brackenwood of Charlsby as a customer gives them inestimable pleasure. You must not deprive them of the happiness of serving a countess."

"I never thought of it in that light," Annabelle said. "It is not natural in me to put myself forward."

"It is not, and I believe your future husband is of just such a retiring disposition," Robin said. "But you will soon be a person of some consequence in this town, and it is as well that the tradesmen recognise it. Ah, there is Lord Brackenwood awaiting us now."

Allan was standing outside the hotel entrance across the street, his nondescript attire attracting no attention from passers-by. Annabelle guessed that he rather liked such anonymity, as she did herself. His face lit up as he saw them, and Annabelle hurried forward to meet him with so little care that she almost collided with a young lady emerging at a rush from a shop.

"Oh, I do beg your pardon!" they said simultaneously.

Annabelle laughed, but the girl curtsied and lowered her head in embarrassment, and Annabelle recognised her at once. "Why, Miss Lorrimer! How are you?"

The girl looked more closely at Annabelle and blushed scarlet. "Oh! Oh... it is Miss Winterton!"

"Pray allow me to congratulate you, and wish you every joy. Mr Keeling is... the most charming and amiable man."

Miss Lorrimer blushed even more fiercely, and nodded. "And... and... to you also."

Annabelle had forgotten just how shy the child was. "Thank you. We have both been most fortunate. But you are not out alone?"

"Oh no... my aunt..."

Annabelle now saw a lady of mature years, rather garishly dressed, standing nearby, smiling and nodding at her, not socially confident enough to ask for the introduction although she clearly wanted it. Her gaze took in Robin and Rosamund, standing a little aside, and there was a certain excitement in her eyes, which Annabelle well understood. Her sister and brother-in-law exuded London style.

"Will you do me the honour of introducing me to your aunt?" Annabelle said.

"Oh... oh yes! Mrs Lorrimer... um, Mrs James Lorrimer. Aunt, this is Miss Winterton. The governess from Charlsby."

The two curtsied politely and exchanged greetings, but Annabelle could see the lady's face change. She knew, as perhaps Miss Lorrimer did not, that Charles had been in love with Annabelle. Perhaps she even knew of his most improper offer to her while still betrothed to Miss Lorrimer.

"Not the governess for much longer," Mrs Lorrimer said unsmilingly. "Congratulations, I'm sure. Who are your friends, Miss Winterton?"

Annabelle turned to Robin with an eyebrow raised in query, but he willingly stepped forward and allowed her to make the introductions. Her voice did not waver, even as she said, "Miss Lorrimer was a guest at Charlsby earlier this year, and is shortly to marry our Brinshire acquaintance Mr Charles Keeling."

"How delightful!" Robin said, making a sweeping bow that brought even more blushes to Miss Lorrimer's cheeks, if such a thing were possible. "And how soon is the wedding to be? Are you bound on the same errand as we are today, that of wedding clothes? I have been most favourably impressed with the warehouses here, for the quality is very near as high as one sees in London, and the prices a great deal more moderate, would you not agree? But tell me, Mrs Lorrimer, is there a fan maker you can recommend, for I have not seen one yet which meets the standard one would hope for."

Mrs Lorrimer instantly launched into an enthusiastic recital of every purveyor of fans in the town, clearly delighted to display her knowledge to a gentleman of such London style. So it was that they did not notice another gentleman approaching, and were quite startled when he burst out, "Annabelle! Good God!"

Mr Keeling! For an instant, Annabelle's heart lurched in shock. She recovered herself instantly, turning to him with a calm smile on her face. He was the one who seemed jittery, apologising and laughing in equal measure, making a jerky bow before tucking Miss Lorrimer's hand into his arm.

As the others returned to the interesting topic of wedding clothes, Charles turned to Annabelle and said quietly, "I wish you joy, Annabelle. He is a good man and will make you happy, I am sure."

She could not help smiling as she thought of Allan. "He will, I know it. And I wish you every happiness, too. She is quite charming."

"Indeed she is." But there was a bleakness in his eyes that affected her deeply. Poor Charles! But he had made his choice, and must live with the consequences of that.

And now she was impatient to be with Allan again, and reminded Robin and Rosamund that he was still waiting for them.

They made their farewells, and crossed the street to where Allan still stood patiently. He watched Annabelle approach with an anxious look, and they entered and went through to their private parlour without a word being spoken beyond the essentials.

A cold collation was already laid out for them, and they had eaten in silence for several minutes before Allan looked sideways at Annabelle and said, "Is he well? Mr Keeling, that is?"

"He is very well, and Miss Lorrimer also. They are looking forward to their wedding very much. Miss Lorrimer grew quite effusive on the subject, when Robin pressed her. She is to have a barouche for summer use, as well as a closed carriage, and her own horse for riding, and their house has something very special in the way of staircases, we must understand."

"Oh, a staircase. How original," Allan murmured, smiling at her in a way which warmed her inside.

"Yes, one must approve of a house with a staircase. And a oriel window, apparently. What is an oriel window?"

"One which projects, somehow."

"Ah. Well, their house has one. Or several, possibly, I am not very clear about that. But it is all very exciting, and Miss Lorrimer's aunt has been so very kind as to give Robin the directions for a fan maker, three more warehouses and positively the best haberdasher in town, so I believe we shall be obliged to return for more shopping on Monday."

He laughed, reaching across the table to take her hand with a sigh of satisfaction. "Oh, excellent, for I want my wife to be rigged out in the finest styles."

"And how about my husband? Is he to be rigged out in the finest styles, too?"

"I am to have a new coat to be married in. Is that not enough for you?"

"For now," she said. "Next year, perhaps, we might venture to persuade you to a new waistcoat, and the year after perhaps a pair of Hessians."

He laughed, and she patted his arm playfully. "That is better. You looked so anxious for a while there. But I am quite done with Mr Charles Keeling, so you need not worry about me."

"Ah, you two are so delightful together," Rosamund said with a sentimental sigh. "Nothing could be more perfect, and as soon as we return to the house, I shall write to Lucy, Margaret and Fanny to reassure them."

"Reassure them?" Annabelle said. "About what?"

"Why, they were worried that you might be still in love with Charles, of course, and marrying Lord Brackenwood merely to obtain a comfortable home, but now that I have seen you with both gentlemen, I can tell them that matters are very much otherwise."

"Oh, yes," Annabelle said happily. "Very much otherwise."

"I am very glad about it, for it is much the most prudent outcome," Rosamund said.

"Oh, very prudent on my side," Annabelle said. "Every young lady should fall in love with a handsome, wealthy earl if she can possibly manage it. But not at all prudent on Allan's side. A penniless governess — how shocking!"

"You are Miss Winterton of Woodside," Allan said with dignity. "You are the daughter of a gentleman, and therefore an excellent match for a poor, lonely earl with no social graces." And he lifted her hand gently to his lips.

Rosamund laughed. "What a pity Fanny is not here to see such romantic behaviour. She would be quite in raptures."

"Poor Fanny!" Annabelle said. "Who knows when we shall see her again?"

"What about Christmas?" Robin said, smiling. "Would that suit you?"

Annabelle squeaked with astonishment. "But how? Allan and I talked about it, but he is not minded to travel so far north as Yorkshire before the roads improve in the spring."

"Would you consider a journey to Brinshire, Brackenwood?" Robin said. "It is my father's idea. He is not well, and, as often happens when a man is confined to his bed for long spells, he has been fretting rather over Rosamund's sisters, scattered about the countryside. He regrets that he did not exert himself more in January to help them to stay together. Now he wishes to invite all four of them to Westerlea Park for Christmas. And there is another reason, also. I have finally found a buyer for Woodside, so there are papers to sign and so forth. The new owners hope to be in by Candlemas, so this will be the last opportunity for the Miss Wintertons to see their old home before it is lost to them, should they choose to proceed with the sale."

Annabelle turned beseeching eyes to Allan.

"You would like to go, I can see that," he said, "and I am not minded to deny you such a pleasure. I know how close you are to your sisters, as the daily avalanche of letters attests. Let it be so, and we must all hope there is not too much snow, for travelling in winter is foul at the best of times, and unendurable in snow. You may write to your father, Dalton, and tell him that the Earl and Countess of Brackenwood would be delighted to visit him at Westerlea Park at Christmas."

"Thank you," Annabelle whispered. His warm answering smile was full of affection.

"And now, if everyone has eaten their fill, let us send for the carriage and go home, for I should like a little walk up to the woods before dinner. Perhaps you would care to accompany me, Miss Winterton? There is a very fine oak tree there where we might rest for a while."

Annabelle blushed so fiercely that Rosamund said, "Now what in the world is so interesting about an oak tree that sets your cheeks aflame, sister?"

"It is a very fine tree," Allan said blandly. "A large, well-grown tree with a bench around its trunk."

Rosamund looked mystified, but Annabelle laughed. "Mistletoe!" she whispered.

"Ah! Then that entirely accounts for it. Enjoy your walk, Lord Brackenwood."

"I believe I shall," he said.

"And so shall I," Annabelle said.

*THE END*

The next book in the series is *The Chaperon*, and features the third Winterton sister, chatterbox Lucy. You can read a sneak preview of chapter 1 after the acknowledgements. For more information or to buy, go to my website: http://marykingswood.co.uk.

# *Thanks for reading!*

If you have enjoyed reading this book, please consider writing a short review on Amazon. You can find out the latest news and sign up for the mailing list at my website: http://marykingswood.co.uk.

Book 2 of the series is *The Chaperon*, featuring Lucy, and you can read a sneak preview of Chapter 1 after the acknowledgements.

**Family trees:** You can see a hi-res version available on my website: http://marykingswood.co.uk.

**A note on historical accuracy:** I have endeavoured to stay true to the spirit of Regency times, and have avoided taking too many liberties or imposing modern sensibilities on my characters. The book is not one of historical record, but I've tried to make it reasonably accurate. However, I'm not perfect! If you spot a historical error, I'd very much appreciate knowing about it so that I can correct it and learn from it. Thank you!

# The Governess: Sisters of Woodside Mysteries 1

**About the series:** *When Mr Winterton of Woodside dies, his daughters find themselves penniless and homeless. What can they do? Unless they wish to live on charity, they will have to find genteel employment for themselves. This book is set in England during the Regency period of the early nineteenth century. Book 0 takes place 5 years before books 1-4, and book 5 ten years later.*

**Book 0: The Betrothed (Rosamund) (a short novel, free to mailing list subscribers)**

**Book 1: The Governess (Annabelle)**

**Book 2: The Chaperon (Lucy)**

**Book 3: The Companion (Margaret)**

**Book 4: The Seamstress (Fanny)**

**Book 5: Woodside**

Any questions about the series? Email me - I'd love to hear from you!

# *About the author*

I write traditional Regency romances under the pen name Mary Kingswood, and epic fantasy as Pauline M Ross. I live in the beautiful Highlands of Scotland with my husband. I like chocolate, whisky, my Kindle, massed pipe bands, long leisurely lunches, chocolate, going places in my campervan, eating pizza in Italy, summer nights that never get dark, wood fires in winter, chocolate, the view from the study window looking out over the Moray Firth and the Black Isle to the mountains beyond. And chocolate. I dislike driving on motorways, cooking, shopping, hospitals.

# Acknowledgements

Thanks go to:

Jane Austen and Georgette Heyer, who jointly inspired me to try my hand at writing a Regency romance.

Shayne Rutherford of Darkmoon Graphics for the cover design.

My beta readers: Mary Burnett, Barbara Daniels Dena, Amy DeWitt, Quilting Danielle, Keti Vezzu.

Last, but definitely not least, my first reader: Amy Ross.

# Sneak preview of The Chaperon Chapter 1: A Journey To Shropshire (January)

'19th January 18— Longmere Priory, Shropshire. My dear Mrs Price, or may I call you Lucy? For I feel sure that we shall be the greatest of friends from the moment we meet. We have heard so much of your amiable and charming nature, and we are all wild to see you, especially my two step-daughters who will be your particular charges. They cannot wait to go back into society again, and I am sure that under your watchful eyes and with your experience in the ways of young girls, they will be perfectly well behaved. I do wish that I could take them about myself, but I am strictly forbidden from exerting myself in any way, and there is no one else who can oblige in this manner. But you, with your experience of social occasions and your relationship to Lord Westerlea, must be of the utmost benefit to my poor dear step-daughters. We are all so grateful to you for rescuing the dear girls from the dreadful prospect of no society but the family. All is prepared for your arrival, so you may *travel here whenever it suits your esteemed brother-in-law to bring you to us. Yours, in great anticipation, Augusta Kingsley.'*

~~~~~

## JANUARY

Lucy waited in the hall, her boxes stacked near the door. She wore her new black pelisse over a new travelling gown, for although she would not normally wear anything fine for travelling, it was important to make a good first impression on her employer. Besides, she would be in Robin's rather fine carriage, and stopping only at the very best inns, so there was little risk of mud.

The pelisse depressed her. For the full year after her husband's death she had managed perfectly well with her old black cloak, for she went nowhere and was seen by nobody. Now she was in black again, for her father this time, but she would be venturing into society and even a chaperon must look respectable.

A chaperon. How lowering at the age of two and twenty to be relegated to the benches reserved for dowagers and matrons. It had not seemed so bad here in Brinshire, for everyone knew her well, but in Shropshire she would be pitied, she knew, and how she hated pity. No one need waste their pity on her, for although she was widowed young, she had chosen her husband with her eyes wide open and regretted none of it.

Margaret crept down the stairs, her face chalk-white, her eyes swollen from crying. Poor Margaret! She, perhaps, would feel the change more than anyone, for she was so shy that new society would quite overset her. Annabelle was so composed that she would be at ease anywhere. As for Fanny, her sweet nature must win her friends wherever she went. But Margaret was not so blessed with an easy manner.

Lucy herself had shed all the tears she had inside her, and now faced the future with fortitude, she hoped. Outward fortitude, at least, for she felt like a jelly inside, her stomach churning with fear. Still, there was nothing to be done about their situation, after all. Papa had mortgaged the house and sold half his land to sustain his gambling habits, and now there was nothing left for his daughters. Woodside itself must be sold to pay the outstanding debts and they must all make their own way in the world.

Annabelle and Fanny appeared as the appointed hour drew near, and then Janet, who was to stay with Lucy as her maid. The four sisters had shared her services before, but the others would not be going into company, so they had all agreed that Lucy would have more need of her own maid. One by one the other servants materialised from their fastness below stairs, the maids weeping and even Mrs Thompson, the cook, blowing her nose fiercely. It was a difficult time for them, too, for the house would be closed up and most of them must look for new places.

Exactly on time, the carriage rattled up the drive, Robin's valet Brast huddled on the seat beside the coachman. Rosamund whisked into the house, then Robin, to supervise the stowing of the boxes. At least Rosamund was safely married, and was not to be tossed out of her home into stormy seas, as her four younger sisters were. Her husband had helped them all find posts, since they would accept no other aid from him, and was now to convey them all to their new homes, first Lucy and Margaret to different parts of Shropshire, then Annabelle to Cheshire and Fanny all the way to Yorkshire.

So far away! The sisters had never been broken apart before, and had not even travelled much. Rosamund had married, but lived most of the year not a mile from Woodside. Annabelle had spent but two brief seasons in London. Lucy herself had lived in the village when she married. And if ever one or two of the five were away, the others would still be at home, in the familiar Woodside routines. Now they would be scattered to the four winds, like seeds blown away from the tree, to land who knew where.

"There now, the boxes are loaded and all is ready," Robin said. "Time to go. We must make the most of the daylight."

Margaret bent her head, tears flowing again.

"Now, now," Rosamund said briskly. "No more crying, Margaret. You are to be living with relatives, after all. Aunt Letty and Aunt Pru will look after you."

But she only cried all the harder.

Fanny put her arms around her. "Never mind, sister, we shall write very often, shall we not? You must tell me all the Shropshire gossip, and I shall tell you about Yorkshire, which is a very interesting county, I believe. And we are all going to very kind, good-natured people, I am sure."

"Come now, Margaret," Robin said. "Lucy, will you go first? We cannot delay."

And so, somehow, between the sisters' cajoling and Robin's anxiety to be off, Margaret was got into the carriage, and Lucy beside her, the hot stones placed at their feet and the fur-lined rug spread over their legs. Robin and Janet sat opposite them, the door was slammed shut and the horses were in motion instantly. Lucy waved, but almost at once the curve of the drive hid the house from view and she could no longer see her sisters or the house that had been their home all their lives.

At first, Margaret's incessant weeping and the lowering winter skies subdued Lucy's spirits, but before long they left behind the familiar roads and views, and she began to feel more cheerful. She, who had never left Brinshire before, would soon be in

Shropshire, seeing new sights and making new acquaintances, and what could be pleasanter? Nothing, surely.

"Oh, look, Margaret! Such a fine stand of elms over there. And is that a windmill in the distance? I believe it is. Why, a windmill, just fancy! We have only water mills in our part of the county, is it not so, Mr Dalton? Oh, such sweet little cottages! I do so love a cottage, do not you, Margaret? And they have chickens! I dearly love chickens. I had twenty two layers and a cockerel at Mill Place, and I so enjoyed feeding them every day. They would peck away around my feet... so charming. Oh, Margaret, do stop crying, dearest."

"Yes, it would be for the best," Robin said. "Your head will ache abominably if you do not."

"That is very true," Lucy said. "You are quite right, Mr Dalton, for it is always so when one cries a great deal. It makes one feel so dreadfully *ill*. You do not wish to be ill, do you, sister dear? Think what a bad impression it would give Aunt Letty and Aunt Pru. Although I am sure they are very kind." She paused, realising that she knew nothing at all about them. They were Mama's older sisters, but she had seldom mentioned them, and Papa not at all, so the image of two kindly elderly aunts was all her own invention.

And then there was Uncle Arthur, Mama's only surviving brother. What did she know of him, except that he had twelve children and lived in Market Clunbury? His wife's sister was the lady whose step-daughters she would be chaperoning.

"Mr Dalton, do you have with you the letter from Uncle Arthur?"

He retrieved a neatly folded sheet from an inner pocket, and handed it to her.

*'West End House, Market Clunbury. 18th January 18— Sir, I am obliged to you for your letter setting out the good qualities of my niece. I had no doubt of her suitability, but your words of commendation will serve to reassure a mother's heart that her daughters will be in safe hands. I am sure Lucy will do very well, and will take admirable care of the girls. It is a pity that my wife and I are unable to be of service in this way, but we are humble people who move in a different level of society from the Kingsleys. I will attempt to answer your concerns regarding the family she will be entering as best I can, although I know little enough of them. Kingsley is a private man, and speaks little of himself, so all that I know is through others. The Kingsleys live at Longmere Priory, the prettiest little estate imaginable with some excellent shooting. We dine there sometimes, and they keep a very good table, with plenty of game and fish every day. Kingsley has his wine sent up from London, from someone who has it from France, and does not go through the local vintner at all, and gets the best coal and candles - wax candles in use even in the servants' hall, if you can imagine it. He is reputed to be worth five or six thousand a year, although not for long with such extravagances, I wager. He married a viscount's daughter, who gave him his twin girls and expired thereafter, and he never took another wife until he saw Augusta, my wife's sister, some four years ago. She is an amiable creature, who will treat Lucy quite as one of her own daughters, to be sure. Beg pardon, but the paper is at an end. Yours, Arthur Tilford.'*

Lucy laughed, and Robin smiled, too. "It is not very informative, is it?" he said.

"Oh, but there is good shooting to be had, and fish every day, not to mention wax candles in the servants' hall. What more is there to say of the Kingsleys?"

"Only the important matter," Robin said. "That Mrs Kingsley is ill and has been forbidden to rise from her chaise longue, so it is for you to take the step-daughters about. Easy work, I imagine."

"With two young ladies of eighteen? Perhaps," Lucy said. "Well, I cannot tell much about the family from this, so I shall just have to discover all their little secrets when I arrive."

"I do not imagine they have any secrets worth the discovering," Robin said. "Some cousins in trade perhaps. A bastard or two, no doubt. They are quite an ordinary family, I think."

"Even ordinary families have secrets," Lucy said, smiling.

They changed horses once and then they were into Shropshire, and the country seen through the windows became noticeably different, although Lucy could not say how. Nevertheless, she exclaimed over every vista brought into view by a bend in the road or a slight incline, admired the empty fields and bare trees, and declared the cottagers the stoutest and healthiest she had ever seen. Eventually, Margaret stopped crying and nodded off to sleep, Janet had been dozing off and on all day, and even Robin leaned back against the squabs, at great risk to his coiffure, and closed his eyes.

He was an odd sort of man, Lucy had always thought. He took prodigious pride in his appearance, and always looked very fine, as if he had been transported directly from the saloons of London without so much as ruffling his hair. Lucy could imagine him strutting about the great houses of the capital, and mingling with the highest in the land. Well, he was to be a baron one day, when his father should quit the mortal sphere, Lord Westerlea of Westerlea Park, so that was appropriate. And Rosamund would be Lady Westerlea — how grand that sounded! And although Rosamund would always be her familiar self and not give herself airs, and Robin had turned out to be a kind brother and a devoted husband, Lucy was a little in awe of both of them.

Late in the afternoon, when Robin was beginning to grow fretful at the slow pace, they came to the bustling town of Market Clunbury, with its fine old buildings clustered around a cross. After a brief stop at an inn to bespeak rooms for Robin, Margaret and Brast for the night, they drove on through the town and into the darkening countryside. But they had not far to go, for the gates to Longmere Priory were no more than a mile from the outskirts of the town, and in no time they were turning in past a lodge with lamps already cheerfully lit, and then rounding a large and very ugly fountain to pull up outside a starkly modern house.

They were clearly expected, for two footmen and a butler emerged from within, and began unloading boxes. While Robin instructed them, Lucy stood uncertainly, looking up at the house in some disappointment. The name of it, Longmere Priory, has excited hopes of a quaint medieval house, perhaps something like Willowbye in Brinshire, all odd, twisting passageways and low ceilings and uneven floors, not to mention a great hall. There was something appealing about a great hall, with its history of ancient barons lording it over the serfs and dogs sitting amongst the straw, the walls adorned with battle flags and musty tapestries. The clean lines of this building looked to be no more than fifty years old.

Three ladies now emerged from the house, bundled up in heavy shawls.

"Come in, come in, Mrs Price, do come inside out of this horrid cold," called one of them, almost bouncing with excitement, and Lucy rushed to comply, for the three were hardly dressed against the winter weather.

All four ladies hastened into the hall, a great echoing room, much adorned with statuary, where several servants waited. There was a blazing fire in a massive marble hearth, which drew Lucy to its welcoming warmth.

"Yes, do warm yourself, Mrs Price. You must be frozen. Travelling in winter is so unpleasant, is not it? There now, how delightful to— Oh!"

Lucy looked at the speaker properly for the first time, seeing a woman of very much her own age, very pretty and dressed in a stylish manner, although perhaps not quite in the latest London fashion. She wore a matron's cap, but this could not be Mrs Kingsley, who was confined to her chaise longue. A relative or companion, perhaps. The other two women were, she now saw, a little younger and wore identical simple woollen gowns. These were presumably the two step-daughters.

"Oh, but my dear!" the lady said mournfully. "You poor dear thing! So young! I had imagined a lady of mature years, but... oh, how tragic to be widowed at such a young age, how dreadful for you."

"No, no, you must not—" Lucy began, but to her dismay two great tears rolled down the matron's cheeks.

"Oh, my dear!" she wailed, enveloping Lucy in a great hug.

The two younger ladies sighed and rolled their eyes.

Lucy's boxes began to be brought into the hall, followed by Robin, who waited politely to be introduced.

"Ma'am, this is my brother-in-law, Mr Dalton, who very kindly conveyed me here."

"Oh, indeed, most kind, most kind. You are most welcome, sir. Which are your boxes, sir, so that the footmen may take them to the correct room?"

"I have engaged rooms at The Lamb and Pheasant for myself and Mrs Price's sister, Miss Margaret Winterton, who travels with us," he said.

"The Lamb and Pheasant? Nonsense! I shall hear of no such thing, Mr Dalton. You will stay here for tonight, and Miss Winterton also, I insist upon it. John shall run to the inn to tell them of the change in plans."

"You are too kind, but we would not for the world inconvenience you—"

"Oh, it is not the least inconvenience, and you will not mind taking your pot luck with us, I am sure. I will not hear of you going off to an inn, it is quite unthinkable. I am quite decided upon the matter, and will entertain no dispute."

"You are most kind, ma'am, to poor, weary travellers." He made her his most respectful bow, and she coloured up like a girl. "I shall bring Margaret in, and arrange for the rest of the boxes to be unloaded." With another small bow, he whisked out of the door again.

"Well... well now... goodness me! Such delightful manners! London polish, I dare say."

One of the twins coughed, and tugged at her sleeve.

"Oh! Oh yes, how foolish of me! Mrs Price, may I present to you my step-daughters, Miss Kingsley and Miss Winifred Kingsley."

The two girls made perfectly demure curtsies, then spoilt the effect by giggling.

Lucy was almost too surprised to make her own curtsy. So this lady, of much her own age, was Mrs Kingsley, the lady whose illness was supposedly so severe that she must not exert herself in the slightest. Yet here she was, in the very bloom of health, fairly exuding energy and wellbeing. It was a puzzle.

Robin returned with Margaret, Brast slinking in behind them, and this time Lucy made the introductions, noticing Robin's eyebrows rise a little as she named Mrs Kingsley. He too had supposed her to be a companion of some sort.

"Let me show you to your rooms," Mrs Kingsley said, and set off directly for the stairs.

"Ma'am, should you not be resting?" Lucy said in some alarm.

Mrs Kingsley turned, her face crestfallen. "Oh dear! I suppose I should, but I was so happy to see you... I keep forgetting, you see. Peter will be so cross with me."

"Perhaps the Miss Kingsleys would be so good as to show us the way, so that I may get to know them a little?" Lucy said.

One of them — was it Winifred? — looked cross, but the other said, "Oh yes, let us show you the way! May I put them in the tower, Mama?"

"Oh, well... Mrs Price, certainly, the Queen's chamber, as we discussed, but Mr Dalton and Miss Winterton... I had thought the blue room and the lilac room? Those are always prepared, you know. There will be not the least dampness in the air, you see, dear. And those narrow stairs in the old house are so awkward for the servants."

Deirdre said silkily, "It will not take a moment to light the fires and make up the beds, and the servants may use the regular service stairs and then along the upper passageway. It is not very much further."

"Oh, very well, very well. Mrs Hapmore, prepare the priest's room for Miss Winterton and the great chamber for Mr Dalton. Oh, I do hope the rooms will be warm enough."

"I am sure we shall be very comfortable, Mrs Kingsley," Robin said smoothly.

Lucy thought so too, and could not help smiling to herself. The tower? A priest's room? The Queen's chamber? That sounded perfect! She was going to like it here.

END OF SAMPLE CHAPTER of *The Chaperon*.

For more information or to buy, go to my website: http://marykingswood.co.uk.

Made in the USA
Coppell, TX
09 September 2021

62063545R00194